"And what is it you think about out here all alone?"

The sexy timbre of his voice washed over her like a soothing rain. She shivered in response.

"Cold?" Misinterpreting her reaction, he closed the gap between them and wrapped his arms around her.

"A little." The mid-sixties temps had nothing to do with her reaction to his nearness, but she had no intention of telling him that.

Mia had only ever been with one man, and he'd turned out to be a ginormous tool; an absolute error in judgment. Not only had he started cheating on her as soon as he got her into bed, but he'd also come damn close to discovering her and Kat's secret. If Mia hadn't immediately scrubbed his memory, she could only have imagined the headlines: *Modern Day Witches Living in Middle America!*

Plain and simple, her instincts sucked when it came to the opposite sex.

And right now, they screamed for her to run as fast as possible in the other direction. But her body dared her to snuggle into his warm embrace and enjoy the moment.

Which is exactly what she did.

Praise for Donna Marie Rogers

THERE'S ONLY BEEN YOU

"Love lost and found is the basis of this wonderfully heartwarming read. Throw in a years-old lie and a strong sense of family and it only gets better and better."

— 4 Stars, RT Book Reviews

"Readers of contemporary romance will be thoroughly delighted...Donna Marie Rogers delivers a tender tale of love, family, and second chances."

— 5 Bookmarks, Wild on Books

MEANT TO BE

"The plot kept me spellbound throughout the entire book. Rogers has the ability to keep her readers on the edge of our seats."

— 5 Hearts, The Romance Studio

"The material is tightly written, well plotted and fast paced, and the characters are unforgettable."

— 5 Books, Long and Short Reviews

WELCOME TO REDEMPTION SERIES

"With their easy, breezy style and skilled characterizations, Rogers and Netzel have created a town that readers won't want to leave."

— 4½ Stars, RT Book Reviews

Dedication

For Audrey, and the rest of my second family while growing up—the Blakes.

I think of you all quite often, and have told my kids more stories than I can count…though, I'm not sure they believe half of them. Particularly, that infamous ride to school. God must have been sitting on the hood of the ol' LTD station wagon that day.

I've used Dawn dish soap (original blue) forever because it reminds me of Cathy, one of the most incredible—and unforgettable—ladies I've ever met, and who we lost way too soon. And Auddie, I know in my heart she's the reason Miranda looks more like you than me.

Thanks for the memories and an amazing childhood. And Cassie, thank you for your service.

In case you're wondering, yes, the Mudcat in this story is my little nod to that gentle beast who, with one welcoming lick, gave me nightmares for years.

Edited by Stacy D. Holmes
Cover art by The Killion Group
Formatted by Author E.M.S.

ISBN-13: 978-1499728958
ISBN-10: 1499728956

Published in the United States of America.

That Magic Touch

Lake Shelbyville Series, Book 1

Donna Marie Rogers

DONNA MARIE ROGERS

One

The crunch of tires on gravel had Jack Sutton glancing up from underneath the hood of the car he'd just topped off with antifreeze. He shielded his eyes against the glare of the mid-July afternoon sun as an unfamiliar black Ford pickup rolled to a stop at the top of the driveway, the front driver's side tire blown. Wiping his hands on a rag, he stepped out of the garage and watched with mild interest as a guy climbed from the truck, an adorable blonde pixie in his arms who couldn't have been no more than four or five years old.

He studied Jack with a pensive frown as he strode up, but an easy smile chased it away by the time he stuck out his hand. "Hey, how are you? My name's Kent, and this is my daughter, Zoe."

"Jack." He shook the guy's hand and winked at Zoe.

The doe-eyed youngster cast him a shy smile before burying her face into the crook of her father's neck.

He returned his attention to Kent and nodded toward the truck. "Blew a tire, hey?"

"Just down the road by the marina. I'm hoping the rumors are true about the garage being open for business again."

"Open a couple weeks now," he confirmed.

The little girl wriggled in her father's arm until he set her on her feet. A loud "*woof*" told Jack exactly what had captured her interest. The owners of the bait shop/convenience store next door had a monstrous black and tan English Mastiff named Mudcat, who loved kids almost as much as he loved chasing birds.

"Daddy, can I buy a treat?" she asked, her big brown eyes lit up with hope.

Kent hesitated. "I don't know. Last time you gave that poor dog an entire bag of potato chips, and he got sick as a...dog." He grinned. "They'll probably lock the doors when they see you coming."

She huffed out an exasperated breath. "Come on, I won't give him nothin'. I promise."

Her father gave in with a sigh and a reluctant nod. "All right. But only one treat or you'll spoil your supper." He pulled a five dollar bill from his pocket and handed it to her.

Zoe clutched it in her little fist and took off like a shot.

Jack smiled as he watched her cross the yard at warp speed, skidding to a stop to let Mudcat sniff her hand before skipping up the stairs and into the store.

After a bemused shake of his head, Kent turned to him and asked, "You must have met the sisters by now. What do you think? They seem nice enough to me, though my wife's convinced they're evil."

"I've been in the store a few times." He shrugged noncommittally. "Don't really know them that well." Jack cast a quick, inadvertent glance next door. Frankly, the sisters had always seemed rather normal to him. But then, he wasn't exactly a good judge of what constituted 'normal.' "Evil, huh?" A grin tugged at his mouth.

Kent let out a self-deprecating laugh. "Yeah, I know. Forget I said anything." He nodded toward his truck. "I was hoping you could check the front brakes for me as well. I noticed they were sticking some before the tire blew."

"Not a problem. You wanna back up so I can pull the Malibu out?"

"You bet. And thanks, I appreciate it."

Zoe returned just as Kent tossed him the keys to his truck.

"Milk Duds?" her father asked with a raised brow.

"Mia said they're her favorite." She held the box up and gave it a shake. "Want one?"

"No thanks. Those things get stuck in my teeth. But maybe Jack would?"

She cast him a shy smile and shook some out into her hand. When she held up her offering, he couldn't resist. He plucked one from her palm and returned her smile. "Thank you."

His enjoyment was short lived as he spied a police cruiser driving by at a snail's pace, the officer staring directly at him.

"Hey, George," Kent called out with a wave.

The officer nodded, gave Jack one last considering look, then drove off.

Great. Looked like Shelbyville's finest finally heard from his parole officer.

It was nearly seven-thirty by the time Jack closed shop for the night. And man, was he ready for it. He'd had a busy day, though most of his jobs had been oil changes, so he hadn't raked in much more than usual. He didn't mind the hard work, but it would be nice to have a bigger job come in once in a while, like replacing a carburetor or tranny.

With a yawn, he flipped off the lights, leaving only the overhead on above the back door. The garage was in need of a good sweeping, but exhaustion had settled into his bones, so he decided to leave it for morning. Hell, it'd be a miracle if he had enough energy to take a quick shower before crawling into be—

An arm wrapped around his neck and he was yanked back as something sharp plunged into his gut. Searing pain engulfed him, and a hard shove sent him crashing to the cold, concrete floor.

"You should've slit his throat," a croaky, male voice complained.

"He'll be dead in an hour," a second assured the first. "Come on. Help me get the cash register open."

Jesus, he was going to puke. *Concentrate, Sutton*, he thought, swallowing hard, choking down bile. He sucked in a breath, but the coppery smell of blood mingled with the noxious odor of gasoline made it worse. And holy hell…the burning in his gut was excruciating, as if he'd swallowed the fucking sun.

Jack lay still as death, praying the bastards would hurry the hell up. If he could crawl to the phone and dial 9-1-1, he might have a chance.

Holding down a groan, he squeezed his eyes shut and listened as his attackers struggled to get the cash register open. He would have laughed at their incompetence if every second didn't mean the difference between his own life and death.

His head spun and his world darkened. He teetered

on the brink of unconsciousness; the voices of his attackers becoming more and more distant. Jack fought with everything he had to remain conscious, but was quickly losing the battle.

The ring of the cash register opening reached his ears, and he nearly groaned his relief. He heard the distinct crinkle of paper as they cleaned the sucker out.

"Should we grab some new tires?" the deeper voice asked.

"Nah, this is good enough. The cops'll see the register open and figure the place got robbed."

Figure the place got robbed? If they weren't there to rob him, then *what* the fuck just happened?

Jack sucked in a shaky breath as he listened to their retreating footsteps, a glimmer of hope flaring to life.

When the back door slammed shut, he struggled to his hands and knees, squeezing his eyes tight as he fought the urge to vomit. Head hung low, he half-crawled, half-dragged himself to the desk, never imagining twenty feet could seem so damn far. He reached up and grasped the metal edge, somehow managing to pull himself to his knees. But as a wave of dizziness hit him, he had to lay his head down on the cool metal of the desk.

Come on, Sutton, focus, he silently commanded, summoning every bit of strength he could. No way in hell he survived seven years in prison only to go out like this.

He took a shallow, ragged breath, lifted his head, and reached out for the old, black-corded phone mounted on the wall. His fingers smacked the receiver hard enough for it to pop off the cradle and drop down to the desk. He fumbled for it, hooking the pigtail cord with his forefinger.

A chill wracked him; he laid his head down again as his strength waned. His knees buckled, and Jack crashed to the floor.

Just before he lost consciousness, he thought he heard an angel's voice calling to him.

"Hello? Jack, are you here?"

Mia Grey pushed the door open and cautiously crept inside the dimly lit auto garage. Her new neighbor had taken the place over a couple of weeks ago and usually closed up shop by now. So, when she happened to see two men slip inside the back door after taking a cautious look around, her hackles rose. When the same two men walked out less than five minutes later, stuffing cash into their front pockets, her uneasiness grew. Once they drove away, she decided to hurry over and investigate.

Mia barely knew the guy, only that he'd called Wisconsin home before moving down to central Illinois. But if she ignored her gut instinct and found out later he'd been injured or worse, she'd never be able to forgive herself.

And if she were letting her imagination run away with her, calling the cops would be a huge overreaction at this point.

She stepped in a small puddle pooling on the cement floor, and lifted her foot to examine her white tennis shoe—soaked red. And Mia was pretty darn sure it wasn't transmission fluid. She clapped a hand over her mouth to stifle a scream and sped up the search for her neighbor.

A faint beeping caught her attention. She listened

intently, trying to determine where the sound was coming from within the darkened bay. Following her ears, she gasped when she discovered him, lying still as death on the floor beside the counter. The beeping she'd heard a busy signal coming from the phone off its hook.

Mia rushed forward and dropped to her knees to feel his neck for a pulse. Weak and faint, but still there. *Thank god.*

Jack let out a low groan as she carefully searched for a wound, his handsome face drained of color.

"I'm sorry," she whispered. "I didn't mean to hurt you."

His eyes fluttered open and his lips moved. He probably meant to tell her where he was hurt. His shirt was soaked; he'd lost so much blood, it was a miracle he was alive, let alone able to speak. He tried to move his head, and she placed a gentle hand on his cheek.

"You need to calm down, okay? I can't help you until I figure out where you're bleeding from," Mia said.

He wore a black T-shirt and navy workpants. Locating the wound would be no easy task, especially with the only light coming from a dim, grime-encrusted overhead lamp that hung above the back entrance door. She skimmed her fingertips lightly across his midsection, sucking in a breath when they encountered the oozing, jagged cut.

Holy Mother, they stabbed him in the stomach!

"P-Please…help…9-1…1…"

Tears burned her eyes. No way would an ambulance make it there in time, and she certainly couldn't just let him die. But the alternative was unthinkable. If *anyone* were ever to find out…

Jack coughed and bloody spittle flew from his mouth, spraying across her hands and arms.

Tears spilled from the corners of her eyes as she wrestled with her conscience—and her demons.

She'd been drawn to the dark-haired brooder since the first time he'd walked into her bait shop, a little over a week ago. And it wasn't only his good looks that caught her attention. She'd sensed an odd sadness about him from the very first. He was polite and courteous to a fault, yet she'd never seen him smile. Not really.

He coughed again, the sound much weaker this time. Mia silently chastised herself for her wayward thoughts. She held this man's life in her hands and needed to make a decision.

Now.

She lifted his T-shirt, gently working it loose from the wound. Another moan escaped him, and she bit her lip as she slid the material up as far as possible without having to pull it over his head. The wound was barely visible in this lighting, but then it didn't need to be in order for her to help him.

Mia rubbed her cupped hands together to generate the initial warmth, then hovered both palms down over the torn flesh.

The first surge of heat nearly overwhelmed her. Sweat beaded across her brow, and then slid down her face in hot rivulets. She tilted her head back on her shoulders, closed her eyes, and concentrated. His injury was bad and would no doubt use up every ounce of strength she possessed.

The heat grew with intensity. Her hands were so hot, she could barely hold her fingers together. Jack groaned and became restless as his strength slowly returned.

Her head pounded. Burning up, she feared she might internally combust before she finished healing the wound. Her hair, face, neck and shirt were soaked with sweat, and she wasn't sure how much longer she could hold the connecti—

Jack lurched to a sitting position and gasped for air.

Mia flew back on her haunches, watching in fascination as he heaved one last breath, then collapsed back onto the floor. Scrambling to her knees, she checked his pulse, nearly crying her relief when she found it—steady and strong. Since he'd shifted positions, the faint light now shone dimly across his stomach, and she could clearly see the wound had closed. All that remained was a two-inch, jagged red line and a lot of dried blood. He was unconscious, but she was pretty sure now that he would live.

She hated leaving him there, lying on the cold, damp concrete, but she couldn't risk him—or anyone else—discovering her secret.

After making sure all the doors and windows were locked, Mia checked his pulse one last time, fought the urge to run a loving hand over the handsome face she dreamt about every night since he'd moved in, then slipped out the back door.

Drained, she kicked off her shoes and carried them home, making a mental note to toss them in the washing machine before her sister saw them. She was startled to find Katarina waiting expectantly on the back porch, arms crossed, her face hidden in shadow as the sun slowly disappeared behind the western horizon.

"I told you to stay in the house," Mia admonished, tossing her shoes aside in the grass before hurrying the fearless teenager inside. She shut and locked the door, twisted the mini-blinds closed after a quick peek outside, and collapsed against the door with a heavy sigh.

Eyes wide with curiosity, Katarina stepped forward and reached for the blinds.

She dodged in front of her. "Open those blinds, and you'll be grounded for a week."

"But you looked!" Kat angrily pointed out.

She steered her sister into the living room and settled her onto the threadbare, brown sleeper-sofa. The moody little stinker rolled her eyes, blew out a dramatic breath, and crossed her arms—as she always did when Mia intended to lecture her.

Well, too bad. This could very well be a matter of life and death.

"I don't want you stepping one foot outside until morning," she said. "Do you hear me?"

"What the heck happened?" Kat leaned forward, her blue-eyed gaze more concerned now than curious. "You tell me to wait inside for you, but then I see you sneaking out Jack's back door."

"I thought I heard something and went to check it out. That's all."

Miss Smarty Pants arched a disbelieving brow. "Yuh-huh. Nice try. Come on, Mia. I'm not a baby anymore. You can tell me." Her eyes lit up. "Did you kiss him?"

"Of course not! I…" She cleared her throat, collecting herself. "The back door of his shop was open, so I decided to make sure he hadn't forgotten to shut and lock it."

"I don't know." Kat eyeballed her with suspicion. "You're awfully freaked out over a door being left open. And you're sweating like a pig." Her eyes widened and her mouth dropped open; she shot to her feet. "Oh, my God, was he hurt? Did you have to—"

"No!" she quickly denied, stuffing her hands in her back pockets to hide the evidence.

Kat's eyes narrowed with suspicion. Mia sighed. Darn the kid's intuitive nature.

"Listen, I have some invoices to go over, and we both have to get up early tomorrow," she reminded her. "Why don't you run up and get ready for bed."

"I'm tired of you treating me like a baby," her sister pouted, arms crossed and hip cocked.

"You're thirteen years old, Kitty Kat. Still a baby in my book."

"I hate when you call me that," the young girl groused. She spun around and stomped up the stairs.

When her bedroom door slammed shut, a reluctant smile curved Mia's lips. *Such a little hothead*, she thought with a shake of her head. But just as fast, her smile faded. Kat's temper had already gotten her into trouble last year at school. Mia needed to make sure she learned to control it before summer was over—or next time she may not wait until her teacher's coffee cools before willing it into his lap.

With a sigh, Mia headed into the kitchen to put a cup of water in the microwave for tea…and scrub Jack's blood off her hands. An image of him lying still on the cold, cement floor brought on a wave of remorse. She wished she had been able to call him an ambulance once she'd healed his wound, but she couldn't risk bringing that kind of attention to herself. And she certainly didn't want to have to answer the many questions the EMTs—and the cops—would no doubt have for her.

She'd simply have to wait until morning and see if he made an appearance. If not, she would come up with a reason to go check on him.

Two

Jack awoke with a splitting headache and a churning stomach. He rolled to his side and pressed his forehead against the cool...concrete? Christ, he felt hung over. Odd, considering he hadn't had so much as a drop of alcohol.

With a groan, he sat up and leaned back against the desk. The coppery taste of blood filled his mouth; the urge to spit it out was strong. He closed his eyes and took a deep breath, trying to get his bearings.

A dull ache just above his bellybutton surprised him, and he lifted his shirt to investigate. But it was still dark out, and the overhead light was so damn grimy it made it impossible to see anything. He frowned, surprised to discover he'd torn his shirt and... Why did it feel so crusty?

He flexed his fingers, and felt something odd that had dried on his hands. What the hell had he been doing before he blacked out?

Climbing to his feet was no easy task, but somehow he managed. Jesus, he felt weak as a baby. He realized the phone was off its cradle a second before his gaze landed on the cash register—wide open and empty.

Sonofabitch, I've been robbed!

He flashed to the cop who'd driven past earlier and wondered if the good officers of Shelbyville had decided to try and scare him out of town. A stretch, he knew, but his trust in the law was nonexistent. Well, maybe with one exception.

Cursing under his breath, Jack dragged himself upstairs to his apartment, staggered into the bathroom, and flipped on the light. Holy shit, he was white as a ghost and...

What the hell?

His hands were covered in dried blood, as was his shirt. He stuck his fingers through the jagged tear in the cloth as his pulse kicked into overdrive.

Then he saw what looked like a scratch, about an inch and a half long, bright red and—he ran his index finger over it—the skin slightly raised, just above and to the left of his bellybutton. Had he attempted to fight the thieving bastards off? While he felt tired and weak, he didn't feel like he'd been beaten. He wracked his brain for any flash of memory, but came up empty. A quick glance at the clock on his nightstand told him it was four in the morning—he'd lost almost *nine* hours.

Frustrated, he braced his hands on the sink and squeezed his eyes shut.

Think, man.

It'd been about seven-thirty, and he'd just started to close up for the night when...when *what*, dammit? Why the hell couldn't he remember?

He washed the blood off his hands, stripped out of his clothes, and trudged into the kitchen to put on a pot of coffee. The cold air flowing out of the refrigerator felt good against his skin. Jack stood there for a moment, letting it wash over his naked body. He grabbed the can of coffee off the top shelf and started a pot brewing before jumping in the shower.

Fifteen minutes later, dressed in a gray T-shirt and jeans, he poured himself a cup of coffee and popped some bread in the toaster. Two cups and four slices later, his stomach finally settled, but his headache had worsened. He knew without looking he didn't have any aspirin.

The sun was just peeking over the eastern horizon when five a.m. rolled around. Recalling the convenience store would be open an hour early all week due to a fishing tournament, Jack stuck his wallet in his back pocket and gingerly made his way downstairs using the apartment's back entrance.

The sign in the shop's front window read OPEN, so he let himself inside and strode toward the register.

Mia, the older sister, crouched over a box that read Mepps-Worlds #1 Lure. She pulled out a handful of carded lures and began hanging them on hooks in the middle aisle. Jack tried not to notice how well she filled out a pair of jeans, but quickly lost the battle. She faced away from him, but he knew just how snug the baby-blue tank top would fit across her ample breasts. His hands flexed just thinking about them.

"Hi, Jack."

He turned and smiled at Mia's younger sister, Kat. She came around the counter to greet him, Mudcat right on her heels, tongue lolling and tail wagging. Jack didn't need to lean over to pat the massive dog's head. It was waist high on his six foot frame.

"Hey, boy. Protecting your ladies as usual, I see."

"*Woof!*"

Kat was a pretty girl with dark blonde hair, blue eyes,

and lots of freckles. He figured she and Mia must be half-sisters since their looks couldn't have been more different. Where Kat was adorable in an All-American way, Mia was so exotically beautiful she took his breath away.

His gaze was drawn back to her. Thick, near-black hair hung all the way down her back, while huge, amber-flecked, dark brown eyes seemed to bore straight into his soul. Her full, rosy lips, high cheekbones and perfectly sculpted nose made him suspect she might have some Native American blood in her, although with her alabaster skin it was hard to be sure.

"So, did you get robbed last night, or just forget to shut the door?" Kat asked, jerking his attention back to her.

Stunned, he could only stare at the young girl. Did she know something about last night? Before he could ask, Mia appeared at her side. She frowned at her sister, clearly upset by her question. Jack crossed his arms over his chest, waiting for one of them to elaborate.

Mia propped her hands on her hips and met his gaze. "You left your back door open last night, so I ran over to shut and lock it for you."

His gaze flickered down to her delectable mouth. He wanted to kiss her so bad he could taste it. He gave himself a mental shake and admitted, "I'm a little fuzzy on last night. If you know something, I'd be grateful if you filled me in."

She exchanged another glance with Kat who gave an apologetic shrug. Mia dropped her arms and walked behind the counter. "I already told you what I know." She poured herself some coffee and stirred in a healthy amount of powdered cream and sugar. "Would you like a cup?"

Jack cast a quick glance at Kat, who frowned openly at her older sister. Something was definitely going on here. He shook his head, wishing the fog would lift already. Maybe he'd figure it out once he got back to the garage. "Just some aspirin, please."

Mia plucked one of the packets of Bayer aspirin off the display behind her. She smiled at him, and his jeans suddenly felt two sizes too small. He shifted from one foot to the other in an effort to relieve the pressure, looking everywhere but at Mia as he paid for his aspirin, muttered a quick thanks, and hurried from the store.

Jack choked down the aspirin dry on his way back to the shop, anxious to take a closer look at the place. Stepping into the garage, the sun now shone in through the windows, and his gaze was drawn to the huge, dark red stain on the floor. *Blood. And lots of it.* A trail led over to the desk where he'd woken up, as well as several bloody footprints surrounding the area. Footprints from a shoe much smaller than his own.

Immediately dismissing the absurd notion that Mia could be his attacker, Jack lifted his shirt and examined his new scar. No way that much blood could've come from a scratch. He searched the entire garage for any other clues that might shed light on what had happened. Nothing. No body lying in the corner, no signs of a struggle other than the phone hanging off the hook.

Okay, so more than likely he'd wounded someone while they were robbing him. The money was a loss he could hardly afford, but no way in hell would he involve the police. He'd rather take his chances with the thief again than put his trust in the cops. Not that a repeat performance was likely. The thief had only gotten away with one day's earning, which couldn't have been more than a few hundred bucks. *And* had been seriously injured for his trouble. Jack ran his gaze around the shop, pretty sure nothing else had been taken.

Still weak and a bit shaky, it took him nearly forty-five minutes to mop up every trace of the blood. After checking to make sure both doors were locked, he headed upstairs to lie down.

Surprised to wake up three hours later, Jack rolled out of bed with a groan and dragged his ass into the kitchen to put on a fresh pot of coffee. His eyes landed on the letter sitting on the table, and he paused for a moment. The moment had definitely waited long enough—today would be the day he looked up his aunt, the only blood family he had. Or, at least, knew of. He'd read the letter he found in his mother's things so many times he knew it by heart.

Karen,

Please come home. This has gone on long enough. I know Mom and Dad have been horribly unfair to you, but if you would just bring that precious boy home to meet them, I know they'd fall in love with him. I have his sweet little face tacked up on the fridge, and mom stares at it every time they visit.

You can stay with Jerry and me until you get back on your feet. I already talked to him about it.

I miss you so much!

All My Love,
Patricia

Jack had no idea why his mother had left home, but

reading between the lines made one thing clear—he'd been the reason she'd stayed away. And since his mother had died a week after receiving the letter, Lord only knew if she'd ever planned on returning home to Shelbyville.

Or if *he* would still be welcomed with open arms.

Jack parked his old, light blue Buick LeSabre on the street and pulled the yellowed envelope from his shirt pocket. Forty-Four Twenty Forest Drive. He eyed the white Cape Cod-style house that stood at the end of the block, and blew out a hard breath.

He knew his aunt and uncle still lived there; he'd looked them up in the phone book his first night in town. He wondered if they knew his mother was dead, and had been for nearly twenty years. And if so, had they ever looked for him? Would they be happy to see him, welcome him into their family? Did they know he'd spent the last seven years behind bars? So many questions... Jack's chest tightened as he suddenly became overwhelmed with self-doubt.

Released from prison only a little over a month ago, he'd been working hard to get his life back on track. But being an ex-con meant people looked down their noses at you. So, it wasn't exactly a subject he planned using to start off the conversation. With any luck, his aunt and her family didn't know about his past, and he'd have a chance to get to know them—and for them to get to know him—before he dropped that particular bombshell.

He swung the car door open and stepped out into the glaring sunshine. Cupping a hand over his eyes, he admired the homey view. Hell, he could easily get used to small town living. The houses weren't built right on top of each other, and people took pride in their homes. The sounds of children's laughter, bicycle bells ringing, a basketball being dribbled down the street, and the loud hum of lawnmowers with the sweet smell of newly mown grass all made his chest ache in an unfamiliar way.

He returned his attention to his aunt and uncle's home just in time to see a little blonde girl, maybe five or six years old, dash out the front door, a young woman, around her mid-twenties and just as blonde, right on her heels. The woman frowned and shook her head at the little girl's antics as she ran circles around the lamp post on the manicure lawn. Jack froze as recognition dawned. The little girl was none other than Zoe, Kent's daughter. Did that mean…could Kent be his cousin? Cousin by marriage?

Heart thumping, he stretched his neck from side to side and started forward. He'd just reached the curb when the woman glanced up and noticed him. She gave him an uncertain once over, then grabbed Zoe's hand and yanked her to her side.

"Can I help you?" she asked.

He stopped several feet away, not wanting to frighten the woman. Before he could speak, Zoe squealed, "Jack!" and tried to break free to run to him, but the woman held firm, which he completely understood.

"Hey, kiddo, nice to see you again." He winked at Zoe before turning his attention to the woman. "Hi, I'm looking for Patricia Kingston. Is she home?"

Her curiosity evident in the slight narrowing of her

eyes, the woman nodded. "I'll go get her." She ushered Zoe into the house ahead of her.

Jack wasn't good at waiting, and at one point nearly raced back to his car and drove off like a coward. But the truth was, part of him craved a family connection—someone he could talk to who knew his mother. Someone to spend the holidays with, someone to share a meal with once in a while.

Someone who gave a damn whether he lived or died.

The front door opened again, and an older woman stepped out onto the porch. Her gaze landed on him, and her eyes widened as she covered her mouth.

His throat constricted. He swallowed past the lump and reminded himself to breathe.

Jack only had two pictures of his mother, and since she'd died before his eighth birthday, his memories of her were faded and few. But there was something so oddly comforting about seeing his aunt, it was a miracle his knees held up under the unfamiliar assault of emotions.

She moved her hand to her throat and called out, "Jackson?"

He nodded, tears burning his eyes. Only his mother had ever called him by his full name. Never had he missed her more than he did at that moment. Then again, seeing her sister was a little like having her back. He found himself craving his aunt's acceptance, her comfort, her understanding.

She reached up and swiped at her eyes before a beautiful, welcoming smile lit up her face. "You going to come give me a proper hello, or do I have to come down there and get you?"

Jack swallowed again and started toward her. He took

several tentative steps, until suddenly he was close enough to gaze into those warm hazel eyes—so much like his own.

With a soft cry, she wrapped her arms around him and whispered, "I knew you'd find us. I always knew you would." She pulled back and gazed up at him, that heartwarming smile returning. "You look like her. These gorgeous curls." She reached up and ran her fingers through his hair, which he knew needed a trim. "Those eyes. Actually, you look quite a bit like my own son, Kent. That was his wife, Sherry, you just met."

Yep, his cousin. Jack held his breath, afraid if he exhaled, a dam would burst. He'd been on his own for so long—no one to care about, no one to care about him—he never imagined he could feel such strong emotion. He wanted to crush her in his arms and never let go. But he'd never known affection like this and wasn't sure how to respond to it.

The last person he'd hugged had been his mother.

"I met Kent and Zoe yesterday. I'm renting Lindala's Auto Garage, and he needed a new tire."

Her eyes widened. "He mentioned that, but not that he'd met you."

"We didn't make the connection. At least, I didn't." Come to think of it, Kent *had* given him an odd look when he'd first laid eyes on him.

His aunt simply stared at him, as if overwhelmed by it all. Finally, she said, "I'm so sorry about your mother. I would've come for you, but we didn't find out about her passing until almost ten years ago. By then, we had no way of looking for you, and we didn't know anything about your father. The only person we knew to contact was your mother's...friend, Beverly. But when we tracked her down, she swore she had no idea where you were or what had happened to you."

That bit of news took him by surprise. "She was telling you the truth, sort of. I got in with a bad crowd once the foster system kicked me out. By the time I showed up on Beverly's doorstep, I had a rap sheet, a reputation, and an attitude, so she told me to get lost. Not that I blamed her."

Fresh tears pooled in his aunt's eyes, but she took a deep breath and smiled through them. "Well, that's all behind you now. You have family here, and I hope the fact you tracked us down means you plan to stay?"

"I…don't know. I hadn't thought that far ahead yet."

Aunt Patricia simply gazed at him. After a moment, she seemed to give herself a mental shake. "There's plenty of time to think about all that later. Can you come in and stay awhile? I'd love to chat, tell you about the rest of the family. Kent and his father are due home for lunch in about an hour. I've got a pot of homemade potato soup on the stove and bread just about to come out of the oven."

He hesitated. His aunt was clearly happy to see him, but would the rest of the family respond as well to his presence? Kent seemed like a decent sort, but then, he hadn't really known who Jack was yesterday when they met. "I don't know…I really don't want to intrude," he insisted. And then his stomach grumbled. Loudly.

A hopeful gleam lit his aunt's eyes. "Please, Jackson, you're already here. What could another hour hurt? And I do make a mean pot of potato soup."

Since he couldn't remember the last time he had a real home-cooked meal, Jack nodded and followed along without complaint.

Before he knew it, he was enjoying a second bowl of the thick, creamy soup while watching Zoe feed some to her doll. The kid was a sweetheart. He could watch her play for hours.

"Adorable, isn't she?" his aunt said as she refilled his coffee cup. "Yeah, I know I'm somewhat partial."

He smiled, still unable to believe he was here, in his aunt's home, being treated like one of the family. Common sense warned him not to get too comfortable, that it was only a matter of time before the novelty of finally meeting him wore off and they tossed him out on his ear.

"You mentioned other family?" he reminded her, anxious to learn if his grandparents were still alive.

"Oh, of course!" She hustled over to the fridge and plucked off a bunch of pictures, then sat down beside him and put them in some sort of order. "You have six cousins. Kent is our oldest, and he just turned twenty-eight. This is our daughter, Cassidy, who's the same age as you." She handed him a picture of an attractive young woman with shoulder length, light brown hair and light blue eyes. "She graduated from the University of Chicago Law School last year, and was immediately offered a position at a prestigious firm downtown," she informed him, pride radiating from her eyes.

She handed him another picture. "These are the twins, Kevin and Kyle. They're twenty-five and identical, as you can see. They're both firefighters. Kevin is in Rockford, and Kyle in Joliet."

She handed him a third picture, and this one stole his breath. The young woman staring back at him looked a whole lot like his mother, right down to the lop-sided smile he missed so much.

His aunt cleared her throat before continuing. "That's Chelsea. She's twenty-three and works at the grocery store with her father and brother. She's my wild child. Smart as a whip, but has no idea what she wants to do with her life. Likes to hang out at the marina on the weekends and party. I think she has eyes for one of the Winston boys. Their father owns the marina."

Aunt Pat handed him one last picture. "Dillon is our youngest. He's thirteen, and as you may have guessed, he was a bit of an *oops*." She chuckled softly. "Though the best kind. He really is a great kid."

Jack wondered if Dillon and Kat knew each other since they were about the same age.

"So, have you met anyone in town yet?" his aunt asked as he handed her back the photos. "I hadn't even heard Lindala's was open for business again, and usually word travels fast around here."

"Just the Grey sisters next door. They stock enough groceries for me to live on, so I haven't had much need to head into town yet."

Sherry strode into the kitchen at that moment, her pretty face screwed up with disapproval. "I'd stay away from those two if I were you."

After what Kent had shared, her advice was of little surprise. "Yeah? Why is that? They seem nice enough."

She cast a glance at Aunt Patricia, who simply shook her head as if to say, 'Not this again.'

Sherry gave a quick eye roll before meeting Jack's gaze. "Because there's something off about them. Ask anyone."

"Nonsense," his aunt scoffed. "They keep to themselves, and that's all it takes for silly rumors to get started. Those girls have never been anything but kind to me. And Zoe adores them."

Interesting. He'd definitely gotten the same strange vibe from the sisters that Sherry described, but still found himself intrigued by them. Particularly Mia, who'd had him tied up in knots since the moment he laid eyes on her. Not that she had any clue. Nor reciprocal interest, from what he could tell.

He glanced at Sherry and found her watching him with narrow-eyed intensity. Her expression cleared, and she smiled before quickly averting her gaze. Huh. Had she...had she been checking him out? He thought about it for a moment and almost laughed at his own ego. Probably she just didn't like him watching Zoe. Hell, she didn't know him from Adam.

The sound of a vehicle pulling into the driveway put Jack on alert.

Here we go—the moment of truth.

He heard male voices a few seconds before the back door swung open. Kent walked in, followed by an older man, both smiling. Kent stopped short when he spotted him, but the older man's smile faded. Uncle Jerry. And if the hardening of his jaw was any indication, he wasn't exactly happy to see his long, lost nephew.

Aunt Patricia raced forward and threw her arms around the older man's neck. "It's him, Jerry! Didn't I tell you he'd find us some day? Didn't I tell you?"

Jack stood as his newly found cousin stepped forward and held out his hand, his smile welcoming if somewhat startled. "Man, I knew there was something familiar about you."

He gripped Kent's hand and gave it a firm shake. Jack had become a decent judge of character over the years, learning to read people pretty well. And there was no doubt in his mind Kent was a good guy.

Aunt Patricia moved to the stove to dish up soup for her husband and son as they both took a seat at the table. Humming happily, she set a bowl in front of each of them.

His uncle didn't touch his soup. Instead, he propped his elbows on the table, clasped his hands together, and glowered across at him. Hell, Jack could feel the heat of the older man's displeasure as if it were a live thing.

"Daddy, Jack is our family. He made Nana cry happy tears."

Kent reached over and chucked Zoe under the chin. "I bet he did. He's our cousin, baby. Aunt Karen's son."

The little cutie smiled up at him and explained, "Aunt Karen is in heaven. Nana said she's an angel."

He returned her smile. "That she is, peanut."

Zoe's face lit up. "Hey, that's what daddy calls me! You kinda look like him."

"He sure does," Aunt Patricia agreed as she set a plate of fresh, sliced bread on the table.

"Handsome men run in this family," Sherry chimed in.

Although her tone had been teasing, he was starting to become uncomfortable under his cousin-in-law's watchful gaze—maybe his initial assumption had been right on after all. Jack got the distinct feeling all might not be well in his cousin's marriage.

Uncle Jerry still hadn't said a word. The older man continued to stare, making it painfully obvious he wasn't a welcome sight in his home. Of course, he could be reading too much into it. Maybe the guy was just the standoffish type. Jack couldn't blame him for that. He was a virtual stranger to these people.

Deciding he'd best make the first move, he stood and extended his hand. "Sir. I appreciate you welcoming me into your home."

His uncle eyed his outstretched hand with contempt.

Baffled, Jack dropped his arm, but remained standing.

"Zoe, honey," Sherry said. "Why don't you head upstairs and set up your Hungry Hippos game. I'll be right up."

"'Kay." Zoe grabbed her doll and skipped from the room.

"Jerry, what in the world is the matter with you?" Aunt Patricia hissed under her breath.

"Yeah, Dad. What the hell?" Kent said, leaning back in his chair.

The older man shot to his feet with a curse, shoving his chair back. "I don't shake hands with cold-blooded killers."

Three

"Jerry Kingston, have you completely lost your mind? You apologize to my nephew, and I mean right now." Aunt Patricia turned to him, shock and confusion reflected in her gaze. "I don't know what to say, I'm so sorry. I have no idea what this is all about, but—"

"He's a goddamn killer, Pat!" Jerry shouted. "Your precious nephew spent seven years in prison for murder. I don't want him in this house, with my kids and my granddaughter." With that, the older man swung his gaze to Jack and jabbed a finger toward the front door. "Get the *hell* out of my house, and don't bother coming back. You're not welcome here."

Aunt Patricia broke down in tears; Sherry stared in stunned silence, as if she'd never seen the old man's temper before.

Jack hung his head as he fought to get his own temper in check. *He* knew he was innocent, but it was still hard to have someone call him a killer, dammit, when he'd never hurt anyone.

His aunt met his gaze again. "Please…what your uncle says, it can't be true, right? There has to be more to the story."

Kent stood and faced his father. "How could you

possibly know that?" he asked, his voice soft. "You swore you couldn't find him, Dad. You swore to Mom, to all of us, that you couldn't find him."

The older man swiped a hand across his balding head, bristling with righteous indignation. "How was I supposed to tell your mother that her sister's boy turned out to be a killer? It would've broken her heart, and you know it."

Jack shot a quick glance at his uncle before returning his attention to his aunt. He hadn't wanted her to find out like this. Of course, he'd planned to tell her about his past. Eventually. Once they'd had a chance to get to know each other. But as usual, fate bit him in the ass, and here he was again, having to defend himself. The thought of watching the affection in her eyes turn to fear and loathing was enough to break his heart.

"It's true," he finally said. "I spent the last seven years in Green Bay Correctional…for murder."

"Oh, Jackson," his aunt whispered, fresh tears trailing down her cheeks. "Why?"

"I was set up. I didn't kill anybody."

Uncle Jerry's brows beetled as his scowl deepened. "You actually expect us to believe that?" He turned to his wife. "Look, I know this isn't easy to hear, but Karen's boy is a murderer. Just because he's your blood relation doesn't make him a good person. We can't have him around the kids, Pat. Or Zoe."

His aunt's eyes turned positively glacier as they landed on her husband. "You've known where he was all these years and never told me. How *could* you do that to me? How could you keep something that important from me?"

"Of course I didn't tell you! I knew it would break

your heart, finding out what a loser he'd turned out to be."

Jack's face grew hot as his anger surfaced. "You don't know a damn thing about me."

He had to get the hell out of there before he really lost his temper and made the situation worse—if that was even possible.

He met his aunt's distraught gaze. "I'm truly sorry. I never meant to cause you any grief." He flicked one last glance at his uncle before he spun around and strode from the house.

He'd just started the car when he noticed his cousin had followed after him. Kent placed his hand on the roof of the Buick and leaned in.

"Come on, man, don't leave like this. Don't do this to my mother. She doesn't deserve to have you walk out on her after all the years she's spent praying for you."

Jack leaned back against the headrest. "You heard your father. He doesn't want me in his home."

"You say you didn't kill anybody, and for what it's worth, I'm willing to reserve judgment. My father…well, he tends to be a bit overprotective when it comes to the family. As a father myself, I can understand. I'm sure he thought he was doing the right thing by keeping us in the dark about you."

"Maybe he's right," he murmured, staring through the windshield at nothing in particular. "Maybe it would've been better for everyone if I'd never come here."

"But you did come, and it's not like you can change history. So, unless you're a coward, you'll just have to stay and make the best of it."

Jack smiled up at his cousin with new respect. "You're a ballsy little shit, you know that?"

Kent chuckled. "You only have a couple inches on me, and believe me, looks can be deceiving. Take care of yourself, Cuz. I'll be in touch." He gave the roof of the car a slap and headed back to the house.

With a shake of his head, Jack put the car in gear and drove out of his aunt's neighborhood.

As he cruised through the quaint small town, admiring the picturesque scenery of lush trees and purple and yellow wildflowers, he decided his cousin was right. He hadn't come all this way only to run back to Green Bay with his tail between his legs when things got tough. He'd never intended to keep the truth about his past from them anyway. He just hadn't expected it to be tossed out in the open so soon.

But Jack had learned the hard way that life rarely worked out the way you expected it to.

As usual, it didn't take long for his thoughts to drift around to his beautiful and enigmatic neighbor. He didn't deserve a good woman like Mia, but it didn't stop his heart from racing or his body from reacting whenever she was in sight. *Hell*, he thought as his jeans grew snug in the crotch, just the thought of her was enough to evoke a response in him.

Looked like another cold shower was in order when he got home.

"He's got the hots for you. Anyone can see it."

Mia rolled her eyes as she tore open another case of root beer. Just what she needed, her baby sister trying to play cupid. Not that *she* hadn't had a few of those thoughts herself. But after last night, she decided Jack Sutton would be more trouble than she could handle.

Especially now with Kat coming into her full powers. It was all she could do to keep the temperamental little witch on the straight and narrow. If she let herself get distracted with their handsome new neighbor, Lord only knew what kind of trouble that girl could find herself in.

And Mia had no doubt there'd be trouble.

She finished stocking the soda cooler, then made some room on the shelves for the new line of crappie jigs that had just come in.

"Come on, Mia, I know you. You get all smiley and stupid whenever he's in the store. You have to be crushing on him, too."

She straightened, ignoring her sister's ramblings. "Can you please go make yourself useful and dig me out the box of extra pegboard hooks in back? I want to get these new jigs and lures out before we close tonight."

With a huff, little sister stomped off into the storeroom, Mudcat on her heels.

The bell above the shop's door jingled, and Mia glanced up to see a burly, graying, middle-aged guy wearing a limousine driver's uniform enter the shop. He headed to the back of the store for a couple of twenty ounce bottles of Pepsi, then grabbed a big bag of Doritos on his way to the register.

She slipped behind the counter and smiled as she rang up his order. "Five eighty-nine, please."

The man's gaze was glued to her chest, and she did an eye roll as she accepted his money. Holding his change up at eye level, she nearly laughed aloud when he met her gaze and turned beet red. She dropped his change into his hand and watched him scurry from the shop. *Perv.* With a shake of her head, she went back to filling shelves.

Kat emerged from the storeroom and handed her the box of hooks she'd asked for. "Hey, there's a limo parked in Jack's driveway," she said, her voice laced with excitement. "Think it's someone famous?"

Mia shrugged. "Maybe. Maybe not." She fished around for hooks of the same size. "We drove around in limos, and we're not famous."

"Yeah, but Mom was."

"Woof!"

Mudcat's nails clacked on the tile floor as he lumbered toward the back entrance. He tried to twist the knob with his mouth, as he always did, with no success.

"Can you *please* let that monster outside so he can take care of business? And don't forget to wipe his drool off the doorknob."

"She didn't mean it, boy," Kat assured the dog as she let him outside. With a smirk, she added, "She's just crabby 'cause she's too chicken to admit she likes Jack."

"Kitty Kat, if you're bored, the dead minnows need to be scooped out of the tanks. There's a sink full of dishes waiting for you at home, too."

With a disgusted *tsk* of her tongue, her little sister slammed out the back door.

"Please, God," Mia muttered as she tore open a small box of lures, "when the time comes, don't let her period run the same week as mine."

The tournament started Friday, but anglers would be arriving all week long, so she wanted to make sure she carried every lure, jig, and rig available. She also had every pound test line the fishermen could want, from eight up to thirty. She'd even stocked a few extra rods and reels, which she normally didn't do since the sporting goods store in town sold them cheaper than she could. But during a tournament, everything sold. Mia planned to use the extra money she brought in over the next week to buy Kat a new wardrobe for school.

She rarely spent money keeping her little sister in the latest fashions, but Kat would be in eighth grade this year, and Mia knew how important wearing the right clothes was to a young girl. Especially since Kat seemed to have trouble making friends. God, what she wouldn't give to have their mother's guidance right now—she'd never missed her more.

The bell above the door jingled again, and she watched as a distinguished-looking gentleman wearing an impeccably tailored, three-piece, navy suit entered the store. His thinning blond hair didn't detract from the incredibly handsome face beneath. He stopped and peered around in dismay until his sharp blue gaze landed on her.

"May I help you?" she asked.

He strode forward and studied her from head to toe. Mia cocked a brow but remained silent.

"I've been waiting almost an hour for a Mr. Jack Sutton to make an appearance. I don't suppose you know when he's due to return?"

She shrugged one shoulder. "I didn't realize he'd left, but then he doesn't clear his schedule with me."

The gentleman's lips twitched. "I see." He extended his hand. "John Whitlow."

"Mia Grey." She held out her own, surprised when instead of shaking it, he grasped it and brought it to his lips.

"A lovely name for a lovely young woman."

He didn't seem to want to let go of her fingers. Mia cleared her throat and gently extricated her hand from his grip. He was a good-looking guy, no doubt about it. A little old for her, but she was flattered by the attention nonetheless. "I... Thank you."

"My pleasure."

She waited for him to say something else, but he remained silent.

"Mr. Whitlow, I don't mean to sound rude, but I have no idea where Jack is, or when he'll be back. And I have a lot of work to get done before closing time."

"Oh." He blinked, and his smiled faltered. "I'm sorry. I didn't mean to stand here gawking at you, taking up your time." He glanced around again. "I actually came in to use your restroom."

Anxious to get back to work, she pointed toward the hallway between the soda cooler and magazine racks. "First door on the left."

His smile returned. "Thank you."

No sooner had the restroom door closed behind him than Kat rushed in the back door, Mudcat on her heels. "Hey, that limo's still sitting there, and Jack isn't home. Wonder where he is, huh? Think they're there to finish the job they started last night?"

She hurried over and shushed her loose-lipped sister, then gestured toward the restrooms and whispered, "He's in the bathroom."

Her sister's eyes rounded with excitement. "Really? Oh, my God, this is awesome."

Mia shook her head, then motioned for her to get behind the register. After gathering up the empty boxes and wrappers, she said, "Stock the batteries and the lake maps, would you? I have to figure out how I'm going to squeeze in one more row of hooks."

"Think he's famous?" Kat asked right as the men's room door opened and Mr. Whitlow stepped out.

"Not in the traditional sense, I'm afraid," he said with a bit of a flourish. "But in the business world, I'm the equivalent to The Rolling Stones."

"As if anyone under sixty even knows who they are," Kat informed him with crossed arms.

"Katarina Alexis, you apologize right now, or you can march your butt next door and stay in your room until you learn how to speak to people with respect." She turned to face Mr. Whitlow, mortified. "I'm sorry. She's...a teenager."

"You don't look much older than that yourself," he informed her through kind eyes.

"Geez, I was kidding," the moody little witch grumbled with an exaggerated roll of her eyes—something Mia was getting awfully tired of seeing. "Can't anyone take a joke?" She stormed out the front door, but not before a boxful of candy bars flew off the shelf and crashed to the floor.

Mia just barely held on to her composure. She bent down to pick them up, praying Mr. Whitlow didn't question how it happened.

"She's a firecracker, that one," he commented as he knelt down to help her.

"With a short fuse, unfortunately." She set the box back on the shelf with a sigh of relief. She had no idea how she was going to rein in that girl's temper. "Thank you. And again, I'm sorry."

He waved it off. "My own fault. I should've said Michael Jackson." An oddly familiar smile lit up his face. "Take care of yourself, Mia Grey."

Well, that was interesting, she thought as he exited the store. With another shake of her head, she returned to her display hooks.

Jack spotted the limo sitting in his lot as soon as he turned onto his block. He drove up the driveway and parked beside it. The driver stood outside, leaning against the door, munching on a bag of chips or something. Jack got out and walked around to greet him.

"Can I help you?"

The guy frowned, then cleared his throat. "You Jack Sutton?"

"That's me. What can I do for you?" He eyed the car, which didn't seem to be sitting at an angle, so he ruled out a blown tire. The engine wasn't smoking either.

The driver set the bag down on the hood and dusted off his hands before opening up the left-side passenger door.

Jack watched as some dude in a monkey suit stepped out. The man straightened his tie, then met his gaze, his expression inscrutable. Besides his three-piece suit, he wore a pair of shoes Jack would bet cost as much as his car was worth. Not that his car was worth all that much.

The guy studied him from head to toe, making him feel like an animal on display at the zoo. There was something oddly familiar, although for the life of him, Jack couldn't place him.

"Is there something I can do for you?"

The older gentleman cast a quick glance at his driver before gesturing toward the garage. "Would it be all right if we went inside to talk?"

Jack paused. He reached up to finger his new scar, and his hackles rose. "Whatever you have to say, you can say it right here."

"It's personal. I'd appreciate not having an audience, if you don't mind."

The man nodded toward the bait shop, and Jack turned to see the younger Grey sister and her monster of a dog sitting on the porch, both watching with interest. He smiled, and Kat did a finger wave, a mischievous grin curving her lips. Mudcat barked.

"Fine. You've got ten minutes." He motioned them both inside.

Once the door swung closed, the driver leaned against it and crossed his arms over his chest, like he was standing guard or something. The older guy walked in and turned a full circle, as if taking it all in and passing judgment in one quick sweep.

"Not much, is it?" he said.

Jack cocked a brow. "It's an auto garage. What were you expecting, lace curtains and doilies?"

"I'd just hoped for better for you." He swiped a handkerchief across the torn, black vinyl chair next to the desk before taking a seat.

Jack shook his head, bemused. "I'm touched. Look, I have work to do, so can we get to the point here? Who are you, and what do you want?"

He did the stare thing again, and Jack's uneasiness grew.

"You must look like your mother," the guy finally remarked.

"All right," Jack muttered, ready to throw the two of them out. "I've had enough of this creepy shit. You either tell me who you are, or get the hell out of my garage."

"Calm down, pup," the driver said, dropping his arms. "And when you speak to Mr. Whitlow, it had better be with respect, or I'll pull you across my knee."

Jack stared in stunned silence for a moment, then let out a bark of laughter. "You lay one hand on me, and they'll have to carry you out on a stretcher. Now, both of you, get the fuck out before I call the cops."

The driver took a menacing step forward, but the older guy must have sent him a signal, because he stopped in his tracks.

"Jack, I'm not here to cause you any trouble," Whitlow assured him. "I just wanted to meet you. See what you're like. Maybe get to know you."

"Good God, would you quit talking in riddles already? I'll ask one more time, nice and slow so you understand. Who the hell are you?"

"I'm your father."

Four

Jack had to have heard him wrong. "Come again?"

"I said I'm your father."

Adrenaline surged through his body, and it was all he could do to keep from tossing them both out on their asses. After the shitty reception from his uncle, he needed this like he needed a hole in the head.

He jabbed a finger toward the door. "Get the hell out of my shop." He had no idea what kind of game they were playing, but his father was dead. He'd died in a car accident before Jack was born.

"Son, you're signed up with the registry, so I assumed you knew."

"Don't call me son, my—" He paused, frowning. "Signed up with *what* registry? What are you talking about?"

The two men exchanged glances. The driver shrugged.

"Jack," Whitlow began, "back during my college days, kids that came from prominent families, especially those with high GPAs, were…encouraged to make sperm donations."

Unable to believe what he was hearing, he could only stare at the guy. A sperm donor? Bullshit. His father was dead. Why would his mom and Beverly have lied about that? And if they *had* lied, why a sperm donor? His mother had barely been in her twenties when he was born. Not exactly someone at the point in her life of wanting to start a family—or needing help to do it.

He gave himself a mental shake and stalked over to the mini refrigerator in the corner to grab a can of orange soda. He cracked it open and drained most of it in one long gulp before turning back to face the man who claimed to be his father. "There has to be a mistake."

The older man gave his head a sad shake. "I'm sorry if this isn't exactly good news, but there's no mistake. Though we'll need to take DNA tests to make it legal."

"Make what legal?"

"To make you my legal heir. You're a Whitlow, son. A member of one of the oldest and richest families in the state of Wisconsin. Hell, in the entire country. You stand to inherit a great fortune."

Jack suddenly felt light-headed. "I don't want a damn thing from you," he snapped, angry as hell. If this man's story was true, then...then his mother had lied to him. But why? It didn't make a damn bit of sense. *No.* Whitlow had to be mistaken. He'd simply mixed Jack up with someone else.

"Look, I don't know anything about this registry, but what you say can't be possible. My father's dead and has been for years."

"Your mother's name was Karen Lawson, correct?"

At his hesitant nod, Whitlow continued. "Then there's no mistake. One of my donations went to a woman named Karen Lawson from Green Bay, Wisconsin. Less than two years later, she listed a Jackson Curtis Sutton with the registry. There's only one

41

reason she would do that. So if we ever chose to, we could find each other."

"Yeah?" Jack crossed his arms over his chest. "So, why today? Why now? You must have plenty of"—he made air quotes—"legal heirs of your own by now. And if you truly are my father, and you're as rich and influential as you claim, why the hell did it take you twenty seven years to find me?"

Whitlow shot a look at his driver, who remained stone-faced. Whitlow sighed. "Because I only decided to look into my donations about a year ago."

"Guess you were pretty damn surprised to find me rotting in prison." Bitterness laced his words, but he didn't care. If all of this was true, then he didn't know what the fuck to believe anymore. His whole life had been one big goddamn lie.

"Of course I was. But I read the court transcripts, and I have no doubt you were set up by that dirty cop, just as you claimed. It kills me when I think about everything you've been through over the years. If I'd just..." Whitlow stopped and blew out a hard breath; he hung his head for a moment. When he met Jack's gaze again, he said, "Thankfully, my lawyers were able to get your parole hearing moved up."

Jack froze as he absorbed that bit of information. He *had* wondered why his parole hearing got moved up a couple years, though he hadn't been foolish enough to ask. They'd released him, and getting out of that stink hole with his sanity intact had been the only thing that mattered at the time. But now...

Could this absurd story be true? He'd never been one to believe in coincidence. But then the question remained: why had his mother lied to him about his father?

A thought suddenly occurred to him, his suspicion piqued. This was a set up, it had to be. He walked around, peering up into every shadowed corner of the garage, into every light fixture, every dark space.

"What are you doing?" the driver asked, glancing around himself.

"Looking for the cameras. This is that *Punk'd* show, right?"

The driver gave a dismissive wave of his hand. "That show's not even on anymore. Besides, they only 'Punk'd' famous people."

Jack stopped and eyed them both. "*Candid Camera*?"

"Nope," the driver said. He scratched his forehead. "That's not on anymore either…is it?"

"No idea," Whitlow replied with a shrug.

"All right," he said. "This crazy conversation is over. Now, for the last time, I have things to do." He strode over to the door and yanked it open.

"Jack, this is no joke. According to the registry, I'm your biological father. I assumed you knew how you were conceived, or I wouldn't have blurted it out like that. But the fact remains you *are* my son."

"Even if it is true, so what? What did you expect would happen by coming here? That I'd throw my arms around you and call you daddy? That we'd start going to ballgames, spend the holidays together?"

"I just thought—"

"Because it ain't gonna happen. Maybe if you'd shown up twenty years ago when I needed…" He took a deep breath and swiped his fingers through his hair, gathering his composure. "I've gotten along just fine without you 'til now, so why don't you hop back in your limo and head the hell home. I have no interest in you or your money."

Whitlow gestured to his driver to leave, who then eyeballed Jack before walking out.

"You *are* my son," the man reiterated, as he turned to face him. "And I'm truly sorry I wasn't there for you when your mother passed, or when...well, when you needed me the most. But I'm here now. If you need anything, don't hesitate to contact me." He tucked a business card in the pocket of Jack's T-shirt, and then walked out the door.

Jack blew out a hard breath, closed his eyes, and stretched his neck from side to side. He had no idea what to think or how to feel about the man.

His mother had gone to a sperm bank to get pregnant?

He simply couldn't wrap his mind around it. She'd only just turned twenty-two when she'd had him, so he'd always assumed he'd been an accident. The reason she'd left home.

But if Whitlow was telling the truth—and Jack suspected that he might be—that meant he'd been planned. But again, why? With any luck, his aunt would have some answers for him, though he'd definitely need to let things cool down there before he contacted her again.

Monday morning started with a bang as three cars arrived promptly at eight a.m. for service. Five oil changes, two brake jobs, a tune-up, and a blown radiator hose later, Jack found himself once again in need of aspirin. The surge of business had been welcome considering the money he'd lost during the robbery, but he still wasn't feeling a hundred percent. By the time his last customer pulled away, he was more than ready for a break. And some lunch. Mia kept the store coolers and freezers well-stocked, and a frozen pizza sounded like heaven right about now.

As he approached the front door, he thought he heard the sisters talking near the back of the building. He switched course and made his way down the gravel path that led to the back entrance. His steps faltered when he saw Mia kneeling on the ground, eyes closed, her hands hovering over something. He crept in closer...a dead bird? What in the world was she doing?

"Come on, Mia, hurry up," he heard Kat urge in a loud whisper.

Jack craned his neck and realized the younger sister was sitting on the back porch, her chin propped in her hands. He swung his attention back to Mia, who had yet to say a word. She just held her cupped hands over the bird and concentrated on whatever the hell she was doing. She knelt under the shade of a stand of tall pines that surrounded the back of the store, but he could see she was sweating so hard it rolled off her nose.

Suddenly, the bird chirped and hopped to its feet, flapping its wings before flying up into the tree. Mia fell back on her haunches and blew out a hard breath.

Shock kept him rooted to the ground. What kind of weird shit had he just witnessed? If he didn't know any better, he'd swear it looked as though she'd brought that bird back to life. But that was impossible...wasn't it?

Christ, this is turning out to be one strange fucking week.

Kat hopped off the porch and hurried to her sister's side. "You all right?"

Mia nodded before climbing slowly to her feet. She wiped her palms on her jeans, then let out a whopper of a sigh. "I'm fine. Get back in the store in case a customer walks in, will you?"

"Fine. Geez." Kat hurried up the back porch, but stopped to add in a heartfelt whisper, "Thanks, Mia," before rushing into the shop.

Stunned, Jack crept quietly back around to the front of the building and entered through the front door. He had no idea what he'd just witnessed, and frankly, he wasn't sure he wanted to know. But it couldn't be what he thought because that was just...*crazy*.

"Hi, Jack." Kat waved from behind the counter, all adorable smiles.

"Hey, Kat." He headed to the back of the store and grabbed a couple of bottles of apple juice, a frozen sausage and cheese pizza, and a half-gallon of milk. He passed Mudcat, who was lying on his side in front of the ice cooler, and stopped short when he realized the big guy didn't look so good. He was panting heavily, his eyes wide open, and... Ah, hell, the poor thing. He'd had an accident all over the floor.

"Kat, can you do me a favor and get your sister for me, please?"

"'Kay."

He quickly put his items back, then knelt beside the dog to give it a gentle stroke. "Don't worry, boy, you're gonna be fine."

The back door opened. "Jack?"

"Over here by the ice cooler. Is Kat with you?"

"No, I asked her to go check on my spaghetti sauce. What's going on?" Mia's eyes widened when they landed on Mudcat. She dropped to her knees beside him. "Oh my God…is he…?"

"He's breathing, but we'd better get him to the vet. I just hope I can lift him."

"You'd have to be Superman to lift him off the floor by yourself. He weighs almost two hundred and thirty pounds. Let me prop the door open, then I'll help. Together, hopefully, we can get him out to my car."

Once she returned, he had her grasp Mudcat under his head and shoulders while he took most of the mammoth dog's weight in back. They managed to lug him outside; he eyed Mia's car, which was little bigger than a go-cart.

"I think we'd better put him in my car, if you can make it that far?"

She nodded, the strain of holding the massive dog's weight evident only in the tightening of her lips. Though Jack was in awe of Mia's physical strength, he hated that he needed her help in the first place.

Mudcat let out a low groan as they carried him across the lawn to Jack's driveway. He somehow got the rear passenger side door open with one finger, and they settled the beast in the backseat of his old Buick as gently as possible.

"Why don't I run him to the vet while you get the floor cleaned up and close shop? Then I'll run back to pick you guys up."

She met his gaze. "How will you get him inside?"

"I'm sure there's someone there who can help."

"I don't know what to say. That's awfully generous of you."

He shrugged. "Kat loves this dog, anyone can see that."

"Still, you barely know us, so this is above and beyond. I want you to know how much I appreciate it."

Jack gave a quick nod as an unfamiliar emotion formed a lump in his throat.

"The vet's about five miles down the road on the left side of the street. Just past Bull's Pub," she explained. "It's a brand new facility with a huge sign, so you can't miss it."

He shut the door and climbed into the driver's seat. "I'll be back as soon as I can."

"Thanks, Jack. We'll be waiting."

His chest tightened with longing as he watched her race back to the shop. He pulled out of the parking lot.

She's out of your league, Sutton. The sooner you realize that, the better.

Mia sniffed back tears as she cleaned up Mudcat's 'mess,' feeling miserable for not having found him first. If only she'd come across the poor thing before Jack had, she could have healed him. Now, she'd just have to wait and pray that he was all right.

"Hey, what's going on?" Kat demanded when she returned from the house. She stopped short and wrinkled her nose. "And what's that nasty smell?"

After one last swish of the mop, Mia propped it in the bucket and met her sister's anxious gaze. "Honey, Mudcat had an accident. It wasn't his fault, but I think he's sick. Jack ran him to the vet while I got the mess cleaned up. He'll be back any minute to pick us up."

"You mean he puked? 'Cause it was probably just that raw hamburger you gave him last night."

She frowned. "I'd never give Mudcat uncooked meat. When did you see him eating raw hamburger?"

"Last night after supper. Remember, he wouldn't come in right away when I called him?"

Before she had a chance to think on it, the bell over the front door jingled and Jack stepped inside. "Ready?"

Making a mental note to question her sister later, Mia nodded and escorted Kat from the store, locking the door behind them.

"Ibuprofen?" Mia repeated, confused.

"Yes. Advil and Motrin are the most common brands. Mudcat consumed at least thirty tablets." Dr. Miller wrote something down, then smiled reassuringly. "He'll need to stay overnight for observation. Luckily, he's a big boy, so he'll be fine. Probably won't eat much for a day or two, but I don't believe he suffered any permanent damage."

Mia stood and smiled at the kindly older gentleman. "Thanks, Dr. Miller. What time should we come pick him up?"

"Let's say ten a.m. If I feel he needs to stay another night, I'll call. And for future reference, make sure you keep your meds up high."

"We'll certainly do that," she assured him. "Thanks again."

They were in Jack's car on the way home when Kat said, "Mia, why didn't you tell him about the hamburger?"

Jack cast her a curious glance. "What hamburger?"

Good question. One she wished she had an answer

for herself. "Kat thinks she saw Mudcat eating raw meat last night."

"I don't *think*, I know. There was a huge pile of it in his dog bowl. And why didn't you tell Dr. Miller we don't have any medicine in the house? Just Tums and that old bottle of pink stuff." Kat turned her attention to Jack. "Mia doesn't keep pills in the house because our mom—"

"Because our mom didn't either," she quickly chimed in, cutting her sister off before she opened a can of worms Mia wasn't ready to explain. "Old habits."

"Oh, my God," her sister exclaimed as she suddenly clutched onto Mia's shoulder. "I know who gave Mudcat the hamburger and pills! That nasty Mr. Bilsky down the road. How much you wanna bet?"

Jack glanced at Kat through the rearview mirror. "Why would anyone want to harm your dog?"

"He keeps accusing Mudcat of pooping on his lawn, but he's the one who's full of shit."

"Katarina!" Horrified, Mia cast Jack a sidelong glance, but he appeared to be fighting back a grin.

An overwhelming urge to feel those full lips on her own caught her off-guard, warming her from the top of her head to the tips of her toes—and everywhere in between. She gave herself a mental shake. The last thing she needed in her life right now was a distraction. No matter how tempting that distraction might be.

"Well, it's true," her sister insisted. "Mudcat never goes on his property."

"I'm not arguing with you, Kitty Kat. But it takes a real sicko to purposely harm an innocent animal. Mr. Bilsky, though odd, seems like a decent guy. He just likes his lawn…poop free."

She cast Jack another quick glance. His small grin had turned into a full-blown smile. Lord, the man was gorgeous.

"Whatever." Kat sat back with a huff.

"We'll have to be more watchful," she added, ignoring her sister's temperamental attitude. "Though it was probably just some neighborhood punks on a dare."

Or a couple of thieves trying to clear the way for a break in.

As soon as they pulled into Jack's driveway, Kat unbuckled her seatbelt and leaned over his shoulder. "Hey, wanna have supper with us tonight? Mia's making spaghetti, and it's really good."

She just managed to hold back a groan. Not that she didn't at least owe the man a meal. But spending time with him was starting to do funny things to her libido. And Kat, darn her keen nature, was already convinced of a mutual attraction between them.

Jack cast her a searching glance, and Mia wasn't sure if he was looking for her approval, or a way out.

"Sounds great, but it's been a long day," he said. "Maybe I should take a rain check."

"Come on, you have to eat. And Mia made enough sauce for freezing, so there's plenty. And we have garlic bread and salad and—"

"Kat, it's not polite to put Jack on the spot. Like he said, we can do it another night, when he's up to it."

"Actually," he countered, those incredible hazel eyes brimming with anticipation and…mischief? "I love spaghetti. If you really do have enough, I'm up to it."

"We have plenty," her matchmaking little sister assured him before she could respond. "Dinner's already late, so we'll probably eat as soon as we get home. Right, Mia?"

She barely managed a nod. A tidal wave of conflicting emotions welled up at the thought of sharing a meal with this man; a meal she'd prepared. Part of her yearned to sit across the table from him while he enjoyed the homemade sauce she'd put so much time and effort into. Which seemed silly, really. Good Lord, it was just spaghetti, not an actual date or anything. On the other hand, every minute she spent in his presence put her one step closer to falling for him.

And *that* was something she definitely wasn't ready for.

"God, what's the big deal? Why do you have to make such a case out of everything?"

Mia blew out a frustrated breath as she smeared the split loaf of French bread with garlic spread. "Kat, you know I have a big day tomorrow. I'd planned to soak in a hot bath tonight and head to bed early."

"So? You can still do that. He's just coming for supper, not to spend the night." Her eyes narrowed. "Unless, of course, you want him to. I bet Jack would be more than happy to wash your back for you."

"You say one more ridiculous word and you can march right next door and cancel. I'm tired, I'm sore, and I don't need any smart mouth from Miss Thirteen-Going-On-Thirty."

"You're also PMSing," Kat muttered under her breath.

"I warned you, kid."

"I'm sorry, okay? It's just...I like Jack. He's nice, and he doesn't treat me like some stupid little kid."

"I'd treat you more like an adult if you acted like one. If you're not giving me attitude about every little thing, you're complaining about your chores, or about how much TV time you get, or—"

"Okay, okay, I get it." Kat huffed her hair out of her eyes. "Can we please just act normal while he's here? I don't want to scare him off."

A grin tugged at Mia's lips. "Act normal? You *do* realize he's too old for you, right?"

Her little sister rolled her eyes so hard it was a miracle they came back down. "Don't be gross."

"Just checking. I've never seen you act this way before."

"What way?"

Mia did a one-shoulder shrug. "I don't know. You pretty much hate everyone you meet."

"Do not!" Kat hotly denied.

She cocked a brow, and the little stinker surprised her with a soft chuckle.

"Well, most of the boys my age are morons, and most of the girls are stuck-up snobs."

Softening her tone, Mia said, "You have to give people a chance, Kat. Quit making snap judgments about everyone, and maybe you'll make some friends."

"Whatever."

Her sister's comeback lacked its usual indifference, and Mia knew she'd struck a nerve. The world was a lonely place without friends, and a young woman Kat's age should have many. But she needed friends her own age, not a twenty-something grown man.

A breathtakingly handsome grown man, with a lean build, rock-hard muscles, and gorgeous hazel eyes that seemed to see straight down into her very soul—

"Hey, Sis, wanna join me back on planet earth?" Kat teased, waving her hand in front of Mia's face.

She cleared her throat and stuck the garlic bread in the oven. "Why don't you set the table while I cook the pasta?"

Ten minutes later, she was pulling the garlic toast from the oven when a knock sounded at the back door.

Kat rushed over and swung it open. Jack stood on the porch looking gorgeous as ever. He'd showered and changed his clothes, and Mia had to force her attention back to putting supper on the table.

"Come on in," Kat said, her tone bordering on giddy. "Everything's ready."

He nodded and glanced around. "Nice place. Homey."

"Yeah, well, *someone's* obsessed with butterflies."

Mia held back a grin over the disgust in her sister's tone. As if an affinity for butterflies was a shameful secret or something.

"Thanks for having me over. I'll have to return the favor sometime." Jack closed the door behind him and held out his hand.

He'd brought flowers—a beautiful mix of daisies, zinnias, and carnations—and her insides warmed with pleasure. Charmed by his shy smile, she accepted the gift and brought them to her nose for a quick whiff. "You can cook?"

He grinned. "Not sure."

Wow, his smile was just as potent the second time. "So, we'd be your guinea pigs?"

"Pretty much."

They gazed at each other until Kat took the flowers

from her hand. "Better get these in a vase. Jack, you can sit at the head of the table."

Mia bit the inside of her cheek to keep from laughing. They had a square table with four chairs.

He took the seat across from the empty place setting. She and Kat finished setting the food on the table, sat down in their usual spots, and they all dug in. The fresh aromas of basil and garlic made the room smell heavenly. And having Jack there made the meal that much tastier.

Twenty minutes and two helpings later, Jack wiped his mouth on a paper napkin and set it on his plate, which he'd scraped clean. "That was the best meal I've had in a long damn time." His aunt's potato soup had also been delicious, and certainly a close second, but in Jack's book, nothing beat a good spaghetti dinner. It was the one meal he remembered his mother making for him.

"Well, thank you. Though I doubt it's true, I appreciate the compliment." Mia cleared his plate away and replaced it with a cup of coffee and a slice of apple pie a la mode. "Mrs. Smith's," she admitted, her smile sheepish. "But I took it out of the box and baked it all by myself."

"Smells like heaven. Thank you, Mrs. Smith."

She met his gaze with a soft laugh.

Jack had never been more grateful to be seated. He couldn't take his eyes off of her. As usual, she looked incredible, with her silky black hair pulled into a pony tail and a sexy pair of large gold hoops hanging from her dainty ears. He noticed she'd also put on make-up, which she normally didn't wear in the store. Her eyes seemed deeper and darker than usual, her lashes fuller. Those luscious lips sparkled and shined.

He'd like to think she'd gone to the trouble just for him. But he hadn't exactly gotten any 'I'm interested' vibes from her. And why would he? Mia Grey was completely out of his league; way too good for an ex-con like him. Not that it stopped him from longing...

A loud crash out back exploded like a gunshot in the silent kitchen. Jack dropped his fork and shot to his feet. "You both stay inside. I'll go check it out."

They nodded as Mia put a comforting arm around her sister's shoulders.

He opened the door and peered into the darkness before cautiously slipping outside. At the bottom of the porch, he found the culprit—an overturned metal garbage can. *Probably knocked over by a hungry animal rummaging for supper.* Just to be safe, he headed a little farther down toward the dock, scanning the area for anything suspicious.

Water lapping against the pier and chirping crickets were the only sounds to break the calm serenity of the evening. A faint sweetness wafted past on a slight breeze—the red flowers Mia had planted along the edge of the property...petunias, he thought she called them. He gazed across the lake into the darkness, but couldn't make out anything other than a few distant lights. When he turned to head back, he slammed right into Mia.

"I told you to stay in the house," he gently admonished, grasping her by the upper arms to steady her. The amber-flecks in her eyes shone in the moonlight, and Jack watched in fascination as her tongue darted out to moisten her bottom lip.

"I know, but I got worried when you didn't come back right away."

He couldn't seem to drag his eyes away from those

lush lips. As if drawn by some magnetic force, he lowered his head, wanting nothing more at that moment than to kiss her. To taste those lips, to lose himself in her moist heat.

Her eyes fluttered and closed, her head tilting slowly back as if in anticipation of his kiss. He relaxed his grip and slid his hands up to her shoulders, then down to the small of her back. His pulse pounded in his ears as she swayed against him and slipped her arms up around his neck. Powerless to resist even a second longer, he lowered his head and—

"Hey, where are you guys?"

Jack and Mia tore free from each other a split second before Kat shined a flashlight in their direction.

Damn, the kid's got rotten timing, he thought as he tried to calm his racing heart.

"Down here!" Mia called out in an unnaturally high voice. "By the dock. Jack thought he heard something."

"I didn't—"

She quietly shushed him with a soft slap on the arm.

Kat reached them and ran the beam of the flashlight around the dock, then the boats gently bobbing in the water. "Really? Cool. What do you think it was?"

"Probably a squirrel or a raccoon." He placed a hand at the small of Mia's back. It took all his self-restraint not to pull her back into his arms and finish what he'd started. "Come on, let's get back inside. I think we've had enough excitement for one night."

Jack absently fingered the mysterious red scratch on his stomach and wondered just how much more excitement he could handle in this crazy town.

Five

Jack had just finished his second cup of coffee the following morning when a whopper of a curse split the silence.

Mia?

He glanced out the kitchen window in time to catch her slowly work off her shoe and examine her foot. Without thought, he hurried from the house and sprinted down to the dock.

"What happened? Are you all right?"

She shot him a quick glance. "I dropped the stupid boat on my foot."

Crouching down beside her, he said, "Here, let me take a look."

"Thanks, but it's fine. Just bruised."

Ignoring her protest, he gently grasped her ankle and examined the fresh, purple welt swelling the top of her foot. She tried to hide a wince, but he caught it.

"Humor me and have it checked out. Just to make sure you didn't break anything."

"I said it's fine. And trust me, I heal fast."

An image of Mia bringing that dead bird back to life flashed in his mind.

It was your eyes playing tricks on you, nothing more.

"Besides, I don't have time for a trip to the doctor. I have work to do, then I have to go pick up Mudcat. Dr. Miller said he bounced back quicker than expected."

"That's great. But maybe I should take Kat to pick him up. Doesn't look like you'll be able to walk for a few days."

She rolled her eyes, and Jack was hard pressed not to grin. The woman obviously didn't deal well with helplessness.

"For the thousandth time, I'll be fine." She attempted to stand, but cried out as soon as she put pressure on her foot.

With a muttered curse, he scooped the stubborn woman into his arms and headed for the bait shop. "You need an ice pack."

"Wait! I have to get the boat in the water and mount a motor on it. It's been rented for the week, and they'll be by to pick it up within the hour."

Jack glanced at the boat, then with a sigh, carried Mia over to the picnic table and gently set her down. "I'll do it. I've never driven a boat before, but how hard can it be?"

That drew a chuckle from her. "Forget it. I'll call down to the marina, and they'll send Jared to do it. He's always been great about helping out."

A surge of jealousy, bitter and strong, hit Jack in the chest with the force of a mule kick. He'd never experienced the emotion before and had no idea what to do with it. When Mia's smile faded, he figured the look on his face must have betrayed his displeasure.

"Jack?" she whispered.

He cleared his throat and met her gaze. "Sorry, I, uh...heartburn." He gave his chest a thump. "Listen, I'm right here and perfectly capable. Just tell me what to do." Though he hated to admit it, he longed to be Mia's hero.

As if sensing his inner turmoil, her mouth crooked into an encouraging smile. "It's easy. And I appreciate your help. Okay, first, you need to get the boat in the water and tie it up in slip A."

Jack dragged the sea foam green, aluminum boat down to the dock's edge and slid it into the water. Once he had it tied up in the first slip, he beamed at her.

She chuckled. "Proud of yourself, eh? Good job, Sutton. Okay, now for the hard part." She stood and limped toward him.

"What are you doing?" he demanded, starting forward. "I told you I can do this."

Her lips firmed with resolve as she threw up a deterring hand. "Relax, I just need to show you where to clamp on the motor. Besides, it doesn't hurt so bad anymore. Probably just bruised, like I said."

Hands on hips, he gave his head a resigned shake. *The woman's stubborn as a mule.* "Fine. Just be careful, please."

She hobbled down to the pier and pointed to the three motors lying on the grass. "Grab the one in the middle, the eight horsepower."

Jack hefted the motor and carried it over to the boat. The thing wasn't light, and his respect for her grew. She may look delicate, but Mia Grey was obviously an incredibly strong woman—in more ways than he had realized. He climbed gingerly into the boat, thankful when he managed to keep his balance and not pitch himself into the lake.

"Now, just slip it over the back of the boat, and tighten the clamps to hold it in place. Propeller side in the water."

He shot her a look. Her returning grin was ear to ear.

Once he had the motor in place, Mia limped forward to inspect his work. "I'm impressed. Okay, now you need to hook up the gas. The tanks are sitting on the dock next to slip C."

He retrieved the gas tank and ever so slowly climbed back into the boat. Mia giggled, a sexy tinkling he longed to hear again and again. He found himself trying to think of ways to make her laugh. No one had ever accused him of having a sense of humor, not that he'd had much to laugh about the last eight or so years of his life. Hopefully, that would change now that he'd found a place to settle down.

Whoa...settle down? Getting way ahead of yourself there, Sutton, aren't you?

"Set the tank down next to the motor. Okay, now you need to hook up the gas line. See that silver button on the connector? Just press and hold it, push the connector into the hole on the motor, then let go of the button. That locks it into place."

Jack tried to work the connector onto the small male receptor on the motor, but couldn't get the friggin' thing to fit. He cursed, which brought Mia hobbling over.

"It can be a little tricky." She got down on her knees, maneuvered so she was sitting on her butt, and slowly slid into the boat. She half-crawled her way to the back and had the gas line hooked up in three seconds flat.

Some hero you turned out to be. Disgusted with himself, he watched her give several quick pumps to the attached black rubber bulb.

"Time to start the motor," she informed him. "Make sure it works. Grab the rope pull and give it a quick yank." She cautiously climbed to her feet and moved back to give him room.

Grateful to have started a lawnmower or two in his life, Jack grasped the rubber handle and gave it a sharp pull. Much to his relief, the motor cranked right over.

She clapped her satisfaction. "That motor's been sitting in the shed since last year, so I wasn't sure it would start on the first pull."

Mia took a step back, and lost her balance. Teetering, arms flailing, and hopping on her good foot, she desperately attempted to right herself. Jack hurried forward to help her, but his body weight only rocked the boat harder.

He caught hold of her arms just as they both pitched sideways into the water.

She came up sputtering, and Jack couldn't help but laugh. He swung her into his arms and waded the short distance to shore. Once she was lying comfortably on the grass, he collapsed beside her, still chuckling. He sobered once he remembered her injury.

"Christ, your foot. You didn't hit it when we fell, did you?"

"No, it's fine" she said on a breathy little sigh. "In fact, it barely hurts anymore."

"Liar."

She turned to meet his gaze, that beautiful face aglow with mischief. "You've never been on a boat before, have you?"

With a reluctant grin, he let the change of subject go. "What gave me away?"

"Haven't you ever heard the expression 'don't rock the boat?'"

He propped up on his elbow as he thought about it. "Isn't that some old song?"

"Yeah, and if you know the lyrics, it says, 'don't tip

the boat over.' You can't have all the weight on one side of the boat or it'll capsize," she needlessly explained, laughter in her voice.

"Why do I get the feeling I'm going to hear about this for a long time?"

She chuckled. "I'm just teasing you. It's my fault. I should've mentioned it sooner. And for the record," she archly informed him. "I would've caught my balance."

He reached over with his free hand and gently brushed a wet lock of hair from her cheek. When her breath caught, he swept his gaze up to hers. He ran a gentle finger across her cheek, down her chin, and back up to trace her lips.

"How old are you?" he asked.

"Twenty-four. You?"

"I'll be twenty-seven next month." He cupped her cheek, stroking his thumb across the tender flesh beneath her eye.

She smiled. "Guess we'll have to throw you a birthday party then."

"I'm not a party kind of guy. Though, if you're planning to jump out of a cake for me…"

"I'm not a jump out of the cake kind of girl."

"Glad to hear it," he murmured before leaning in to kiss the side of her neck.

A low moan rumbled in her throat. She slid her arm around his waist, her hand stroking his back as she arched her neck, giving him better access to her delectable throat.

Jack wasted no time in accepting her offer. He kissed and nibbled a moist, hot path up to her ear, trailed his lips across her cheek, and finally claimed her sweet mouth—

Mia tore her lips free with a squeak.

His eyes shot open. "Mia? I—"

"Um, excuse me," said an unfamiliar male voice. "I'm here to rent a fishing boat…? I called earlier. The name's Steve Connors."

Jack shot to his feet, then reached down and helped Mia up. Mr. Connors' knowing grin didn't faze Jack, but if the blush staining her cheeks was any indication, Mia wanted to crawl in a hole.

Mia stuck out her hand, praying her face wasn't beet red. "Mia Grey, Mr. Connors. We spoke on the phone. I have your boat ready to go."

Connors grasped her hand, then shielding his eyes from the glare off the lake, cocked his head to the side. "Would that be the one driving itself in a circle?"

Mia craned her neck back toward the lake. "Crap!"

She stood and took a step forward, but as soon as she put pressure on her foot, a lancing pain buckled her legs. Jack caught her before she collapsed and helped her over to the picnic table. He had his shirt, socks, and shoes off in record time, and before she knew it, he was in the water, swimming toward the boat.

Thankfully, the boat chose to troll rather than show off its speed, and Jack pulled himself over the side before she could work herself into a full-blown panic. Until she remembered one very important detail—Jack had never driven a boat before.

"Just kill the engine and row back in," she shouted, afraid he'd try to pull it into the slip and take out her entire dock in the process.

The engine cut off, and Mia sent up a silent prayer as she watched him maneuver toward the pier. She hobbled to her feet just as he coasted close enough to grab the dock. The boat bounced against the wooden pier, but not hard enough to cause any damage. He didn't make it into the slip, but close enough that he could reach the nylon rope and secure the boat.

She limped down to meet him and had to wonder if her hormones were out of whack, because it seemed as if Jack walked toward her in slow motion, like in some hokey eighties movie. Wet denim clung to his legs, his movements sure and confident. Broad shoulders capped long, sinewy arms, and a muscled chest that would put any bodybuilder to shame, though he wasn't bulky. More whipcord lean, with a light sprinkling of dark hair that covered his chest and ran down his washboard abs to disappear into the waistband of his jeans.

As he got closer, Mia realized he had a few tattoos. The only one she could make out was right over his heart. It appeared to be the initial M with a single red rose. Mia's heart sank. He must have loved her very much, whoever she was, to have tattooed her initial on his chest.

A throat clearing brought her attention back to her customer, and she gave herself a mental shake. No one had ever been able to ruffle her composure like her new neighbor, and it was starting to concern her.

Once Steve Conner had the paperwork filled out and his fishing gear packed into the boat, she and Jack waved him off. The sun was so hot her clothes were just about dry, if a bit stiff.

"Thanks for all your help. I don't know what I would've done if you hadn't come along."

He glanced off toward the far shore, his expression hard to read. "You would have called the marina, and ten guys would've raced down here to lend a hand."

"They *are* a helpful bunch," she teased with a playful grin.

No response. Hmm. Though his body was definitely on the Pros list, she could add sudden moodiness to the Cons side. "Listen, I really appreciate everything you did today. But like I said, I need to go pick up our dog. Kat's probably already waiting in the car."

He turned to face her, a slight frown marring that handsome face. "And like I said, I'll drive your sister down to the vet. You should go inside and rest your foot for a while."

"I appreciate the offer, but I don't have time to put my feet up. As soon as we get back, I have tons of stocking to do. Next week is one of the busiest times of the year for us."

He propped his hands on his hips, making his biceps bulge. Cripes, she had it bad. She realized his other tattoo was some sort of symbol, and it looked crude, as if he'd done it himself.

"No way can you maneuver around on that foot."

"Don't have much of a choice." She gave a one-shouldered shrug. "The work has to get done, and Kat's more helpful when she stays out of my way."

"Tell you what. I won't open the garage today. Works been slow anyway. You can stay off that foot while I do the lifting and stocking. All you have to do is order me around."

That idea pleased her—on many levels. "If you're sure, then I have one condition."

"Name it."

"You have to let me pay you."

He gave his head a shake. "Not a chance."

"I wouldn't feel right, you losing a day's pay to help me."

"That garage was sitting empty for almost two years before I got here. Trust me, the rent's cheap."

Mia didn't know what to say. Jack Sutton was turning out to be a pretty great guy. "I…thanks. That's the nicest thing anyone's ever done for me."

"Maybe you could pay me back by having dinner with me tonight. You and Kat both."

A grin tugged at her lips. "The guinea pig experiment?"

"Yep. Fried pork chops, nuked baked potatoes, canned corn, and Hostess Cupcakes for dessert."

Mia laughed. "I'm game. And I'd do just about anything for a cupcake."

"Good to know."

Kent had just finished sending the dairy order when Sherry stormed into his office. Recognizing the tight-lipped determination on her face, he rubbed his eyes, hard, with his thumb and forefinger. *Get ready for round three, buddy.*

"Can we do this later tonight?" he asked, returning his attention to his order logs.

"Asshole."

"So you keep telling me."

"Dammit, Kent, I want out. I don't love you, you don't love me. Why won't you just agree to the divorce?"

He threw his pen down and reluctantly made eye contact. "I told you, sign over custody of Zoe and your rights to the store, and you can have your divorce."

"Bastard!" She yanked open the door and stormed out of the office. Halfway down the produce aisle, she spun around and announced, "No way you're going to screw me out of what's rightfully mine, and no way you're getting my daughter!"

Several people turned to stare, eyeing Kent with pity. Pretty much everyone in town had witnessed a 'Sherry tantrum.' Didn't matter where they were or what they were doing, she had to make a big frigging scene over something.

What in God's name had he ever seen in her? He gave his head a rueful shake. An easy lay at a convenient time, that's what.

The first time he and Sherry slept together had been during their last year of college, after they'd caught their significant others in bed together. They'd headed back to his dorm room, commiserated over two bottles of cheap wine, and had comfort sex.

A friendship born out of mutual disdain for relationships developed, and before they knew it, Sherry discovered she was pregnant with Zoe. After some gentle urging from his parents, he did the right thing and asked her to marry him. She'd balked at first—there was no, nor had there ever been any love between them. But after some prodding from her own parents, she'd agreed to be his wife.

Kent had truly believed they were doing what was best for all three of them. He'd been attracted to Sherry, they'd had fun together, enjoyed each other's company, and he figured that and caring for their child together would lead to love.

He'd never been more wrong.

Kent pushed up from the desk and followed his wife out of the store—mainly to make sure she didn't cause any more trouble than she already had.

He suspected she was having another affair. Her sixth, that he knew of. She'd started sleeping around about four months after Zoe was born, and every time she thought she was in love, she begged him for a divorce.

Frankly, he couldn't wait to be rid of her, but no way in hell was she getting his daughter *or* a chunk of the family store. But as he headed back to the office to balance the afternoon cash drawers, he decided it really was time to end things, one way or another.

Six

"You actually met him? Spoke with him?"

John Whitlow strode over to the sideboard and poured himself a splash of brandy. His sister, Carol, stood gazing out into the courtyard, her expression inscrutable.

With a sigh of contentment, he sat down on the leather arm chair. "Yes. Ah, Carol, you should have seen him. So proud, so defiant. He's a Whitlow through and through."

His sister absently ran one lacquered finger nail across the glass. She seemed especially preoccupied this evening, and John knew it was something more than just her natural worrisome self.

She turned to face him without so much as a bounce of her perfectly coifed, salon-bought, platinum blonde hair. "I'm happy for you, John, you know I am. But truly, what do you know about this young man other than he spent seven years in prison for...murder?"

A frown furrowed his brow. "I know that he's my son. What else is there to know? He's not responsible for the cards life dealt him. And I've read the court transcripts. I truly believe he was framed, just as he's always claimed."

Carol nodded, but again, her expression betrayed her real thoughts.

"What is it? Why are you so flustered over this? You've known for months about Jack, that I'd planned to contact him, have him legally declared my heir. You said you were happy for me."

"And I am," she insisted, her blue eyes, so like his own, reflecting her sincerity. "But John, truly, he's...he's an *ex-convict*. What could he possibly know about running a corporation the size of Whitlow Industries? And I don't need to remind you who's been doing a fantastic job of just that."

John got up and strode over to her side to gaze out over the meticulously maintained gardens below. "Phillip has done a good job, no one is denying that. But he's not my son, he's yours."

He spoke kindly, but knew it was a sore subject with his sister, who was two years his senior. The first son of the first son had been running the company for more than a hundred and fifty years, and until this generation, there'd never been any chance of that changing. If he was unable to produce a male heir, Carol's son, Phillip, would take over the reins.

John's first wife had died in a car accident early in their marriage, before they'd had a chance to start a family. And his second and present wife, Alexandra, had so far proven unable to conceive. The fact that John had fallen out of love with her wasn't helping. Frankly, he wasn't sure what he'd ever seen in her.

Okay, that wasn't true. He'd been enamored by her bleached blonde hair and bountiful double Ds. But the thrill had started to wear off a couple of years ago. If he hadn't been so anxious to start a family, he would've started divorce proceedings long ago. His own fault for marrying a younger woman.

It had come as quite a shock to everyone—particularly Alexandra—when he'd announced his intent to look for any offspring that may have resulted from those donations he'd made back in college. And now that he'd met Jack, he felt a level of excitement he hadn't known in years.

Particularly since time might very well be of the essence. John had been to four different specialists in the past six months, and not one could tell him what was wrong with him. And without a diagnosis, he had little hope of recovering from whatever had caused several seizures, and had him vomiting each morning.

"This Jack may not have any desire to helm this family, John. Have you even thought about that? He would be like a fish out of water, ridiculed by—"

"No one would dare do something so foolish as to insult my son, Carol," he asserted, quickly losing patience.

He loved his sister dearly, but her dream of having Phillip head the company was exactly that—a dream. Phillip, although competent, was not focused enough to head the corporation permanently, and certainly lacked the business finesse needed for such a position. The boy had been caught screwing his secretary twice already, for crissakes. Last time by John himself.

Carol laid a hand on his arm, her perfectly painted face screwed up with concern. "I didn't mean to imply…I'm sorry, it's just been a long day. I think I'll go lie down for a little while."

With a heavy heart, John watched her leave the room. He hated how this affected her, but there was no help for it. Especially now that he'd met his son. Somehow, John would make Jack understand he was destined to head the family, to take his rightful place at the helm of Whitlow Industries—not run some dirty little garage in the middle of nowhere.

And soon, while there was still time.

"Come on, Mia, Jack's waiting!"

"All right, calm down, I'm done." Mia gave herself a final look in the mirror, fixed a mascara smudge beneath her right eye, and flipped off the bathroom light.

Kat leaned against the wall in the hallway, staring at her with a knowing smile.

"Thought this was just a casual dinner?"

"It is." She tucked her house key into the front pocket of her jeans and slowly limped past her sister to the back door. Life would be so much easier if she could use her gift on herself—though she truly was a fast healer, just as she'd told Jack. By morning she'd be fine.

"Then how come you put on so much make up and redid your hair three times?"

"Is there a law against wanting to look decent?"

Kat snorted. "Whatever. Let's just go. Hey, can Mudcat come with us?"

"No." Mia opened the door and ushered her sister outside into the fading sunlight. The night was warm, but not muggy, and the sweet scent of petunias hung heavy in the air. She loved the flowers and planted dozens of them every spring, filling the big whiskey barrel planters out front, plus several pots and hanging baskets out back.

"Why? He'll be good. And he's just gonna cry if we leave him home alone."

"He'll be fine, Kitty Kat. He's been left home alone plenty of times before."

"Yeah, but…"

Mia stopped and blew out a hard breath, having momentarily forgotten someone may very well have tried to put Mudcat out of commission permanently. Dammit, already she was losing focus thanks to her rapidly growing infatuation with their handsome neighbor.

"Honey, Mudcat needs to rest tonight. We'll lock him in the house where he'll be perfectly safe. And we won't stay for more than an hour or so, all right?"

With a curt nod, Kat ushered Mudcat into the kitchen and locked the door.

They walked across the yard in silence. Mia hated the fear that gripped the younger girl and kept her from skipping along as she usually did. What really sucked was she couldn't even go to the cops with her suspicions of foul play. She and Kat were the only ones who knew something had happened at Jack's the other night, and only she knew the full truth. As much as it pained her to keep silent, she couldn't risk anyone discovering their secrets.

Jack appeared at the top of the stairs and came down to meet them. "How's the foot?"

"Not bad. A little sore, but I'll be fine by tomorrow."

He cocked a doubtful brow. "You probably shouldn't even be walking on it."

Before she knew what he was about, Jack swung her up in his arms and motioned for her sister to lead the way back up. Kat opened the door that led into his small apartment over the garage, and held it open, her grin a mile wide. He strode inside, carefully depositing Mia on an old brown leather recliner that had seen better days. He pulled the lever, bringing the foot rest up, and winked at her. "Comfy?"

The chair was surprisingly soft, like lying in a big, fluffy cloud. "Very. Thanks."

She glanced around the sparsely furnished apartment and wondered if anything belonged to him, or if the place was exactly as it'd been left by the old man who'd owned it last. Mia had no idea since this was the first time she'd set foot inside. But Jack hadn't arrived with a moving truck.

"I know it's not much," he said, glancing around. "But then, I don't need much."

Crap, she hoped he hadn't mistaken her surprise for dismay. "Oh, it's fine. Perfect for a bachelor. And you've only been here a couple of weeks, so it's not like you've had time—"

"Forgive her, Jack. Mia gets stupid when she's hungry."

He placed a hand on Kat's shoulder and gently admonished, "You shouldn't call your sister names. Besides, this place *is* pretty pathetic. Not warm and homey like yours."

Kat rolled her eyes at her, then turned on the sun as she smiled up at their host. "Thanks. I mean, I could do without all the butterflies, but Mia and I do have a lot of cool stuff. Mia has a painting in her room worth—"

"It's a paint-by-numbers, Kitty Kat, worth about $9.99 in any department store." She cast her big-mouthed little sister a warning glance, then said to Jack, "I did do a pretty good job on it, and Kat's always thought it looked just like a painting you'd see in an art gallery."

"I'm sure it's beautiful. So, who's ready for supper? Kat, think you could give me a hand?"

"Sure thing." She stuck her tongue out at Mia, then flounced into the kitchen behind Jack.

Mia couldn't help but chuckle. The little stinker sure did have it bad for their new neighbor.

But then, so did she. Which could become a real problem if they weren't careful.

"Well," Mia said as she set her fork on her plate, "I'll never complain about being a guinea pig again. That was delicious."

Jack tilted his bottle of beer to his lips, unable to take his eyes off of her. Was it just him, or did she get more beautiful by the hour? He frowned over the direction of his thoughts and set his drink down with a thunk. *Christ, Sutton, get a grip. She's just being polite.*

"You all right?" she asked, her brow knit with concern.

"Fine, sorry."

"Heartburn?"

He couldn't help but grin. "Something like that."

"Are you two having one of those private joke moments?" Kat asked as she tore open the box of Hostess cupcakes. Before Jack could come up with a reply, she said, "Hey, can I turn on the TV? *Wheel of Fortune* is on."

"Sure," he said, relieved by her sudden change in subject. "You want a glass of milk to go with your cupcake?"

"Yes, please."

He got up to carry their plates into the kitchen and pour Kat that glass of milk. He could hear a special news report in progress, and when the name 'Kingston' filled the room, the hair on the back of his neck stood up.

"...has been confirmed that the car being pulled from the Kaskaskia River belongs to Sherry Kingston. Ms. Kingston is the wife of Kent Kingston, whose family owns Kingston Supermarket in Shelbyville. It has also been confirmed that Ms. Kingston did not survive as, according to reports, the car had been underwater for several hours. It appears that Ms. Kingston was alone in the vehicle. No word yet on a definite cause of death, although an autopsy is expected. More on this story at ten. In other news..."

Holy fucking shit.

"My God..." Mia leaned forward and pressed her fingers to her mouth. "Poor Kent."

"Poor Zoe," Kat added.

Jack nodded absently, glancing at the phone. Should he give his aunt a call, see if...see if what? They needed him? Hell, he'd probably be welcomed at the door by Uncle Jerry holding a shotgun. And it'd be a miracle if Aunt Patricia didn't spit in his face the next time she saw him. But he wanted to lend his support to his new cousin. Jack couldn't even begin to imagine what the guy must be going through. And that sweet little girl of his...Jack knew exactly how devastating it was to lose your mother, especially at such a young age.

"You met Kent and Zoe the other day," Mia reminded him. "Kent's a great guy, and Zoe's a little sweetie. Sherry doesn't...didn't work at the store very often, so we never really got a chance to know her."

"Other than that time she threw a hissy fit in the bakery."

Mia frowned at her sister before meeting his gaze. "Sherry had a bit of a reputation for...public displays of temper."

"I didn't like her." Kat popped the rest of her cupcake in her mouth, then chased it down with a gulp of milk.

Jack recalled Sherry hadn't been too fond of the sisters either. He wished he could tell them that the Kingstons were his family, but now wasn't the time to get into everything.

"Kitty Kat, it's not fair to judge someone based on one incident. Besides, show a little respect. The woman just died."

Kat shrugged, then her eyes bugged, as if she'd just remembered something. "We gotta get home! Mudcat's all alone."

"She's right, we'd better go check on him." Mia sent him an apologetic smile and climbed to her feet, wincing when her bad foot hit the floor.

Jack rushed forward and swung her up into his arms.

She chuckled. "You're going to spoil me, you know. And honestly, it's not so bad."

Unable to resist the pull, his gaze dropped to her luscious lips. He wanted to kiss her more than he wanted his next breath, had, in fact, been fantasizing about it since he'd carried her up to his apartment. His pulse kicked into high gear, and he wondered if she could feel the rapid drumming of his heart as he held her against his chest.

Kat swung open the back door and held it expectantly. With a reluctant smile, he took the hint and carried Mia from his apartment, down the stairs, all the way to their back porch. He set her down with infinite gentleness, resisting the urge to lean in and capture that delectable mouth of hers.

Another time, he promised himself.

"Thanks for supper. It was very good."

"Much to your surprise?"

"Well, it's hard to have high expectations when the name of your dish is 'the guinea pig experiment,'" she teased.

"True." He held her gaze in the ensuing silence, finally coming to a decision. Watching the sisters care for each other, whether they griped at each other or not, made him realize how much they needed each other. And right now, his family needed him. "Listen, I have something to do, somewhere to go. Is there anything you need before I leave?"

Curiosity glowed in her eyes, but she didn't question him. "I'm good, thanks. 'Night, Jack."

"Sweet dreams, Mia."

Jack headed back, hopped in his truck, and drove across town to his aunt's house. He almost turned back at one point, but the thought of what his cousin must be going through spurred him on.

Sherry was dead. Yesterday, she was vibrant and alive; today she was nothing but a memory. The unfairness of it made him want to put his fist through the damn windshield.

And Zoe.

Jack had only been a couple years older than her when he'd lost his own mother, so he knew just how hard this would be on her. And on Kent, who now had the unenviable task of telling his daughter that her mommy was never coming home.

For a split second, he feared he was a jinx, that maybe he'd brought some kind of bad karma with him from Wisconsin. But he gave himself a mental shake and got that ridiculous notion out of his head. As if *he* was so damn important.

He pulled up to the curb and killed the engine, then sat for a moment, questioning again whether or not he belonged here. Oddly enough, it was Kent's own words that got Jack's legs moving.

"But you did come, and it's not like you can change history. So, unless you're a coward, you'll just have to stay and make the best of it."

Before he knew it, he was striding across the street and ringing the doorbell. Aunt Patricia peeked out the curtains before opening the door with what seemed to be a welcoming smile.

"I'm sorry to intrude, but…well, I heard about your daughter-in-law on the news, and I thought I should come by, see if there was anything I could do."

The older woman stepped onto the porch and grasped his hand. "I'm so glad to see you." Silent tears rolled down her cheeks, and she teetered, as if her knees had given out. Jack wrapped an arm around her to steady her before helping her back into the house.

She sniffled against his shirt before pulling back to swipe at her eyes. Her hair had come loose of its bun, her nose was red from crying, and those big hazel eyes were dull with grief. Jack hated that she had to deal with the heartbreak of losing another family member—that they all grieved over a woman who'd been much too young to die. So damn unfair. But then, life was rarely fair. Jack had learned that the hard way.

"I'm truly sorry. I…I wish I knew what to say." He cleared his throat. "What exactly happened?"

She motioned for him to take a seat at the kitchen table, then poured him a cup of coffee. He didn't really want one, but sensed that going through the motions was probably helping her to cope.

His aunt dropped wearily onto the chair across from him and gave her head a slow shake.

"I still can't believe it. This just…this just can't be happening." She gazed up at him, the anguish in her eyes nearly taking his breath away. "Sunday is her birthday. She would've been twenty-seven. Zoe and I were planning a party."

Her voice broke on the last word, and Jack shot to his feet. But she waved him back down before swiping a wad of tissues off the table and dabbing at her eyes. "I'm okay, honest. It's just so hard. I feel helpless here."

"Where are Kent and Uncle Jerry?"

"They raced out of here as soon as the police called. It looks as if she drove off the Main Street Bridge, like maybe she fell asleep behind the wheel or something."

"Zoe?"

"Up in her bed, sleeping like a log." His aunt's face crumpled again, and she pressed the wadded lump of tissues to her eyes. "How are we supposed to tell that precious girl her mommy isn't coming home?"

The question was, of course, rhetorical. Jack merely reached across the table and grasped the older woman's fingers.

She gave his hand a squeeze and attempted to smile through her tears. "Maybe you could head out to the bridge? I know Kent would really appreciate your support right now."

"I don't know. I have a feeling your husband wouldn't exactly be happy to see me."

"Maybe not. But it would show him that you care about this family, and that's a start."

She had a point, even if he'd rather drink battery acid than face that angry old man again. "Let's hope you're right."

The bridge in question was about ten minutes outside of town; one of those old wooden numbers. By the time Jack arrived, Sherry had already been taken away by the coroner, and her car about to be towed to the impound lot. Kent and his father stood talking with a police officer, all three looking at Sherry's car as if they could somehow glean the answer to what had happened if they stared hard enough.

Another cop walked up and placed a hand on his cousin's shoulder, no doubt offering condolences. Kent nodded, propped his hands on his hips, and hung his head for a moment. When he straightened, he headed Jack's way.

"Hey, man," Jack said giving him a thump on the back. "If this is too much for you, I can stay here with your dad and—"

"No, I'm all right. I appreciate it, though. You barely know me, yet here you are. Means a lot."

Jack gave a brisk nod, unsure of what to say—which seemed to be a common theme with him lately. He'd never been one for strong emotion, but the urge to hug his cousin was powerful. He cleared his throat and crossed his arms over his chest, uncomfortable with those unfamiliar feelings. "Least I could do. So, listen, I don't mean to pry, but...what happened?"

Kent exhaled a hard breath and stared off into the distance. "The police found two bottles of alcohol in her car—half a bottle of whiskey and half a bottle of vodka. I told them there had to be a mistake. Sherry never drank anything stronger than white wine. But they said facts were facts." He met Jack's gaze and lowered his voice. "Something's definitely not right here. Sherry was...well, she'd been seeing someone recently."

My God...talk about out of left field. How much was one man supposed to have to go through? "You sure?"

Kent nodded and took a step closer. "Our marriage wasn't a happy one, and most people in town knew it. Hell, most people had witnessed one of Sherry's temper tantrums first hand. She's embarrassed my family and me more times than I can count."

Jack recalled Kat's earlier comments, which he hadn't put much stock in at the time—the kid did seem to be a bit cynical for her age. But it appeared she had better intuition than he'd given her credit for. "Sounds like you had your hands full with her."

A soft snort preceded, "You have no idea what an understatement that is. We tried to make it work, for Zoe's sake. Sherry's a good mom, she really loves..." Kent's words trailed off and he reached up to massage the back of his neck. "How the hell am I supposed to tell my five-year-old daughter her mother's dead?"

"I wasn't much older than Zoe when my mom died. Her friend was the one who told me. Said God needed another angel, and my mom was next on his list. She said it was a huge honor and that I shouldn't be sad."

"Damn...I'm sorry." His cousin swiped a hand

through his hair. "So, what happened to you after your mom…I mean, if you don't mind me asking?"

"My mom's friend, Bev, kept me until the foster care system took me away. About a week before my ninth birthday."

Kent gave his head a disbelieving shake. "You didn't have it easy, did you?"

Jack thought about the gang bangers he used to hang around with, many with drunken, abusive parents who didn't give a damn about their kids one way or another. At least he'd had his mother's love, even if only for a short time. "Wasn't an ideal life, but a lot of kids had it harder than I did."

Uncle Jerry strode up, the cop they'd been talking to when Jack arrived at his side. The tow truck with Sherry's car attached pulled out onto the two lane highway and drove off into the night.

The cop approached his cousin. "Taking what you said into consideration, we're going to have your wife's car checked for any tampering, just to rule out foul play. I'll be in touch soon."

Kent gave a brusque nod and shook the officer's hand. "Thanks, Hal. I appreciate it."

The officer walked away and exchanged a few more words with his partner. They both cast an indescribable look in his cousin's direction before climbing in their car and driving off in the wake of the tow truck.

Jack watched until they were out of sight, a bad feeling blooming in his gut.

Without sparing him even a single glance, Uncle Jerry gripped his son's shoulder. "Come on. We'd best be getting home."

Kent gave a weary nod before refocusing on Jack.

"Thanks again for driving out here. I appreciate it more than I can say."

"Whenever you need me, I'm here." He gave his cousin a quick pat on the back and shared a brief nod of acknowledgment with his uncle.

When he pulled into his driveway a short time later, Jack realized the overhead light in the auto garage was on. The hair on the back of his neck stood up as he got out of the car. He crept around back, careful to stay in the shadows until he reached the window to the right of the back door. But when he peered inside, the garage seemed to be empty. He tried the back door…locked. Suddenly, a flash of memory returned. Someone coming up behind him, an arm around his throat and—

Seven

"Hey! Jack, is that you?"

She heard a softly muttered curse.

"Mia?"

"Yeah, it's me." She stepped out from behind the trees, hungry for the sight of him. "Sorry, I didn't mean to startle you."

He strode forward until they were only a couple feet apart. So close Mia could smell his unique scent—masculine and spicy.

"I just got home and noticed the light on in the garage, which I swear I turned off." He stuck his hands in his front pockets. "How's the ankle? And what are you doing out here in the dark?"

"Still a little tender, but better." She flexed her foot to show him. "I had some last minute preparations for the tournament. I had a late call for a boat, so I needed to make sure my extra motor turned over. Plus, I like to sit out by the lake sometimes at night after Kat's in bed. It's quiet. I can think in peace." *Think about you, which I can't seem to stop doing.*

Jack reached out and tucked a stray lock of hair behind her ear, sending her pulse racing.

"And what is it you think about out here all alone?"

The sexy timbre of his voice washed over her like a soothing rain. She shivered in response.

"Cold?" Misinterpreting her reaction, he closed the gap between them and wrapped his arms around her.

"A little." The mid-sixties temps had nothing to do with her reaction to his nearness, but she had no intention of telling him that.

Mia had only ever been with one man, and he'd turned out to be a ginormous tool; an absolute error in judgment. Not only had he started cheating on her as soon as he got her into bed, but he'd also come damn close to discovering her and Kat's secret. If Mia hadn't immediately scrubbed his memory, she could only have imagined the headlines: *Modern Day Witches Living in Middle America!*

Plain and simple, her instincts sucked when it came to the opposite sex.

And right now, they screamed for her to run as fast as possible in the other direction. But her body dared her to snuggle into his warm embrace and enjoy the moment.

Which is exactly what she did.

Satisfaction rumbled in Jack's chest. He tightened his arms around her and whispered against her temple, "I'm glad you're still up. I was hoping we'd get a few minutes alone tonight."

Me, too. She pulled back and gazed up at him. "I don't mean to pry, but…"

When she didn't finish her thought, he supplied, "But why did I have to run off earlier tonight?"

"You don't have to tell me. It's really none of my business."

Moonlight washed across the bottom half of his handsome face and she watched, spellbound, as he licked his lips. Those gorgeous, full lips she couldn't wait to feel against her own again.

"No, I want to tell you. I would have earlier, but I didn't have time to fully explain."

Keeping one arm wrapped around her waist, Jack slowly led her down to the picnic table closest to the water. He grasped her hand and took a seat, giving her a gentle tug to sit down beside him.

"Kent Kingston is my cousin, though I'd never even met him until he pulled up with that blown tire. Our mothers were sisters. That's why I came here to Shelbyville, to look up my family."

She gazed at him in mild surprise, though somehow she could see it. "You and Kent do resemble each other now that I think about it."

He laughed softly. "So we've been told."

"Wait...I wasn't even thinking. Sherry was your family, too. Jack, I'm so sorry." She rested her head on his shoulder, tamping down the many questions running through her head. She wanted him to be able to confide in her, not only about the tragedy that had just befallen his newly found family, but about his past, his childhood, his parents, whether or not he had siblings. She really didn't know much about him, even though, in an odd way, she felt closer to him than she had anyone in a very long time.

He cleared his throat and kept his gaze fixed across the lake into the inky darkness. "You know Zoe. She's a great kid."

He turned to face her, and although she couldn't see his expression, the sorrow in his tone was unmistakable.

"And now her father has to tell her that her mother is never coming home."

"That poor girl. I was an adult already when my mom passed, but I know how hard it was on Kat."

"It's…not easy, that's for sure."

Mia searched his face in the soft glow of the moon. "You lost your mother at a young age, too?"

"I was seven, a little older than Zoe."

"Jack…" Her heart lurched at the thought of a young Jack being told his mother had passed. She knew exactly how it felt, but she'd been mature enough to handle it, grieve, and help her little sister through it. How does a five or seven year-old child move on when they can't possibly understand the enormity of what happened?

"The cops found open booze in Sherry's car," he continued. "They said she'd been doused in it, but Kent swears she didn't drink the stuff."

Jack gazed back out over the lake and seemed to become lost in thought. She drank in the sight of him, his handsome face creased with a combination of grief and frustration. Mia ached for him, wanted to wrap her arms around him and offer whatever comfort she could. But uncertainty held her back. They still barely knew each other, and she'd never done anything so bold before.

They sat in silence for a minute or so before he said, "It's weird to imagine my mom living here in Shelbyville, growing up here."

"What about your father? Does he live in Wisconsin?"

There was a long pause before he spoke. "I never met my father."

Great job, Mia, open mouth, insert foot. "I'm sorry, I didn't mean to be nosy, or bring up painful… Okay, I'm shutting up now."

He chuckled and turned slightly so they were facing each other again. Her heart bounced around her chest like a super ball when he leaned in and whispered, "That would be good since I'm dying to kiss you."

Without waiting for her response, Jack cupped her face and captured her lips. She melted against him, having dreamt about this moment all day. His soft lips tasted wonderful, like he'd just eaten something minty. He groaned and deepened the kiss, teasing her mouth with his hot tongue, sliding in when she opened for him.

One hand gently caressed her face as his other settled at the small of her back and coaxed her closer. Mia slid both arms around his neck and flattened herself against his broad, rock hard chest. *He must lift weights to have such toned muscles*, she thought. Her nipples pebbled on contact; she wanted this man more than she'd ever thought possible.

Which is exactly the problem, her inner party pooper reminded. *You don't know a thing about him other than someone tried to kill him.*

But that was a robbery, she argued back. *Hardly Jack's fault. Besides, he's been nothing but great to Kat and me. Kind, helpful, thoughtful.*

He could be trouble. Something isn't quite right—

Jack broke off the kiss and rested his forehead against hers. "You all right? Feels like I lost you."

She took a deep, shuddering breath and gave herself a mental shake. "Sorry. My mind wandered."

He leaned back to peer into her face. "Well, that's not good, is it?"

Horrified to think she may have pushed him away, she was quick to explain. "It's not you, I swear. I've just been super stressed this week with worrying about the tournament and…I wanted you to kiss me. You have no idea how much."

He held her gaze as he slowly skimmed his hand up the curve of her waist, over the swell of her breast, until his thumb rested against her puckered nipple. Mia's breath caught as he stroked a slow circle around it.

"And you have no idea how much I want you. I've never wanted a woman more, and that's the God's honest truth."

"Can I…ask you something then?"

"Sure, anything." He dropped his hand back to her waist.

She pressed hers lightly over his heart, curiosity having been eating her alive since the boat incident. "You have a tattoo. An M with a rose. You must have loved her very much to…" She pulled her hand back, suddenly feeling like a jealous girlfriend. As if she had any right to ask him about his past. They weren't even really dating…were they? "I'm sorry. I had no right to—"

He grasped her hand and brought it back to his chest. "The M stands for Mom. I was nineteen, had been drinking with some friends, and one of them said, 'Hey, let's all get tattoos.' I'd been missing her, and it seemed like a nice tribute."

"Jack—"

He swooped in and caught her lips again, giving her no time to protest—not that she would have. He pulled her onto his lap so she was straddling his hips and cradling the proof of his desire. She gasped against his mouth, wanting nothing more than to move against him, let him know she wanted him just as desperately as he wanted her. Need gripped her hard.

"Hey, Mia? Are you out here?"

Tearing her mouth free, Mia swung back to see Kat standing on the back porch, Mudcat right beside her. "Crap," she whispered to Jack, "I told her I wouldn't be too long." Aloud, she said, "I'm here, just talking to Jack. I'll be right in."

"'Kay. Night, Jack." Kat hustled Mudcat back inside and shut the door.

Jack stood and helped her to her feet. "I swear, that's girl's timing is uncanny."

Saturday morning dawned overcast and misty. After a quick shower and a bowl of corn flakes, Mia hurried outside to get the last boat ready. Her foot had healed quite fast; she barely limped as she headed down to the dock.

Kat had asked to sleep in, and Mia allowed it since she really didn't have anything for her to do anyway. Soon enough, she'd be waking up early to get her chores done before school, so she wouldn't begrudge her little sister the extra sleep.

The motor took a little longer to mount with her foot slowing her up, and she breathed a sigh of relief once that last detail was taken care of. The tournament would last until Friday, keeping her and Kat both so busy they'd be lucky to keep the soda and snacks stocked, let alone get anything else done until the store closed at six p.m.

She glanced toward the second floor of the auto garage, half-hoping to catch a glimpse of Jack coming down the stairs and heading her way.

Holy moly, did she have it bad or what? Thank God Kat couldn't read minds or she would never get another moment's peace.

After watering all of her flower baskets and her small vegetable garden behind the shed, Mia decided to pick what would probably be her last batch of green beans for the season. She had a little extra time that afternoon to blanch and freeze them, so she may as well get it done while she cou—

A blood-curdling scream rent the air.

Mia spun around, her heart dropping into her stomach with a sickening splash.

Kat!

She knocked the bucket over in her haste to get to her sister.

The back door burst open before she could reach it, and a man stumbled out, his hair in flames. Mia watched in horror as he tripped down the stairs and landed in a heap at the bottom of the porch. He slapped at his head while staggering back to his feet, then raced around the front of the building and out of sight.

She'd just made the corner when she caught sight of Jack out of her peripheral vision. He stood outside the open bay of the auto garage, staring for a moment in stunned silence before springing into action to give chase. Mia heard squealing tires and spitting gravel as the guy tore out of the driveway and drove off. Jack let out a whopper of a curse, then turned and rushed over.

He gently grasped her arm. "You all right?"

"I'm fine. I was out back picking beans when he... Oh my God, Kat!"

They both raced around back, stopping short at the

sight of Kat standing on the porch staring off into the distance, eyes huge, stance rigid, as if in shock. Mia ran up and threw her arms around her, giving her a tight squeeze before leaning back to search her for injuries.

"Kat, what happened? Who was that guy? Did he hurt you? Did he—"

Kat's eyes finally focused, and her angsty scowl returned. "I'm fine. Geez, exaggerate much?"

"After what just happened, how can you talk to your sister that way? I think you owe her an apology."

Mia glanced back at Jack, astonished by his harsh tone. Not that she didn't appreciate his support, but she knew it would kill Kat to have Jack upset with her. He stepped up behind her and placed a hand at her waist. She turned back to Kat who looked so miserable Mia wanted to pull her back into her arms. The younger girl's eyes grew suspiciously bright and she sucked her bottom lip in, as she always did when trying not to cry.

"It's all right. She doesn't have to apologize, although I *would* like an explanation. Who was that, and how did he get in the house?"

"I-I don't know. I came down to use the bathroom and he...he surprised me. Grabbed my arm and tried to put some rag over my mouth."

"Dear God." Mia's legs went limped, and Jack wrapped his arms around her, saving her from falling to her knees.

"Do you remember anything about him that would help the police—"

"No!" Kat shouted, shaking her head emphatically. "No cops. Nothing happened, and he's gone now. I don't remember anything about him anyway."

When Mia cocked a brow, her sister exclaimed, "I

don't, I swear! He was just some guy who probably wanted to rob the place, only I came downstairs before he got the chance to."

"So then, how did his hair catch fire?" Jack demanded.

Eight

With a huffed-out sigh, Kat turned and headed back into the house, Mia on her heels. Jack followed them inside where the scent of a burning candle clung heavy in the air. The wind was out of the north, which is probably why he couldn't smell it until they stepped inside the kitchen.

"He, uh, tripped when he grabbed for me and fell against the counter. His hair caught fire on the candle."

Mia glanced at him as if gauging his reaction.

Frankly, he doubted Kat was telling them the entire story, though he couldn't figure out why she'd lie—or why Mia's suddenly cagey manner made him suspect she *knew* her sister was lying. "If you just came down to use the bathroom, then why go into the kitchen to light a candle?"

Kat caught the corner of her top lip in her teeth and shot Mia a quick frown. Jack knew her story held little—if any—truth. But why lie? Someone broke into their home and, worse yet, tried to kidnap Kat. Why wouldn't they want to call the cops?

"It's my fault. I must have left it burning," Mia said, earning a smile of gratitude from her little sister. "I'm so sorry, Kitty Kat."

"I'm sort of lucky you did," Kat was quick to reply. "I'm sure that guy'll think twice before breaking into someone's house again."

Jack's gaze shot back and forth between them, no doubt in his mind they were lying. Kat had been so adamant about not involving the police. Not that he was anxious to see the men in blue, but the sisters' safety was the most important thing right now.

"We should call the cops. At least let them know what happened so they can be prepared should this guy try to rob someone else."

"I think you're right," Mia said after a moment, earning a scowl from her sister. "In fact, we have to run into town anyway; we can stop at the station on the way."

The sisters shared another meaningful look.

Yep, the two of them were lying all right. But with four vehicles waiting to be serviced, Jack would have to wait until later that night to get to the bottom of it.

"You have three brothers and a sister, all younger than you."

Jack clutched the phone so hard it was a miracle it didn't crack in two. "Come again?"

John Whitlow gave a soft, almost nervous chuckle, and he got the distinct feeling the old man wasn't as relaxed as he seemed.

"The oldest is Scott Leeland. He's eight months younger than you and lives in Minneapolis. Logan James is also twenty-six, and lives in Redemption, a small town east of Green Bay. The youngest boy is Trevor Gannon;

he's twenty-five and lives in Pulaski, also just outside of Green Bay. Your sister's name is Samantha Banks. She'll be twenty-one in late October and lives on the east side of Green Bay."

Four siblings—half-siblings—more family than he could have ever imagined. Hell, Jack had no idea what he was supposed to feel. He didn't even know if Whitlow was telling the truth about being *his* father. For all he knew, the guy was just some rich, bored nutjob.

"What happened to me being your only kid?"

"You were the only one signed with the registry, but money has a way of opening up doors—it just takes a little longer."

"Why are you telling me this? And what makes you think I give a damn?"

Whitlow blew out a frustrated sigh. "Come on, son, you can quit the tough guy routine. These are your siblings we're talking about. Why wouldn't you want to meet them? And I can make it happen. I—"

"If you start bragging about how rich you are, I'm hanging the hell up right now. And don't call me son. I still don't even know if it's true."

"Then take a DNA test so I can prove it to you. Jack, you *are* my son, there's no question in my mind. Especially now that I've met you."

He snorted. "I think the first words out of your mouth were 'You must look like your mother.'"

"True, you don't look like me, but you do have Whitlow characteristics. Even Dudley noticed."

"Dudley?"

"My driver. He said you walk like me and make certain facial expressions I do."

Jack choked back a laugh. "That dude does *not* look

like a Dudley. Sal, maybe, or Vito. Don Corleone—"

"Yeah, yeah, I get it. Dudley looks like he walked off the set of *The Godfather*. Can we focus now?"

"Look," he said as he rubbed his eyes, having had enough of his 'father' for one day, "I have several vehicles waiting to be serviced, so thanks for the call, but—"

"Jack, your brothers all have good families, good jobs, good lives. But your sister needs you. Needs *us*. Her mother divorced when she was only a toddler, and then passed away from cancer a decade later. The father's never been in the picture. Samantha spent most of her life being passed from one relative to another, until one of her uncles purportedly, uh…"

When the older man's words trailed off, Jack's blood ran cold. "Raped her?"

Whitlow cleared his throat as if choked up, and Jack had to wonder if he was telling the truth after all, about everything. "Yes. She lives with some friends in a nightmare of an old house on the east side of town, working two jobs to pay her way. I don't want her living like that, Jack. I don't want any of my kids living like that. I'm thinking about driving up in the morning, introducing myself. See if I can talk her into coming home with me."

"Yeah. That doesn't sound perverted and creepy as hell."

A slight pause. "Good God, I didn't even think of that."

Jack puffed his cheeks and blew out a hard breath. "Listen, I know a cop up in Green Bay. I'll give him a call, have him check on her, make sure she's safe. Satisfied?"

"No, but I'll take it. Thank you. And please let me know what this officer has to say."

"I'll be in touch."

"Jesus, Sutton, you've been busy," Officer Garrett Jamison teased. "Seriously, man, congrats on all the family. Let me make some calls. I'll let you know what I find out."

"I'd appreciate it if you stopped by, saw her with your own eyes. I just… I want to make sure…ah, hell."

"Don't worry about it, I understand. Got a sister of my own, remember?"

"Thanks, I appreciate it. And give your wife a kiss for me, will ya?"

Garrett snorted. "Like hell, asshole."

Jack chuckled as he hung up the phone. But when he thought about his sister and the garbage life had thrown at her so far, he quickly sobered.

Holy shit, I have a sister and three brothers. He'd gone from having no family to having more family than a person could handle in a matter of weeks. Not that he'd likely meet his brothers. Like him, they may not know how they'd come to exist. And he certainly didn't want to be responsible for tearing anyone's family apart.

But his sister was a different story. She didn't have anyone.

Hopefully, Jamison would have news for him soon.

Jack was torn.

Part of him wanted to hop in the car and drive up to Green Bay, meet his sister and bring her back to Shelbyville with him. Crazy to think they'd been living in the same town all those years. Not that they'd have met seeing as how he'd spent the past seven years behind bars.

Thanks to Garrett.

Ah, hell, he knew it wasn't really Garrett's fault he'd been convicted, although he'd certainly nursed quite a grudge over the years. But Jack had gotten mixed up with some shady people, and that was all on him. Jamison just happened to be the unlucky rookie who'd 'stumbled' upon the crime scene. The staged crime scene set up by a crooked cop who'd long since transferred to New York City. One day Jack hoped to find the evidence needed to clear his name, not that it would be an easy task. The cop in question was chin deep in organized crime, and Jack would have to tread carefully if he started swimming around in those waters.

But right now, he had more pressing matters. Like finding out once and for all who the hell his father was. And there was only one person who might have the answer for him.

"Jack, I'm so glad you called. I swear I don't know where my head is."

He enfolded Aunt Patricia in his arms for a quick hug before following her inside. "Your head is exactly where it should be, busy thinking about your son and your granddaughter."

She motioned for him to have a seat at the kitchen table, and then poured him a cup of coffee. "Your uncle is at the store. He's just no good in situations like these. And Kent is busy making arrangements with the funeral home. I wanted to go with him, but he said this was something he needed to do with Sherry's parents." She poured herself a cup, stirred in some sugar, then leaned tiredly against the counter. She gave her head a shake as if to say she still couldn't believe this was happening.

"Where's Zoe?"

"At a friend's house down the road. We told her this morning about…" The older woman gestured helplessly, as if she couldn't bring herself to say the words. "She doesn't understand, really, but then, neither does any of us. This is such a nightmare."

Jack nodded. He took a sip of his coffee and watched as a million expressions crossed his aunt's face. Strange as it was, he drew comfort from it. His mother had also had a very expressive face. "If you need anything, all you need to do is ask. I hope you know that."

Her smile was bittersweet. "You have a kind heart, just like your mother. She was such a gentle soul. She took it so hard when mom and dad…well, they didn't agree with her lifestyle."

"Which is sort of what I wanted to talk to you about. Do you know who my father is? I've always assumed he lived here in Shelbyville, but something happened recently to make me rethink my assumption." He let out an uncomfortable laugh and reached up to massage the back of his neck. "I have no idea if there's any truth to it, but some rich guy was waiting for me at the garage the other day. He claims he's my father. Says I was conceived through a sperm donation."

The truth was written all over his aunt's face, and Jack suddenly felt lightheaded. Christ, it *was* true. John Whitlow was his father. He was the product of what

102

amounted to a science experiment. As was his brothers and sister. Talk about fucked up.

"Jack, your mother was very young when she made that decision, which is why our parents were so angered by it, and why Karen and Beverly decided to move so far away."

"My mom knew Beverly in Shelbyville? Were they best friends or something?"

His aunt's face grew somewhat flushed, confusing him further.

"Karen met Beverly at college. They... My God, I assumed you knew this. They were lovers."

Whoa... Holy shit.

Talk about out of left field. He didn't know how he felt about *that* revelation exactly. What surprised him, though, was that he hadn't put the pieces together himself. Of course, he was too young to remember his mom and Beverly 'together,' but after his mother died, Beverly had lots of female friends.

He cleared his throat and managed to meet his aunt's gaze. "I, uh...no, I didn't know."

"Don't judge her, Jack. Your mother was an amazing person, and she loved you so much. Enough to give up the life she knew to make sure you grew up in a happy, loving environment."

He stared at his aunt, trying like hell to process everything she'd told him. "For the record, I have no problem with the lifestyle my mother lived. I loved her, she was my world, and nothing will ever change that. I just wanted to know who my father was, and now I think I do."

The smile that lit up his aunt's face brought an ache to his chest, but a good ache.

She took a seat at the table and pushed a plate of cookies his way. "If you've got a minute, I'd like to hear about this man claiming to be your father."

John Whitlow escorted his sister into Mignon, Green Bay's finest dining. He hadn't planned to look up his daughter right away, much less bring Carol along when he did. But after meeting Jack, he felt more alive than he had in years. And, after years of wondering if he'd ever have a family of his own, the thought that he had four more children out there was an exhilarating one indeed.

Once their orders had been taken, Carol snapped her linen napkin open and draped it across her lap, her smile as bright as the noonday sun. "John, what a lovely idea, driving up to Door County for a little shopping. We haven't done this in years. And I'm glad you suggested we stop for dinner in Green Bay on the way home. This place smells divine."

They'd always been close. Thick as thieves, their mother used to say. Unfortunately, Carol had never gotten along with his second wife—his soon-to-be *ex*-wife—which had put a major strain on their relationship. Especially since they all lived together on the family estate. Now that he'd finally decided to file for divorce, he'd noticed a remarkable difference in Carol's demeanor. It felt wonderful to have his vivacious sister back, and happier than he'd seen her in years.

"I'm glad you accepted my invitation. You haven't been out of the house in weeks."

"My new granddaughter has kept me very busy."

His sister and her husband, Steven, had three

children. Phillip, who was twenty-six and single, Addison, twenty-five and married with two beautiful little girls, Mary Elizabeth, three, and Teresa Ann, two months, and Kimberly, twenty-one and a senior at Columbia University. John was almost as proud of Carol's children as she and Steven themselves.

"She's a charmer, that's for sure. The entire staff has been acting like fools arguing over who gets to change her diaper." He shook his head in disbelief, and Carol laughed.

The waiter returned with the bottle of cabernet he had selected and poured them each a glass.

Carol raised hers in a toast. "To a new generation of Whitlows, whatever their last name may be."

John clinked her glass and waited until they'd both taken a sip before commenting. "Funny choice of words considering what I have to tell you."

She eyed him warily. "Please don't tell me you've changed your mind about divorcing Alexandra. I don't think my heart could take it."

He gave his head a decisive shake. "Not a chance. I've stayed in that loveless marriage years longer than I should have." John took another quick, fortifying sip of his wine and blew out a 'here it goes' breath. "So, as it turns out, Jack isn't the only offspring that resulted from my…donations. It seems I have three more sons, and a daughter. My daughter lives right here in Green Bay."

His sister merely stared at him for a moment, as if struggling to take it all in. Then her mouth pursed, and she thunked her glass down on the table. "So, this little trip today really had nothing to do with me, did it? You simply wanted some company for the ride."

"Of course not. I wanted to spend time with you, get

you out of the house. But I also needed to tell you about my children."

"Your *children?* John, these aren't *your* children. You're a sperm donor, nothing more. Don't you understand that?"

"Of course I understand that. My God, Carol, is it really necessary to be cruel?" He swiped a hand down his mouth and took a deep breath, desperate to get his temper under control. "You're in shock. Once you've had a chance to get used to the idea—"

"You make it sound as if you've bought a new puppy. Within the space of a few months, you've discovered you have five offspring out there, and you act as if it's...as if I should just welcome them into the family with open arms."

Okay, now he *was* getting angry. "And why shouldn't you? Because my 'offspring' will inherit controlling interest in Whitlow Industries, not yours?"

Carol gasped and lifted a delicate hand to her throat. "Now who's being cruel?"

Dammit, how had his happy news turned into such a war of the words?

He took a deep, calming breath, a third sip of his wine, and met his sister's wounded gaze. "I'm sorry. I truly am. I honestly thought that since the shock of learning about Jack was over, you'd be more receptive to this news."

"It's just...I feel like we finally got back to a good place after that...*woman* did everything in her power to turn you against me, and my family. And now..."

"And now?" he prompted.

She sighed and fussed with her hair, a true sign that she was uncomfortable with the conversation. Meeting his gaze, she shook her head as a small smile curved her lips. "And now I'm ashamed of myself. Of course I'll love your children, regardless of how they entered this world. It's just...the last couple of years have been so incredibly strained between us. It's been so wonderful to not be at each other's throats anymore."

"I agree. I hate that I let Alexandra drive a wedge between us. No," he said when she opened her mouth to argue. "Don't let me off easy. I was an idiot. Smitten by a pretty face and a great...well, you know." He finished with a grin.

Carol let out a reluctant laugh and rolled her eyes. "Men."

"Predictable to a fault, eh?"

"You said it, little brother, not me."

"And I'm also saying this: Once that gold-digging tramp is out of our lives, I'm dedicating the rest of my days to my family. To *our* family."

She tilted her head, a curious smile curving her lips. "Well, don't sound so ominous. We have many years left ahead of us to enjoy our children, our grandchildren, and maybe even our great-grandchildren."

Tears stung his eyes, and he quickly blinked them away.

If only that were true, sister dear. If only that were true.

"All right, Kat, I've waited patiently for you to calm down and come talk to me. Now, I want the truth, and I want it now," Mia demanded as she tossed the last bag of green beans in the freezer. "Who the hell *was* that guy?"

Her gaze glued to the TV, Kat sprawled out on the couch, one hand flipping through channels, the other patting Mudcat's head. "I told you already, I don't know. I came downstairs to pee and there he was, standing in the kitchen staring at me."

"You're lying and we both know it. Was...was it Tim?"

Her stricken expression was all the answer Mia needed. My God, the SOB had found them! And obviously a restraining order wasn't going to keep him away. Deep down, she always knew the bastard would find them. She'd just hoped he'd be using a walker by the time he did. "He'll be back, Kitty Kat."

Her sister's expression grew smug. "No, he won't. Not if he knows what's good for him."

She stalked over and tore the remote from her grasp. "Don't you dare make light of this. Tim is dangerous, and he's determined to get his hands on you. We have to be careful. As much as I hate to say it, it might be time for us to move on."

"Nuh-uh, no way!" Kat shot to her feet. "I like it here, Mia. So does Mudcat. It's our home. And we can't leave Jack. He's all alone, too. He needs us."

Taken aback by her sister's insight, she could only stare in stunned silence. And of course, Mia was loathe to give up the only man she'd ever felt a connection with. A real connection.

But nothing was more important than Kat's safety. They just simply couldn't take any chances.

"Look, I don't want to leave either. But we have to be practical. Tim—"

"Tim won't be a problem anymore, trust me. I scared him good." Her smug smile returned. "Oh, Mia, you should've seen his face. I bet he about pissed his pants."

"You're not invincible," Mia insisted, fear for her sister's safety so strong it was damn near tangible. "And your powers are useless if he blindfolds you and binds your hands, which he very well knows."

The phone rang, startling her. Swallowing her fear for her sister—and for herself—she tossed her back the remote and hurried into the kitchen. "Hello?"

"So, what did the cops have to say? Any idea who that guy might've been?"

Jack. "No, they, uh, hadn't had any other incidents reported, so they had no leads."

He muttered a soft curse. "Listen, I don't want you to worry about this. I'll take care of it."

Not the least bit surprised by his chivalrous take-charge attitude, a reluctant smile tugged at her lips. But as easy as it would be to lean on him, let him be their protector, Mia knew she couldn't risk him getting hurt—or worse. No one knew better than she did how dangerous Tim could be.

A thought suddenly occurred to her. My God...could Tim have had something to do with Jack getting stabbed the other night? Neither of the men had been Tim's size, but he could've hired someone. *He's probably the one who tried to poison our dog, too.* With Jack and Mudcat out of the way, he'd only have had one obstacle standing in his way of grabbing Kat—Mia.

"I appreciate your macho offer," she said, striving for a teasing tone, "but we'll be fine. I have a feeling the guy's hair getting scorched off will be enough to keep him away...whoever he was."

"Macho offer?"

She chuckled. "You know what I mean."

"I know there's not a chance in hell I'm letting anything happen to you or Kat."

Mia squeezed her eyes shut, Jack's words like a soothing balm on her troubled mind. "I know you won't. You're a great guy, Jack Sutton."

He cleared his throat, and she got the feeling he was uncomfortable with her praise.

"Listen, I have a few more jobs to finish before I can call it a day. How about some pizza later at your place? Around seven?"

Mia glanced at the clock, twenty to five. "Sounds good. Tell me what you like on yours and I'll order them."

"Anything's good with me except anchovies. Wait, no garlic or onions either."

A reluctant smile tugged at her lips. "Got it. See you at seven."

She hung up the phone and stood for a moment, wrestling with her subconscious. She knew allowing Jack into their lives could wind up being a huge mistake. Common sense reminded her that if anyone discovered real live witches lived among them, life as they knew it would be over. They'd both be in danger, and not only from Tim, but any two-bit thief greedy enough to try and capture them. And she could only imagine what would happen if the government took them into custody.

She broke out into a cold sweat just thinking about it.

But what if Jack's able to handle our secret? her heart argued back. They were growing closer each day, and he cared about Kat, that much she knew. She also knew he'd never let anything happen to them if he could help it.

But time was no longer a luxury now that Tim had

found them. She'd simply have to depend on her gut whether or not Jack could be trusted—with their very lives.

Mia grabbed her purse when she heard a car pull into the driveway. Half-hour delivery, as always. But when she opened the door, Jack was already exchanging money for the familiar cardboard boxes.

"I wanted to pay," she protested as he carried them past her into the house. "We have to eat anyway."

"So do I, and it was my idea." He stopped in the middle of the living room. "Kitchen?"

"No, I think we'll eat in here. Kat and I ran out and rented a few movies. Hope you don't mind?"

He set the boxes on the coffee table and plopped down on the couch with a sigh of contentment. "Not at all. I'm starving, and relaxing in front of the tube sounds good to me."

Kat came out of the kitchen carrying plates, napkins, the pizza cutter, and three twenty-ounce bottles of cola. Mia took the sodas from the crook of her sister's arm and set them on the table. Kat passed out the plates, set the napkins on the table, and hurried over to the other end of the couch, leaving Mia the only other seat in between them.

With a reluctant smile, she stuck a movie in the DVD player before squeezing in between her sister and Jack.

Jack *mmmed* as he opened the first box, and immediately slid a thick, pie-shaped slice onto his plate.

"All the new releases were checked out," Kat

explained as she grabbed a slice. "So we rented three of our favorites."

Mia grabbed a plate and flipped open the second pizza box. A twelve-inch Mario's Special deep dish stared up at her, and her mouth watered as the delicious aroma wafted up, mingling with the sausage and mushroom thin crust Kat favored. Mario's Pizzeria was a definite favorite in the Grey household.

Jack peered into the box. "That one looks good, too."

"It's the best. Sausage, mushrooms, green peppers, ricotta cheese, topped with mozzarella." She slipped the pizza cutter beneath a slice and lifted it, waving it temptingly in front of him. "Wanna try it?"

"Don't mind if I do."

He held up his plate, and Mia slid it on, amazed to see he'd already finished his first slice.

When the previews ended and the movie finally started, Jack let out a surprised chuckle. "And here I figured I'd be watching chick flicks all night."

With a delicate snort, Kat assured him, "Not in this house. Mia and I like horror movies. Comedy, too, but mostly horror. Figured you'd probably like *Halloween*, the original. Most people do."

He shrugged. "Never saw it."

Her sister's eyes fairly bugged out of her head. "You've never seen *Halloween*? Get outta here!"

He grinned, and Mia's heart gave a little jump. The man was much too sexy for her peace of mind. Every facial expression he made gave her the chills—in a very obvious way. Her cheeks heated, and she hoped to God he didn't notice.

It was far from cold in the house.

"I didn't get to watch a lot of TV growing up."

"Were your parents strict?"

Mia inwardly groaned at her sister's innocently asked question. She hadn't thought to tell her about Jack's mother.

He shrugged. "My mom was. She died when I was pretty young, but I remember she encouraged me to play outside a lot."

"Crap…sorry." Kat's face pinkened.

"Nothing to be sorry for. You didn't know."

"Our mom's dead, too, so we know how you feel."

He cast Mia a quick glance. "Your sister mentioned that. I'm sorry."

"It's been about five years now," she continued, as if suddenly needing to talk about it. "She was famous. I bet you even heard of—"

"Kitty Kat, that's enough." Okay, so she'd owe him an explanation later. But the last thing she wanted to get into right now was the past.

"But Mia, we can trust Jack."

He smiled his appreciation at her sister, which only made Mia feel like a bigger bitch than she already did.

"You two can definitely trust me," he assured them. "But maybe we should save this conversation for another time. Come on, eat up and let's watch the movie."

"Fine." Kat shot her a 'what's up with you?' scowl before curling up in the corner of the couch.

Mia carefully avoided Jack's gaze as she, too, settled in to watch the movie.

By the time the credits rolled, Mia was ready to get up and put some distance between her and Jack. Sitting thigh to thigh with him for an hour and a half had done funny things to her libido, and she needed to get the sucker back under control. It hadn't helped that he'd spent a good amount of the movie caressing the back of her neck.

"Kat, would you take the dishes into the kitchen, please, while I take out the garbage? Jack, can I wrap up the leftovers for you to take home?"

He drained the rest of his soda and screwed the cap back on. "I wouldn't mind a slice for breakfast if there's enough to spare, but I'll be the one to take the garbage out. No way I'm letting you walk outside alone at night."

"It was late morning when that guy entered our house," she reminded him, though touched by his protectiveness.

"Exactly my point. Whoever he was, he sure as hell isn't working with a full deck—which makes him dangerous and unpredictable."

You don't know the half of it. "Thanks, Jack. We appreciate you looking out for us."

"And don't worry, we have your back, too," Kat chimed in..

Nine

Jack tossed the garbage bag in the black, wheeled trash can on the side of the shed, and when he turned back around, two men stood in front of him, each holding a gun aimed at his chest.

Fuck.

"Something I can do for you boys?"

"Naw, we're good. *You* might wanna say your prayers, though."

Now, why the hell did that voice sound so familiar? Hard as he tried, Jack couldn't place it. "Never been one for praying. Any chance you're gonna tell me what this is about? I know I don't owe anybody money, and I don't have any enemies that I'm aware of."

"Let's just say you were born unlucky and leave it at that."

They both raised their guns and pointed them at his head. Before Jack could react, a pair of oars rose up behind his attackers and cracked them each on the back of their head so hard they pitched face first into the grass.

Stunned by what he'd just witnessed, Jack sprang into action a second too late. His attempted murderers staggered to their feet and ran like hell for the road. Jack was about to give chase when light spilled out from the Grey sisters' back porch and caught his eye. He turned in time to see Mia pull Kat back into the kitchen and shut the door.

What the hell...?

A car sped away in a frenzy of spewing gravel, and Jack cursed a blue streak as he raced after it, desperate to get the license plate number. Blinded by the headlights, he watched in helpless fury as the car drove off and disappeared from sight.

He stalked back to the house and strode in without knocking. Kat stared at him in wide-eyed uncertainty while Mia carefully avoided his gaze as she wiped the counter.

"I wanna know what the fuck just happened out there."

"Th-they were gonna shoot you! I—"

"Kat, go up to bed, please. It's late."

"But Mia—"

"Now, young lady. No arguments."

"Fine!"

Jack held his temper while Kat stormed from the room and stomped up the stairs. Once her door slammed shut, Mia pinned him to the wall with her narrow-eyed gaze.

"Don't you ever use that language in front of my sister again, do you understand me?"

While Jack respected her bravado, her tone pissed him. "Dammit, Mia, I want answers. I just saw..." Frustrated, he stabbed his fingers through his hair before dropping down on a chair. What the hell *had* he seen? Christ, he had no idea. When he looked up, she was staring at him expectantly.

"You just saw…?"

Now why did he get the feeling she was taunting him? "You know damn well what I saw. Those oars…I don't know what you two did, but…well, you did something." Just like with that bird. A sudden chill trickled up the back of his neck.

"You *do* know how crazy that sounds, don't you? What could we have done?"

Watching him with her hands on her hips, those big brown eyes so deep he could easily drowned in them, those full rosy lips just begging to be kissed, the woman was breathtaking. He couldn't have pulled his gaze away if he'd tried. The anger whooshed from his chest as if an elephant tramped on it. "I'm not crazy. I know what I saw."

She dropped her hands to hers sides and took a step toward him, the tiniest smile playing about her lips, her gaze growing oddly intense. "I know you're not crazy. But it's pitch black out there, and the wind's whipping pretty good."

"That was no wind and you know it." His hands itched to touch her, to pull that slip of a tank top off and capture both those beautiful breasts. He imagined stripping her naked and taking her right there against the counter. His cock swelled painfully and…*whoa*. His thoughts had turned sexual so quickly, so…unexpectedly.

"All I know is that I don't want to fight with you."

She took another step toward him, those sexy lips spreading slowly into a come-hither smile. Jack fought the pull for all of two seconds before shooting to his feet and closing the distance between them. He cupped her cheek and gazed down at those luscious full lips, imaging all sorts of wonderful scenarios. "I don't want to fight either. But I won't be lied to or patronized, got it?"

Mia closed her eyes and leaned into his palm for a moment, then pulled back and gazed up at him, and Jack, honest to God, felt as if he were being hypnotized. The need to kiss her overpowered him and cleared all other thoughts from his head. He crushed her in his arms at the same moment she linked her hands behind his neck and kissed him with a passion that nearly buckled his knees.

He picked her up and carried her into the now dark living room without breaking the kiss, then plopped down on the couch. Mia chuckled softly as she straddled his lap. He marveled over how soft her lips were and couldn't seem to get enough. He stroked his hands up the gentle curve of her spine, across the silky skin of her back. Jesus, he was half-crazed with lust and knew it had little to do with the fact he'd been celibate for seven years.

What he was feeling bordered on something he was loathe to put a name to. The thought of becoming emotionally involved with anyone after all these years scared the hell out of him.

Though not enough for him to back off.

She leaned into him, pressing the tight buds of her nipples against his chest with a soft, sexy moan. Christ, he was about to go up in flames. He slid his hands beneath the hem of her top and cupped both of her breasts. She gasped into his mouth as his thumbs rolled over her nipples, and he grew hard as stone beneath her.

He broke off the kiss to murmur, "I want to taste you."

"I want that, too."

Her voice was a breathy little whisper that sent blood rushing from one head to the other. Jack peeled her bra up and lifted her tank top, baring her beautiful breasts to his hungry gaze. He took one pebbled nipple into his mouth, and Mia cried out softly, tunneling her fingers into his hair, urging him on. Shit, it'd be a miracle if he didn't come in his pants.

He lavished both nipples with equal fervor. He'd been dreaming about what she'd taste like since the first moment he laid eyes on her, and the reality was so much better than his imagination.

She moved against him, her hips rolling slowly, stroking his granite length with exquisite gentleness. He abandoned her glistening breasts to reclaim her lush lips again. Grabbing her butt with both hands, Jack urged her to move faster against his straining erection, while his tongue plundered her sweet mouth with urgent abandon. Good God, he'd give anything to be inside her right now. And he was pretty damn sure she wanted it just as much as he did.

Mia deepened the kiss, her hot tongue mating with his, stoking the flames of his desire to a fevered pitch. He worked one hand between them and slipped inside her shorts, under the elastic of her panties, needing more than anything to touch her. She rose up higher on her knees, giving him better access. With a groan, she caught her bottom lip between her teeth as he slid one finger between her slick folds, her hips moving in silent plea. Jack wanted to pleasure her more than he wanted air.

"You're so beautiful," he whispered, stroking her swollen flesh.

"Jack...I need—"

"Mia, is Jack still here?"

They tore apart so fast it would have been comical under normal circumstances. But he was rock hard and throbbing, and he knew Mia had to be drowning in frustration. She worked her clothes back in order and then grabbed the remote to flip on the TV.

"Yes, he is. We were just saying goodnight."

Footsteps padded down the stairs, and then Kat appeared in the living room.

"You're supposed to be in bed, Kitty Kat."

"I know, but I wanted to say goodnight to Jack. And say I'm sorry for—"

Mia sat up and fixed her sister with an odd, meaningful look. As if she were trying to convey a message. "There's nothing to apologize for. I'm sure Jack isn't holding a grudge because you snitched the last slice of pizza."

Confused, Jack swung his gaze from one sister to the other. Oddly, his memories of the night, with the exception of the last ten minutes, were a bit fuzzy. They'd eaten pizza, watched a movie... "Did I fall asleep during the movie?"

"You did, for about fifteen minutes. And when you woke up, you reached for the last slice of pizza, which my sister had already wolfed down. Right, Kat?"

"Uh, yeah. I felt bad, so I'm going to make it up by fixing dinner another night."

He swiped his fingers through his hair and stood, unnerved to not remember having fallen asleep. "Sounds good. Listen, I think I'd better head home, catch a few extra zees." He let out a self-deprecating chuckle. "And I'd probably better start taking vitamins, too, seeing as how I can't stay awake for one movie."

"I'll walk you out. *Goodnight*, Kat."

Jack waited until they were outside on the back porch before taking her into his arms. "Sorry I fell asleep. I must've been more tired than I thought."

Mia snuggled in his arms and let out a lusty sigh. "I'm sorry Kat *didn't* fall asleep." She lifted her head and met his gaze. "I'm falling for you, Sutton. If you don't feel the same, I'd appreciate you letting me know right now. I'm not the 'one night stand' type."

Don't feel the same? Christ, he was already half in love with her. He placed a gentle kiss on her lips, then her brow. "I'm crazy about you, lady. Figured it was written all over my face. And neither am I, by the way."

The smile she bestowed on him was so spectacular it rivaled the moon. "Good. Then I'll see you tomorrow?"

"Absolutely." He turned to go.

"Jack?"

He stopped and glanced back, surprised by the frown suddenly marring her brow.

"Don't forget to lock your doors. I heard there's been a few break-ins on this side of the lake."

Something bothered him about that bit of news, besides the obvious, but he couldn't figure out what. He gave her a reassuring wink. "Will do. And be sure to do the same. 'Night, Mia."

"Hey, Garrett, what's up?"

"Sutton, you aren't going to believe this, but your sister's roommate was killed last night."

A chill went through Jack, though he wasn't exactly sure why. "What the hell happened?"

"Your sister was working a double shift at The Nines. It's a gentlemen's club. Her roommate asked if she could sleep in your sister's room since the air conditioner in her own room had conked out. Samantha got home this morning from work and found the girl dead in her bed. Shot to death."

A tiny flash of memory caught Jack by surprise: Two men, both pointing a gun at his head. Only that never happened. Maybe he'd dreamt it one night? "How is she?"

"She's fine, don't worry. But there's something else I need to tell you. It seems she had a visitor yesterday before she left for work. A man claiming to be her father showed up with a woman. His sister, I believe. The woman was less than friendly, and your sister sent them packing. I doubt he knows what happened to the roommate."

Jack leaned his head back against the wall and closed his eyes. He massaged the bridge of his nose, an ugly suspicion growing in the pit of his stomach. "I'll fill him in. So, where is Samantha now? She can't stay at her place. I think it's pretty obvious whoever killed her roommate meant to kill her."

"The roommate's boyfriend is being checked out, but yeah, we came to the same conclusion. Your sister is as ornery and bull-headed as her big brother, by the way, so instead of tucking her somewhere safe, which she flat out refused, I have her under twenty-four hour surveillance."

A grin tugged at Jack's lips. "Thanks, man, I owe you."

"Damn right you do. So can I expect you in town anytime soon? And yes, I already cleared it with your parole officer."

"Appreciate it. I'll drive up tonight. Won't hit Green Bay 'til late, though. I still have a couple of jobs to do."

"I'll have Jess ready the guest room."

"You don't have to—"

"Save your breath. She'll kick my ass if I let you go to a motel. But if I even catch you trying to kiss my wife, I'll drop kick your ass back to Illinois so fast it'll make your head spin."

A full-blown smile replaced Jack's grin. "Got it. And thanks. I appreciate…well, everything."

"See you tonight."

As soon as Jack hung up, he pulled out the card John Whitlow had given him and dialed his cell phone.

"Whitlow here."

"It's Jack."

A slight pause. "Good to hear from you. I hope all is well?"

"Not really. Got a call from my friend in Green Bay. Samantha's roommate was murdered last night."

"What? My God, what happened?"

"While she was sleeping in Samantha's bed."

There was a pause. "Excuse me?"

"There's a very good chance that whoever killed the roommate thought she was Samantha."

"B-but I was just there yesterday, and everything was fine. Well, not fine as far as I was concerned. She told me to go scratch."

Jack snorted. "Smart girl."

"Jack, she's a stripper, for chrissake. I hate the

thought of her having to take off her clothes to pay the bills. I can't imagine it warms your heart either."

"I don't like it any more than you do. But not all of us were raised with a silver spoon in our mouth. We do what we have to do to survive. That's life."

"Well, not anymore. I've already set up accounts for both of you. As soon as you take a DNA test, the money is yours. You can buy yourself a hundred auto garages if you want."

Jack's knees went weak at the thought. Never having to worry about money again? Hell, he couldn't even imagine. He'd been poor his entire life, and having lived the last seven years of it behind bars had been a huge lesson in humility. Made him appreciative of every little thing he had—most especially his freedom. Jack had walked into prison a good-for-nothing punk, and walked out a man. A hardened, prideful, somewhat cynical man, but a man nonetheless. A man who had a lot to prove—most especially to himself. And becoming self-sufficient was at the top of his list. "I like the one I have, but thanks anyway."

Whitlow chuckled. "You're as stubborn as they come, Jack. A Whitlow trait, I'm afraid." He let out a sigh. "I hope you plan to drive up to Green Bay and check on your sister, make sure she's all right? Maybe talk her into moving to the family estate in Madison where I can make damn sure she's safe?"

Jack was pretty sure the Whitlow estate was the last place his sister would be safe, but he kept that opinion to himself since he had nothing to go on but his gut instinct. "I'll give you a call as soon as I know what's going on."

"I could meet you—"

"Not a chance. I don't want her to feel ganged up on. Like I said, I'll give you a call."

Jack hung up without giving the older man a chance to argue. It would be hard enough getting her to listen and agree to relocate to Illinois until they could figure out who the hell wanted her dead. Last thing Jack needed was dear old dad tagging along.

And maybe leading the killer right back to Samantha's doorstep.

When Jack came by to inform them about his little trip to Green Bay, Mia did her best to hide her disappointment. He'd said he was going to see a friend and that he wouldn't leave if it wasn't important, but somehow Mia knew he hadn't been telling her the whole truth. Which hurt a bit; obviously he didn't fully trust her. Seeing as how she was doing the same thing to him, however, she had no right to complain.

"I still can't believe you wiped his memory. Good thinking. I was worried he—"

"I hated doing it, Kitty Kat. It's not right. But damn it, he saw you. I had no choice. No one can ever discover what we are."

Kat's freckled face screwed up. "You make us sound like freaks or something."

"We're different, whether we like it or not. If the wrong person finds out and I can't wipe their memory, life as we know it would be over. I'd probably wind up as a lab rat somewhere and you'd end up in foster care…if not in the cage next to me."

She hated the fear that blossomed in her sister's eyes,

hated that she'd put it there. But what choice did she have? Kat was young and impetuous, and if Mia didn't constantly remind her of what exactly was at stake, it'd only be a matter of time before their world was torn apart.

"I'll never let it happen, honey, I promise you. Even if it means we have to pack up in the middle of the night and move again. We have to be more careful than ever, especially now that Tim's found us. I can't wipe his past memory, only his recent. And I'd have to be able to get close to him to even do that."

Her sister was silent for a moment, pensive. "But I don't wanna move. I like it here."

"I don't want to move either, sweetie. But we may not have a choice." The thought of never seeing Jack again was something Mia didn't even want to contemplate. More than once, she'd toyed with the idea of telling him everything. But in the end, it always came back to the same thing—could she trust him with their lives?

Kat opened the freezer and pulled out two fudge pops, handing her one before taking a seat at the kitchen table and kicking her feet up. "Mia?"

"Yeah?"

"Tim said he's been in town for months. If that's true, why did he wait so long to come after me?"

The thought of that man watching them all these months, just waiting for the perfect time to pounce, was terrifying. And with Jack out of town until tomorrow, her anxiety was starting to grow into full-blown panic.

She tore the wrapper off her frozen treat and gave a nonchalant shrug, hoping to calm Kat's fears with her lack of concern. "He's probably lying. Trying to creep you out, that's all. If Tim had been here all that time, he would've made a move before yesterday." When Kat merely stared at her, she added, "My offer to move still stands. Just say the word, and we're out of here. I promised I'd never let that man hurt you again, and I meant it."

Kat nodded and turned her attention to her fudge pop, but Mia knew something else was bothering her. The young girl rarely let Mia see her vulnerable side. She'd definitely have to keep a closer eye on her until she figured out a way to get Tim out of their lives, once and for all.

By the time Jack arrived at Garrett and Jessica's place, it was nearly eight o'clock in the evening. Not much time for socializing before he went off to find his sister, but there was no help for it. Jack hated leaving Mia and Kat alone for even an hour, let alone overnight, with that nutjob on the loose. He'd wanted to ask Kent to take a ride past the bait shop while he was gone, but his cousin had plenty of his own problems at the moment— like planning his wife's funeral. Jack would have to take care of business and get his ass back home ASAP.

Back home? When had he started to think of Shelbyville as home?

He'd just raised his hand to knock when Jessica swung open the door and threw her arms around him with a surprising squeal. "I was so glad when Garrett said you were coming! You left Green Bay while I was in Seattle," she gently scolded.

He gave her a quick squeeze, then stepped back to

look at her. Gorgeous as ever, with those big blue eyes gazing up at him and that waist-length blonde hair piled in a loose bun on top of her head. Barefoot, she barely made his chin, which put her at about the armpit of her six-foot-five husband.

Once upon a time, Jack had considered using her to get revenge on the big cop. Instead, he'd ended up befriending them both. "I know, and I'm sorry about that. But I needed to get the hell out of this town, and Lord only knew how long it would take him to pull his head out of his ass and go after you."

"Looks like someone's itching to sample my left hook," Garrett said as he came up from the basement.

"Uh, no thanks, Jamison. I've tasted your right, and I still have heartburn from it."

His friend laughed, then walked up and thumped him on the shoulder. "Good to see you. Jess tell you the good news yet?"

Jack gazed down expectantly at Jessica whose cheeks had gone pink. "I'm pregnant."

"Damn, you guys work fast," he teased, earning a slug on the arm from the glowing mother-to-be. So, that's what that extra sparkle was about. "Seriously, congrats to both of you."

"Thanks, man." Garrett leaned down and gave his wife a kiss. "Sutton and I need to take a ride. We'll pick up Chinese food on the way back. Sound good?"

"You know it does." She grinned at Jack. "Pregnancy cravings."

Once they were outside, his friend informed him, "We eat sesame chicken and fried dumplings like four times a weeks."

"You don't sound all that put out about it," Jack

observed as he climbed into Jamison's black Dodge Ram.

"Hell, it's fine with me. Whatever makes her happy."

Jack gave his head a shake and feigned a look of disgust. "Dude, if you plan to start singing love songs, let me out so I can walk."

The big cop grinned as he backed out of the driveway. "I may do that anyway, pal. Don't tempt me."

"So, where are we heading?"

"She's staying at a friend's house since her place is being swept for evidence. Besides, the Nines is closed on Sundays."

Jack turned a teasing smirk on him. "You seem to know a lot about this gentlemen's club. Bet Jessica wouldn't appreciate that."

"Get over it, Sutton, Jess loves *me*. Time to admit defeat and find your own girl."

Jack cleared his throat. He wasn't usually the type to share personal stuff with anyone, but he liked the guy, and he trusted him, regardless of the unorthodox way they'd met. "Maybe I already have."

Garrett cast him a quick, sidelong glance. "Damn, talk about working fast. So, how about a few details?"

"She runs that little bait shop/convenience store I told you about next to the garage. And she's raising her younger sister, who, let me tell you, is gonna be a helluva handful someday."

"Like her big sister is right now?"

Damn cop's intuition. Jack gave his head a rueful shake. "Between the two of them, it's a miracle I haven't lost my mind yet."

"Women, hey?"

Jamison made a left onto Baltimore and drove down

to the second to last house on the right. *Christ*, Jack thought, *what a dump*. Even worse than the auto garage, which was really just a step above a rat trap.

They parked on the curb right in front of a rather dilapidated looking house. Jack took a deep breath, threw open the door, and stepped out onto the street.

"Don't worry. It looks much better inside than it does out."

Jamison had a sister, so figured he'd know exactly what kind of thoughts were running through Jack's head. Brotherly concern. Something he never thought he'd experience. And the funny thing was, he hadn't even laid eyes on his little sister yet.

Jack and Garrett had just reached the walkway leading up to the house when the front door flew open by a young woman who, with that blonde hair and those light blue eyes, could only be his sister.

She stepped out onto the porch, hands propped on her hips like Wonder Woman.

"Step one foot on my property, and I'll kick both your asses."

Ten

"Shit, she looks just like him." A reluctant grin tugged at Jack's lips. And she had brass ones, that's for sure. Maybe having a little sister wouldn't be so bad after all.

Garrett cast him a quick glance. "Like who, your father?"

"Yep. Bet Whitlow about peed himself when he laid eyes on her."

"Obviously, you take after your mom's side."

"Funny, that's what he said."

They stood there staring at the blonde spitfire in a showdown of wills. After a full minute, Garrett pointed out, "She can't take us both. I say we rush her."

Jack laughed.

"I don't know what you morons think is so funny. I'm a fourth degree black belt in Taekwondo."

Garrett snorted. "Lotta good that'll do you when I pull out my gun."

"Dude, you're not allowed to shoot her, no matter how big a pain in the ass she is," Jack informed him.

"Hey, she started in with the threats, pal, not me."

Samantha rolled her eyes heavenward. "Look, I just don't like cops, all right? And I already gave my statement yesterday, so I have no idea what you guys are doing back here."

"Do I look like a damn cop to you?" Jack scowled, insulted.

She scowled right back. "How the hell should I know what a cop's supposed to look like? I would've taken Paul Bunyan here for a wrestler, but I know *he's* a cop."

Jack grinned despite himself. He chanced a glance at Garrett who was glaring daggers at little sister. "Samantha, I just need to talk to you. It's important, trust me."

She hesitated, her gaze bouncing back and forth between them. Finally, with a 'fine, let's get this over with' wave of her hand, she beckoned them forward. "You've got five minutes," she advised as they strode past her into the ramshackle house. "Make 'em count."

Jack realized with a small measure of relief that Jamison was right. The inside of her friend's place was clean, well-furnished, and quite homey. Not as homey as Mia's butterflies, he thought, missing her like crazy, but definitely nice.

Samantha plunked down on the sofa and tucked one leg beneath her. Garrett stood sentinel beside the front door, his dour expression and set jaw screaming *hurry the hell up*. Jack didn't take it personally. If he had Jess waiting for him at home, he'd be in a rush to leave, too.

He swiped a hand through his hair and sat down beside his sister.

"Well?" she prompted.

He almost smiled. Patience wasn't his strong suit either. He sobered over the thought of what he had to tell her. "I'm sorry about your roommate."

"Yeah, me, too." Genuine remorse darkened her eyes.

"I didn't know her well. She'd only just moved in a few weeks ago. But she had a lot going for her. Just started a new job at the bank, classes at Rasmussen." Sam leaned forward and added, "Now, you wanna tell me why you're really here since I doubt it's to offer condolences for someone you don't know."

Without preamble, Jack replied, "I have reason to believe whoever killed her, thought she was you. I think you were the intended victim."

Her brow lifted, but not in surprise. "Well, duh. Why do you think I'm not too eager for visitors today?"

He exchanged a look with Garrett, then to his sister asked, "Well, then why won't you let the police help you? They can put you in a safe location until the killer is caught."

"No one knows I'm here except the cops. And I can take care of myself much better than they can," she boasted. "Besides, why do you even care? We don't know each other. How does my safety concern you in any way?"

"It concerns me because I'm your brother."

She stared at him for a moment, then cocked a brow. "Funny, the family resemblance is uncanny."

Smartass. Though she was right; they couldn't look less alike. Where Jack had his mom's wavy, brown hair and greenish-hazel eyes, Samantha had Whitlow's piercing blue eyes and blonde hair. Only hers was lighter, longer, and straight as an arrow. "I look like my mother. You look like our father."

"You mean that nutty rich guy who showed up here yesterday with the sperm donor story?"

"You look just like him. Didn't you notice the resemblance? It's pretty...*uncanny*."

She made a face over his choice of words.

He nearly smiled again, but fought it off. Something told him she wouldn't appreciate it.

Samantha cast a quick glance at Garrett who was watching them with amused interest. With a hearty sigh, she shot to her feet and marched into the kitchen. She returned with three cans of soda, tossing them each one before they could respond. Jack caught his, but Garrett was unprepared, and the can hit him square in the chest before dropping to the hardwood floor.

"Thanks," he muttered.

"No one can ever say I'm not a good hostess." She pulled back the tab of her cherry cola and took a sip. "Okay, so someone wants me dead. Why? I don't have any enemies. I mean, not that I'm aware of."

Jack clasped the cold can between his palms and considered how much he should tell her of his suspicions. He'd wanted to discuss them with Jamison first, but he supposed now was as good a time as any. "Someone tries to get rid of you the day after your über rich father shows up to claim you. And…" He cast a quick glance at Garrett, who quirked a brow in response. "Well, I'm a little fuzzy on the details, but the night before Whitlow showed up on my doorstep with the same dear old dad story, I was robbed. And I think I was…stabbed."

"You *think* you were stabbed?" his friend repeated, staring at him as if he'd lost his mind. "That's not exactly something a person would be unsure of, Sutton."

"You don't think I know how crazy that sounds? But I have about a nine hour window of time that I can't remember, and a fresh scar above my belly button with no idea where it came from."

"Maybe you'd better start from the beginning." Garrett tapped the top of his soda can a few times before popping it open.

"Yeah," Samantha chimed in, leaning forward with interest. "I agree with Paul Bunyan."

Jack filled them in on everything he could remember, from closing up the garage that night, to waking up the next morning without a clue, to the pool of blood he'd had to clean up. He decided to leave out the Grey sisters' odd behavior the following day since Jack didn't think for a second either of them meant him any harm. Whatever was going on with them had nothing to do with him, of that he was certain.

"Why the hell am I just hearing about this now?" his friend demanded, setting his soda down on the coffee table with a thunk.

"What was I supposed to say? 'Hey, by the way, I woke up on the concrete floor of my shop with a fresh scar and no recollection of how I got it?' You would've thought I was drunk."

Garrett massaged the back of his neck and started pacing. "We can't tell Jess about this, not in her condition."

Samantha turned to Jack. "Who's Jess?"

"Jamison's pregnant wife. She's a little overprotective when it comes to the people she loves."

Garrett stopped short and scowled at him. "She just has a soft spot for strays, Sutton. Don't flatter yourself."

Jack grinned. "She adores me and you know it."

Samantha's forehead screwed up in puzzlement. "Are you two friends or what?"

"Or what."

Jack gave her a 'don't worry about it' wave. "He's

just cranky 'cause he's hungry. So, why don't you pack up what you need, and we'll get the hell out of here. "

She quirked a brow. "'Scuse me?"

He got up and set his unopened soda on the table. "You're coming home with me. At least until this nut is caught."

"Uh, no, I'm not."

"Look, it probably won't be for long, and a change of scenery will do you good. Trust me on that."

Her gaze shot between the two of them. "So, where do you live? De Pere? Ashwaubenon?"

"Central Illinois. A little town called Shelbyville."

She stared at him for two heartbeats, then let out a bark of laughter. "Guess the old man's not the only one who's crazy. I'm not moving all the way to friggin' Illinois. I have a house here, friends, two jobs. A *life*."

"You rent the dump you live in on a month to month basis, you're a waitress and a stripper for chrissakes, and you won't have a *life* for very long if you stay in that house." For a second Jack thought she was going to cry. He hadn't meant to be so blunt, but this was a matter of life and death—hers.

"Don't you dare judge me! I work my ass off. Two full-time jobs, five days a week. And I won't be doing it for long, only until I finish beauty school. Thanks dancing, I'll own my own salon within five years."

"Look, I'm sorry," he said, wishing he'd used more tact. "I'm the last person to be judging anyone. I just...well, I don't want anything to happen to you, all right? I've been an only child for twenty-seven years, so this is all new to me, caring about someone else."

"It's new to me, too," she pointed out. "Although I

don't know how you can say you care about me when you don't even know me."

"Fair enough. So let's take this time to get to know each other while we keep each other safe. Maybe you can even teach me a few moves."

A hesitant grin settled on her lips. "I don't know about that. I don't really have the patience to teach."

"Yeah, I kinda picked up on that."

They continued to eyeball each other. Finally, she shot to her feet and let out a whopper of a sigh. "Fine. Give me twenty minutes. My stuff's mostly packed, but I have to make a couple of calls before I can leave."

"Hey, look, Jack's home!"

Mia glanced up from stocking the empty soda cooler and blew out a silent breath. As much as it bothered her to admit it, she'd been watching for his car to pull into his driveway all day.

Thankfully, the shop had been as busy as she'd hoped it would be, so she hadn't had much time to dwell on the real reason for his trip to Green Bay. Not that he owed her an explanation. It was just hard to figure out where she stood when he obviously didn't trust her enough to share...

There she went again. As if she'd been nothing but open and honest with him. Seemed they both had trust issues to work on if they had any chance for a future together.

Cripes, getting ahead of yourself, or what? They'd what, kissed a few times, ate a few meals together? Sure, they had boatloads of chemistry, and a powerful sexual attraction going on. But that didn't spell future.

And let's not forget she and Kat might not be around much longer anyway thanks to her evil stepfather.

With a rueful shake of her head, Mia closed the cooler and headed into the storeroom. She grabbed a box of weights and bobbers, thrilled by how well things were selling, and on the first day, too. Funding for Kat's new school wardrobe was looking pretty good at the moment.

When she returned to the store, her sister was standing at the front door, hands on hips, eyes narrowed, obviously unhappy by whatever had caught her attention. Mia tore the box of weights open as she headed her way, more than a little curious to know what had her so upset.

"What's going on?"

Kat spun around in surprise. "Nothing."

Hmm. With a frown, Mia stepped around her so she could see for herself. And immediately wished she hadn't. Jack and a beautiful blonde were busy pulling luggage from the trunk of his car. Her heart lurched painfully when the blonde laughed at something he said, then did a little hoochie dance as they headed around back and disappeared from sight.

"Want me to make her fall down the stairs?"

"Don't be ridiculous, of course not. Besides, I don't own Jack. He can see whoever he wants to."

"Yuh-huh, right. You don't care at all."

"I didn't say that." Damn right she cared. "Look, I have lots to do today, so just…don't get in my way."

"Whatever." Kat stormed past her and strode straight out the back door.

Okay, so she shouldn't have taken her frustration out on her sister. From the look of things, Kat had probably done her a huge favor by interrupting them last night. How humiliating it would be to discover Jack had gone from her bed to that bimbo's in less than twenty-four hours.

Doing her best to put the fickle man out of her mind, Mia busied herself with the shop. The new shiners needed to be dumped into the holding tank, the five and eight pound test lines needed to be restocked, and she had to get the pot roast in the oven for supper.

Once she finished with the first two chores, she decided to have Kat watch the register while she started supper. She found her down by the dock watching one of the marina boats head their way. Mia jogged down to join her and smiled when she recognized the driver.

Jared Winston, whose father owned the marina, had been flirting with her since the day she and Kat arrived in town. He was the second youngest of four brothers and a bit of a player, she'd heard, so he always laughed good-naturedly when she shot down his advances. Not that he wasn't a decent guy, and he certainly was a hottie. But Mia had always been singularly focused when it came to Kat and keeping a low profile.

He pulled up to the dock and tied off his boat. "Hey, how are the two prettiest girls on Lake Shelbyville?"

Kat crossed her arms. "Jared."

Was it her imagination, or did her sister's tone border on hostile? "Hey, Jared. What brings you down here?"

He stepped onto the pier and headed her way. "Let's just say I was hungry for the sight of you."

She rolled her eyes, and he grinned.

"Okay, seriously. I came down to see if you needed any help. Word is you hurt yourself a few days ago."

"Yeah, I got careless and dropped one of the aluminum boats on my foot. But it's much—"

"She doesn't need your help, she has Jack."

Mia shot her sister a quelling glance. "Jack is otherwise occupied, or have you forgotten?"

"Who's Jack?" Jared's expression grew slightly puzzled as he looked from Kat to Mia.

"Sutton. He's renting the old auto garage next door."

"Ah, got it. I didn't realize you were seeing someone."

"She is."

"I'm not."

Kat glared at her. "I'm sure that'd be news to Jack. Maybe I should go get him and see what he has to say."

Mia cleared her throat, embarrassed beyond words. Oh, she was going to throttle the little witch when she got her alone. She managed to meet Jared's amused gaze with a sheepish grin. "Sorry. Will you excuse us?"

He nodded, his smile curious, and made his way over to the picnic tables. Mia grabbed her sister by the elbow and led her into the shop without breaking stride.

"Hey, that hurts!" The little shit had the nerve to complain as she rubbed her arm.

"Do I need to remind you who the adult is here, Kitty Kat? You really need to learn when to just shut your mouth."

"But you love Jack, don't you?"

Taken aback by the softly spoken question, she could only stare in shock. Love? Good Lord. Relaxing her posture—and her frown—she placed a hand on the young girl's shoulder. "Honey, I like Jack. He's charming, handsome—"

"And sexy."

Mia blew out a silent breath. "Okay, I'm going to forget you said that. Listen, I like Jack, and I thought he liked me—"

"He does!"

"But that's just it, Kitty Kat. You saw the woman he brought home with him. I didn't just imagine her. Obviously, our neighbor isn't as into me as you think." *Or as he claimed to be.*

"But Mia—"

"This subject is closed, and I mean it. If Jack wants to be a man and come explain himself, fine. But right now, I have a very nice guy outside who came all the way down from the marina to offer his help. And I'm going to take him up on it. I need you to watch the store for a while. I have to put supper on."

Kat's face screwed up with frustration, but she wisely chose not to argue. "Fine. Whatever. It's your life." She whistled for Mudcat, then flounced off in a huff.

Mia shot a look heavenward before heading back down to the picnic tables where Jared waited. He stood as she approached, and she shook her head silently acknowledging, 'she's a handful, that one.'

"Why do I get the feeling she doesn't like me?"

His lopsided grin was teasing, and Mia had to admit the guy was gorgeous. Thick, near-black hair brushed the collar of his white pocket T-shirt, while startling sky-blue eyes twinkled with mischief. He was tall and muscular and, suddenly, she had no idea why she hadn't noticed before.

Because you were waiting for your soul mate.

"Kat doesn't like anybody, please don't take it personally. She's…well, she's a teenager."

Jared grinned his understanding. "Just wanted to

make sure I hadn't done or said something." He nodded toward her foot. "So, what can I do for you? I'm here, might as well use me."

Would you be willing to go beat some sense into Jack for me? Mia almost laughed out loud at her ridiculous thought. "If you really don't mind, I have a stack of boxes I need put up on the shelf in the storeroom. My foot is still a little tender for me to lift that kind of weight." Okay, so that wasn't entirely true, her foot had healed quite nicely. But like he said, he was here, and she could certainly use the help.

"Lead me to it, sweetheart."

After explaining to Jared where everything went, she ran into the house to get supper started. The pot roast would take a couple of hours, and as she quickly peeled the carrots and potatoes, she decided to invite him to join them. Kat wouldn't be happy, but it was the least she could do after his generosity.

Okay, so she knew his motives weren't entirely selfless, but then neither were hers, if she were being honest. Part of her wanted to gauge Jack's reaction to seeing another man in her home. And it wasn't like she planned to lead Jared on or anything. Just supper and some light conversation. She deserved that much after all her hard work this past week getting ready for the tournament.

She no sooner slid the pan in the oven than a knock sounded at the back door. Jared stood on the porch, hands on hips, smiling as he stared out across the lake. Fishing boats dotted the lake for as far as the eye could see. Lake Shelbyville boasted a hundred and seventy-two miles of shoreline and, with an average depth of nineteen feet, was considered by many to be one of the best lakes to fish in Illinois. Mia found the view quite beautiful, situated between rolling, steep wooded bluffs, and had known she and Kat found their home the first time she'd laid eyes on it.

The thought of possibly having to leave this wonderful place brought a fresh ache to her chest.

"You look a million miles away."

She hadn't realized he'd turned to face her and quickly plastered a smile on her face. "Sorry. Thought of something I have to take care of later. Come in, I was just putting supper in the oven."

Jared stepped inside and took a seat at the table. "So, what are we having?"

Mia grabbed a couple of sodas from the fridge and handed him one before taking the seat across from him. "Believe it or not, I was just about to ask if you'd like to join us. Nothing fancy, pot roast with potatoes and carrots. And it'll be a couple hours before it's ready."

"I love pot roast, thanks. I'd love to stay."

He popped the tab on his soda and took a long drink, his tanned throat working and…and the vision that formed in her mind was of Jack, damn him. Why was it when she had a hot guy sitting here, all she could think about was that two-timing… Well, okay, to be fair she didn't know for sure he was seeing Miss Blondie, she only suspected. But really, why else would he bring her home with her suitcases—

"Penny for your thoughts?"

Mia grew flushed and prayed it was only internally. "Nothing worth that much," she teased. "Just thinking about Kat."

He peered at her for a moment in contemplation. "You sure you want me to stay? I mean, if you haven't run it by your sister, I can take a rain check. Maybe you'll let me take you out for dinner sometime instead?"

"I don't have to run my dinner guests past Kat. And she'll be on her best behavior, don't you worry." *Or else she'll be grounded for the rest of the summer.*

"In that case, I'd love to stay."

He smiled, but there was an odd, almost disappointed look in his eye, and Mia realized he'd asked her out on a date again. Crap. As much as she wanted to say yes, she had to talk to Jack first, figure out what, exactly, was going on between them. If anything.

"Hey, I almost forgot, Pop wanted me to ask if you could use some crappie fillets or some bullheads. They're already cleaned," he assured her when she blanched.

Bullheads could sting you if you didn't know what you were doing, which Mia discovered last summer when she'd attempted to scoot one back into the lake with her foot. The darn thing had stung her right through her tennis shoe, leaving her big toe swollen for days.

"I'd love some crappie fillets. I found a recipe last week for a cornmeal batter I'd like to try. Please thank your dad for me."

Jared guzzled down the rest of his soda and set the empty can on the table. He waved her thanks away. "He's got crappie coming out of his ears. A lot of the out-of-towners come for muskie and white bass, so they give the crappies to Pop. And mom's so tired of finding new ways to cook 'em, she'll be thrilled to have you take a few off her hands."

He grinned, and Mia once again wondered why her heart didn't melt the way it did whenever their fickle neighbor set eyes on her.

"Well, I'm grateful. Lord knows I'm not much of a fisherwoman, and Kat loves fried fish." She got up and grabbed his empty can to rinse out for the recycling bin. When she turned to toss it in, Jared was standing right behind her, his gaze intent.

Trapped between him and the kitchen sink, she playfully rolled her eyes and tried to make light of their close proximity. "Well, hello there."

"Hello yourself." He reached up and trailed his fingertips across her cheek, down the column of her throat, then back up to gently tip her chin. His face lowered, and Mia froze, stunned to realize he was about to kiss her.

The back door flew open and banged against the wall. Mia's heart shot up to her throat as Jack stepped inside, his handsome face contorted with rage.

"Unless you wanna lose a limb, you'd better get your fucking hands off of her."

Eleven

Shock quickly turned to anger, and Mia pulled back out of Jared's reach to glare her displeasure at Jack. "Are you crazy? You don't just barge into my home as if you have the right—"

"I have every damn right. Or do you make a habit out of kissing every guy who lands on your doorstep?"

Jared took a step forward. "I think you'd better apologize to the lady."

Jack flexed his fingers, and Mia swore she saw a muscle tic in his jaw.

"One more step, asshole, and you'll be leaving here on a stretcher."

Exasperated by his macho display, she stabbed a finger toward the door. "Get the hell out of my house, Jack, and I mean right now."

Barely sparing her a glance, he kept his gaze centered on Jared, the look in his eyes feral. A frisson of alarm tingled her senses, and for a split second, she feared what might happen. Truth was, she didn't know Jack that well, not really, and had no way of gauging his potential for violence.

After what seemed like forever, he dismissed Jared and settled his gaze on her. "Would you like to tell me what the hell's going on here?"

"Not that I owe you an explanation, but Jared is a friend who came down to offer a hand."

Jack shot her guest a contemptuous glance. "Looked like he was offering a lot more than a hand. Try again."

"Hey, man," Jared chimed in, stepping forward. "You want to know what was going on here? None of your damn business. Now, get the hell out, like the lady asked."

"Smart-mouthed, sonofabitch." Without warning, Jack swung, clipping Jared in the side of the head, sending him crashing into the counter.

Mia managed to save the ceramic butterfly soap dish as it went flying. She set it down and demanded, "Dammit, Jack, what the hell's the matter with you?"

Jared righted himself with a muttered curse and lunged at the mechanic, tackling him to the floor. He threw a punch, but Jack dodged it, and Jared cracked his knuckles on the faded linoleum. He swore again; Mia winced as he clenched his teeth and shook his hand. Jack tossed him aside and jumped to his feet. Jared was a bit slower in finding his footing.

"I warned you, asshole." As soon as he got up, Jack swung again, catching him in the midsection. He quickly followed it with a jaw-crunching blow.

Mia cried out as Jared hit the floor a second time. Much to her surprise, he climbed right back to his feet, albeit a bit wobbly.

Desperate to defuse the situation before Jared ended up at the emergency room, Mia threw herself between them and half-demanded, half-begged, "Jack, I want you to stop this right now. Kat could come in any minute." Having zero experience with fighting males, she prayed the mention of her little sister would snap her neighbor out of his destructive mindset.

He swiped his fingers through his curls and stepped back to lean against the counter. "Fine. Tell him to get the hell out of here. We need to talk."

Jared eyed him in wary anticipation as blood seeped from his split lip and a cut above his left eye. He brushed his knuckles across his mouth and shook his head as if in disbelief. "I'm not leaving you alone with this psychopath."

Because of her, the man was broken and bloody, yet he still insisted on playing the protector. She started forward, but Jack stepped between them, blocking her path. And as much as it shamed her to admit it, his jealous reaction sent a small shiver of excitement coursing through her.

"I'll be fine, don't worry." She cocked a brow at Jack, and he reluctantly released her arm as she addressed Jared. "Thank you so much for coming down to help. I'm…I'm just so sorry."

He gave a curt nod, his gaze never leaving Jack's face. "I'll call you tomorrow," he assured her as he started for the door. "Raincheck on supper?"

"Absolutely."

No sooner had the door closed behind him then Jack spun to face her. "I'm gone one goddamn day, and you're already making dinner plans with someone else? Real fucking nice, lady. And he was about to kiss you when I walked in, don't waste your breath denying it."

"I don't have to confirm or deny anything," she informed him, hands on hips. "You don't own me. And after today, I'm not so sure I even want you in my life anymore. Or around my little sister."

Jack stared at her in stunned silence for almost a full minute. Slowly, he straightened and tucked his hands in his front pockets, hunching his shoulders in a non-threatening manner. "Please don't say that. Look, I'm sorry, it's just... Hell, I'm about to knock on the door when I see some schmuck with his hands on you, about to kiss you. How was I supposed to react?"

"Oh, I don't know, like an adult? Maybe you could have knocked instead of barging in? Or if you'd waited two seconds you would've seen me pull away, and that would have been the end of it. My God, you could've broken his jaw. Or worse."

"If the asshole had kept his mouth shut, I wouldn't have laid a hand on him. And it sure as hell didn't look like you were about to 'pull back' from where I was standing."

She shook her head, a combination of disbelief and sadness filling her chest. Tears stung her eyes. "Your temper scares the hell out of me, Jack. If it were ever directed toward me or Kat..." She turned around, choking back a sob, hating the ugly place they found themselves in.

Suddenly, his arms were around her, squeezing her gently, his lips feathering along the shell of her ear.

"Sweetheart, until I met you, I had no idea what jealousy even felt like. I know I handled it badly. Seeing another man's hands on you...it was like a knife in the gut."

Mia blanched at his choice of words. A tidal wave of guilt washed over her.

"But there's one thing I can promise you without a moment's hesitation," he continued. "I would never, *never*, lay a hand on you, or Kat, in anger. I'm so sorry I

149

scared you, baby. It's the last thing I wanted to do. We've known each other all of three weeks and I'm so friggin' crazy about you I can't see straight."

She didn't want her anger to dissipate, not after what he'd done to Jared. But he sounded so sincere, like the Jack she'd come to know and...love? God help her, she was dangerously close to falling in love with the man. Whether she wanted to or not was irrelevant. Mia craved his touch, his kisses, his sexy, masculine scent. More confused than she'd ever been in her life, she disentangled herself from his embrace and moved beyond his reach, wrapping her arms around herself in self-preservation.

"You owe Jared an apology, at the very least. He didn't know I was seeing anyone, and most certainly didn't deserve to be attacked."

"So, why didn't you tell him about me...about us?"

"I was just about to when you showed up and lost your damn mind," she informed him.

Silence. After a few moments, he blew out another hard breath. One of the chairs scraped against the linoleum as he took a seat at the table. "I've never been in a relationship before, Mia. And I have zero experience with jealousy; the emotion is completely foreign to me. But I swear to you, I'll find a way to deal with it that doesn't include my fists. Just please don't give up on me. I need you in my life, sweetheart. The thought of losing you scares the hell out of me."

The desolation in his voice tugged at her heartstrings, and all she wanted to do was throw herself back into his arms. Instead, she turned and eyed him with wary caution. "Who's the bimbo?"

He frowned. "You lost me."

"I watched you and some *blonde* get out of your car earlier. She had a suitcase, Jack. Care to explain?"

A slow grin curved that sexy mouth, which annoyed the hell out of her. "You mean my sister?"

Well, hell. She hadn't expected that. "Your sister? You don't look a thing alike."

"I hate to break it to you, but neither do you and Kat."

True. "But… Okay, I realize we still have a lot to learn about each other, but why didn't you mention you have a sister? Do you have any other siblings you'd care to tell me about?"

He got up and, before she realized his intent, drew her back into his arms. "You were jealous."

Yes, dammit! "Was not."

He chuckled and pressed a soft kiss to the top of her head. "I know this is going to sound strange, but I just learned yesterday about my sister. In fact, I have three brothers, too. Though I don't know if I'll ever meet them."

She pulled back and gazed up at him, wanting to know everything there was to know about Jack Sutton. "I'm all ears."

He cupped her cheek, and Mia turned into the warmth of his palm, his gentle touch like a healing balm. "I want to tell you everything, and I will. But it'll have to wait a little bit. I told Sam I'd be right back."

"Your sister's name is Sam?"

"Samantha, actually. And just to warn you, I'm not the only one in the family with a temper."

Great. Just what she needed, another hot-headed female to deal with. "Well, since you already chased off my dinner guest, how would you like to have supper with us? And of course, your sister is invited."

Jack tilted her chin up and kissed her on the lips, a slow, toe-curling kiss that left her craving so much more. "We'd love to."

"Good. Supper'll be ready in a couple hours."

"That's right. She's here with me in Shelbyville."

John Whitlow dropped his head back against the leather armchair and breathed a sigh of relief. "Thank you, Jack. I was worried sick about her, all alone, no family to protect her. Now she has you."

"And you. You dragged me into this situation; I fully expect your help in keeping her safe. I have my hands full with…other things."

A smile tugged at John's mouth. "That beautiful young woman who works in the shop next door?"

"Yeah. And her little sister who's a bit of a handful." Jack cleared his throat, and even though John couldn't see him, he'd swear his son was smiling.

"I picked up on that. So, is this serious?"

"What? I don't know. Look, since you have the resources, I want you to assign someone to watch my place while Sam's here. That won't be a problem, will it?"

"Of course not. In fact, Dudley and I will be flying down tonight. I bought a house in Shelbyville, so I'll be staying there until this nightmare is over."

There was a pause. Then Jack said, "Something else we need to talk about. Any idea why someone's trying to eliminate your offspring? Any enemies you know about? Could this be about money?"

A chill wracked John's shoulders. The thought that someone had tried to kill the daughter he'd only just found was sobering. "It *is* odd that someone targeted Samantha the very day I arrived on her doorstep, but we can't be sure the attack was due to her relation to me."

"I don't think Sam was the only one targeted."

"What are you saying?"

"I'm saying I was attacked as well. The night before you showed up at my door."

John's heart skipped a beat. "My God...what happened?"

"Look, we'll have to talk about it later," Jack said. "Just make sure you hire someone to watch my place. You may want to do the same for your other...offspring."

"I just can't believe this is happening."

"Relax, Whitlow. We'll catch the bastard."

John tossed the phone in its cradle and leaned back, pinching the bridge of his nose. Before he had a chance to dwell on who might be behind the attacks on his children, Dudley entered the room.

"We can leave whenever you're ready, Mr. John."

"Thank you, Dudley."

When his chauffeur didn't move, but continued to eye him, John inquired, "Was there something else?"

"Just wanted to make sure you're all right. You don't look so good."

He didn't feel so good, either, but his own health issues would have to wait until he made sure his children were safe from whoever had decided to target them. "I appreciate your concern, but I'm fine. Just stressed." He chewed the inside of his cheek in contemplation. "I think I may need your help down in Illinois. Any chance you'd be willing to stay there with me for a few weeks or so?"

"Sure." Dudley shrugged. "Not like I got a family to get home to. Why? What's going on?"

John blew out a hard breath. "I need to hire twenty-four hour security for Jack and Samantha, and also the others. I was hoping you might take care of this since you were in the business before you came to work for me. You'll be well-compensated, of course."

Dudley propped his hands on his hips. "You know I'd do anything for you, Mr. John."

With a grateful nod, John rose from his chair and crossed the gleaming hardwood floor. He gazed out across the expanse of his property, a view he'd never grown tired of over the years. He wished he could bring all of his offspring home where they'd be protected, but knew the chances of that happening were slim to none.

Jack and Samantha were both incredibly headstrong and independent—two excellent traits under normal circumstances. Like Samantha, Scott, Logan, and Darrin weren't signed up with the registry, but unlike their sister, they all seemed to have wonderful and supportive families. Chances were none of them even knew they were the products of sperm donations, and the last thing John wanted to do was disrupt their lives. However, that didn't mean he couldn't make sure they were all safe.

"Dudley, please call the pilot. I'd like to leave within the hour."

"The wake is tomorrow from two until six, the funeral immediately follows." Kent gripped the phone as he watched Zoe play with her doll, feeding it pieces of the pound cake his mother had made that afternoon.

"I can't even begin to tell you how sorry I am," Jack said. "How's Zoe doing?"

"She's a tough kid, but I'm not sure she really understands what's going on. And Sherry's parents are already making noise about wanting custody."

"No Shit? Damn, that's cold-blooded. They haven't even buried their daughter yet."

"I can't entirely blame them. Thanks to Sherry's lies, they think I'm the devil incarnate and that my parents treat Sherry like some kind of servant. We live with them right now, and Sherry only works part-time at the store, so my mom has her help out around the house a bit, like anyone would, you know? Only Sherry made it sound like she's some sort of slave, and her parents, of course, believe everything she tells them." Kent squeezed his eyes shut. "Listen to me, talking about her as if she's still alive."

"Give yourself a break; she's only been gone a couple days." Jack was quiet for a moment. "So, is that something you're considering?"

"Giving them custody of Zoe? Hell no! My daughter is my life, Jack. The thought of being parted from her... No way. I can't even imagine it. And her parents would do everything in their power to turn her against me, of that I'm certain. Sherry's been poisoning them against me for years. Since the first time I refused her request for a divorce."

His cousin muttered something under his breath. "I'm really sorry, man. That's the last thing you need to deal with right now, grieving, angry in-laws."

Kent was silent for a moment as a wave of sorrow

overwhelmed him. Not for the loss of his wife—which he'd worry about the ramifications of later—but for the loss of his daughter's mother. "You'll be able to make it, right?"

"Yeah, I'll be there. Something I have to tell you, though. I, uh, have a sister. Met her last night for the first time. She'll be staying with me for a little while, so would it be all right if she accompanied me to the wake? If it's a problem—"

"Of course it's no problem. I'd like to meet her. I know Mom would, too. I hope you don't mind, but she filled me in on your father situation."

"I'd have told you soon enough anyway. A lot has happened in the last few days." Jack cleared his throat. "I'll meet you at the funeral home. If there's anything you need, just let me know."

"Thanks, man. I appreciate it."

Kent hung up the phone and stuck his hands in his front pockets. Watching his daughter play, knowing that very soon she'd need him just as much as he needed her, was the only thing keeping him sane.

Suddenly, the guilt eating at his soul nearly choked him. Guilt that all he felt over Sherry's death was immense relief.

What the hell kind of a man feels relief over his wife's death?

His little girl had lost her mother; his in-laws had lost their daughter.

And he'd lost the woman who'd been making his life a living hell for the past five years.

All he could do to make up for his moral shortcomings was to be the best father to Zoe that he could be. And he could start by reminding himself

Sherry had done one thing right—she'd given him his daughter, the greatest gift he could've ever asked for.

"Daddy, are you mad at me?"

Startled by the question, Kent looked down, surprised to discover Zoe standing before him, her little face screwed up with concern. He scooped her into his arms and squeezed her tight. "Oh, honey, of course not. Why would you think that?"

"'Cause you're making the mad face."

He playfully relaxed his features before catching her chin between his thumb and forefinger. "Sorry, I didn't mean to. I was just thinking."

She cocked her head. "Were you thinking mad thoughts?"

For the first time since finding out that Sherry was gone, Kent felt an almost overwhelming urge to cry. For his daughter's sake, he kept it together. "No, but I smelled something yucky, so maybe that's why I made the mad face."

"It's a skunk," she kindly explained. "They stink."

He grinned. "That they do, peanut."

The doorbell rang. Kent set Zoe down and gave her nose a playful tweak. "Why don't you go finish feeding Annabelle her cake?"

"'Kay."

She skipped back into the kitchen, and Kent headed for the front door. He swung it open and came face-to-face with the last person he expected to see that day. "Hey, Sheriff. Something I can do for you?"

"Can't I just stay here and order a pizza?"

Jack managed to hide a grin as he pulled on a clean, white T-shirt and tucked it into his jeans. "No."

Samantha huffed the hair from her eyes and leaned back against the wall, arms crossed in annoyance. "Look, I don't get along with other chicks, okay? They take one look at me and dismiss me as some blonde bimbo."

He smiled over her word choice, which earned him a shot in the arm. "Hey, what are you getting mad at me for?"

"I'm *not* a bimbo, dammit. I can't help the way I look."

"Mia and Kat aren't the judgmental types." Well, maybe a teensy bit—though Mia's comment had stemmed from jealousy, not meanness. "So quit being a baby, put a smile on your face, and let's go. I'm starved."

Sam pushed away from the wall with an eye roll. "Typical man. If you're not horny, you're hungry."

He grinned. "You're the expert."

Another eye roll was followed by a reluctant smile. "Idiot. Fine, if you're going to force me to be social, let's get this over with. I'd like to get back in time to watch *Jeopardy*."

Mia had just set a platter of food on the table, and Kat was busy pouring milk for everyone, when they arrived. Jack's mouth watered as he surveyed the sliced beef, baby carrots, and oven-roasted potatoes. The table also held a bowl of green beans, a basket of rolls, and a jar of some kind of relish. Basic food to most, but after seven years of prison slop, it was a feast fit for a king.

Ignoring the call of his stomach, he made the

introductions. "Mia, Kat, I'd like you to meet Samantha Barnes, my sister. Samantha, Mia and Kat Grey."

Mudcat let out a loud "*Woof!*"

Jack laughed as he scratched the massive dog's head. "Sorry, boy. And this is Mudcat."

After a quick "Hey" to the Greys, his sister made a big to-do over petting the Mastiff. The dog immediately rolled to his back and started kicking his hind leg. Sam laughed, a genuine tinkling of sound which, for some odd reason, warmed Jack's heart.

Ah, shit, he was growing soft already.

Mia wiped her hands on a terrycloth towel before waving everyone to have a seat. It was already after five p.m., and Jack hadn't eaten since breakfast, so he had to remind himself not to shovel the food in like a pig. But after one bite of Mia's tender, flavorful roast, he couldn't help but dig in with enthusiasm.

He caught her eyeing him a time or two, and made a concerted effort to slow down.

"Mmm, this is yummy," Sam said around a mouthful of food. "I can see now why Jack practically dragged me over here."

He looked up and met Mia's amused gaze. She surprised him with a playful wink.

Sam set her fork down and bounced a look between the sisters. "I'm sorry, I didn't mean that the way it came out. It's just...well, to be honest, I wasn't in the mood to socialize. But you two seem pretty cool." With a shrug, she picked up her glass and sipped her milk.

Kat eyeballed his sister with teenaged annoyance.

"Thanks," Mia said with a pleasant enough smile. "And no worries. We don't always feel like socializing either."

"Like right now," Kat muttered under her breath.

Jack coughed to cover up a laugh. Sam would get used to the little hellcat's surliness soon enough.

Mia merely shook her head at her sister before casting Sam an 'ignore her' eye roll. Thankfully, the rest of the meal was eaten in silence.

Blowing out a loud, satisfied breath ten minutes later, Jack leaned back in his chair and laced his fingers over his swollen stomach. "I can't remember the last time I ate so much."

"I can. The other night when we had spaghetti," Kat pointed out with a cheeky grin.

He chuckled. "You got me. Heck, at this rate, I'll be spoiled for anyone else's cooking in no time."

"You just don't want to have to cook for yourself," Mia teased as she got up to clear the table. His sister surprised him by jumping up to help.

"True." He grinned. "But since you've tasted my cooking, you can hardly blame me."

"True," she tossed back at him, scooping the leftovers into a large plastic container.

They exchanged a look, and a crackle of sexual awareness jolted his lower region into high alert. The need to get her alone nearly overpowered him as he watched her swish around the kitchen, her sweet ass encased in a snug-fitting pair of red jogging shorts. His fingers itched to pull her into his arms and reacquaint himself with her soft curves, to taste those sweet lips, delve into that luscious mouth…

Ah, hell, he was growing hard. Not good in the company of their sisters. He cleared his throat and stood to help…and to relieve the pressure behind his zipper.

Mia took the bowl of beans from him. "Relax. I'm just going to put the food away, and Kat can load the dishwasher. Sam, thanks for helping."

"No problemo. Thanks for supper." She turned to Jack. "You don't mind if I head back, do you? I have a couple of calls to make."

"'Course not. Make yourself at home, I'll be there soon."

Mia smiled. "Nice to meet you, Sam."

"Same here. You, too, Kat."

"Uh-huh. Later."

As soon as she left, Jack got up and strode over to the fridge, where Mia had her head buried. He wrapped his arms around her from behind, causing her to jump. She turned in his embrace and smiled up at him, heating his blood to a slow simmer. He dropped a quick kiss on those sexy lips, then leaned back so she could close the fridge door.

"I can finish up in here if you guys want to take a walk down by the dock," Kat offered, her offhanded tone belying the twinkle in her eye.

Although he wasn't sure why, Kat seemed to have taken a liking to him, and for that he was grateful. "You sure? I'd love to take a walk down by the lake, maybe toss in a line." He glanced down to see what Mia thought.

"Sounds good to me. Wanna do some crappie jerking off the pier?"

"Crappie jerking?"

She laughed. "Fishing for crappie. You just drop a line in with a sinker, no bobber, and when a crappie bites, you jerk him out of the water."

Unable to help himself, he leaned down for another

quick kiss. "Sounds easy enough. Lead the way." He caught Kat's gaze and winked. "Thanks."

Mia grabbed a small, plastic container with holes poked into the cover from one of the coolers in the bait shop, then stopped at the shed for two fishing poles and tackle box. She led him down to the pier, all the way to the last slip, and took a seat with her legs dangling over the side. Jack followed suit.

Once she'd removed the bobbers from the poles and tied on what she called weights, she peered at him in contemplation. "I suppose I'll have to put your worm on for you."

"You mean a live worm?"

Mia tossed her head back and laughed.

"It's not that funny," he grumbled, tempted to lean over and tickle the shit out of her. "I've only been fishing a couple of times when I was a kid, and we used those metal lures."

"Sorry," she said, bringing it down to a giggle. "For some reason, that struck my funny bone. Yes, a live worm. And I know some people are squeamish about putting them on their hook, which is why I asked."

"Woman, if I didn't know better, I'd think you were questioning my masculinity." When she pushed the container of worms his way, he suddenly wished his masculine pride had minded its own damn business. Of course, he had no clue how to put a worm on a hook…but how hard could it be?

Figuring he could watch Mia do it first, Jack frowned when she set her pole down and reclined back, tipping her head up toward the sun, her eyes closed, smile serene, as if she were simply enjoying the beautiful day.

After watching her for a moment, he blew out a silent

breath and reached into the container for a worm. The damn things were slimier than he'd expected, and he must have chosen the most pissed off one of the bunch. He could barely hold onto the squirmy little bastard; he dropped it on the pier twice, the second time just catching it before it slipped through the cracks. He shot a quick look at Mia, who seemed oblivious to his plight as she continued to bask in the warmth of the sun.

Finally, he got a good hold of the slithery devil and attempted to wrap it around the hook. Only the stupid thing refused to grab on, and Jack was starting to feel like an idiot.

"You have to pierce it through. The worm isn't going to hang on for the ride when you drop it in the water."

She hadn't even opened her eyes, the smartass. As if she'd known exactly what he'd try to do. Finally taking pity on him, she sat back up and gently took the hook from his grasp. Swallowing his pride—along with a couple of curse words—Jack handed her the spastic wiggler and watched as she deftly worked him onto the hook.

"Okay, now we just drop it in and, I swear, within half an hour, we'll have a bucketful of crappie." She handed him the pole and readied her own, dropping her line in right next to his.

"You know, the only fish I've ever eaten are fish sticks."

She made a face. "Trust me, you'll never eat another fish stick once you've tasted some good fried panfish. I'll cook 'em up tomorrow, if you'd like."

Jack met her gaze, but his eyes were instantly drawn down to her luscious lips. "I'd like."

He cleared his throat and looked out across the lake.

The sun had just started its downward descent, and the view was amazing. He leaned back, holding the pole with one hand while propping himself up with the other. He enjoyed the breeze coming off the lake, heavy with the sweet scent of the purple flowers that grew wild along the bank.

"Here we go!" Mia abruptly shouted as she 'jerked' her pole up to reveal a wriggling fish, maybe eight to nine inches in length. "Fill that five-gallon bucket about halfway with lake water."

She removed the fish from the hook like a pro, dropped it into the bucket he'd filled as instructed, and put another worm on her hook, all in less than a minute. Her love of fishing was obvious, and for the umpteenth time since they'd met, Jack found himself unable to take his gaze off of her. The woman was amazing, easily the most fascinating person he'd ever met. Not to mention the most beautiful.

Jack had spent seven long years believing once he got out of prison, his life would be shit. Who the hell would want to hire an ex-con? And what woman would want to hook up with a man who couldn't give her more than the bare essentials in life? Sure, he'd managed to earn a mechanic's certification while in prison. But a woman deserved more than what a guy like him could give.

Then he'd met Mia, and that happy future he'd only dreamt about actually seemed like a possibility. He was crazy about her, well on his way to falling in love. An emotion he'd thought himself incapable of until he'd met the raven-haired beauty. And she was attracted to him, too, for which he thanked his lucky stars. They were far from making any declarations, but he knew in his heart and soul that Mia Grey was his destiny. He'd never believed in fate before, but maybe, just maybe his mother had guided him to Shelbyville for more than a family reunion. Maybe she'd delivered him to his future.

A sharp tug on his fishing pole snapped Jack from his musings. He jerked the pole from the water, just as Mia had, and barely caught himself from letting out an excited squeal as he eyed the fat crappie dangling from his hook. Mia yanked her pole out of the water a second after him, and just like she'd said, they had a bucketful of fish in no time at all.

"That was a blast," Jack said as they gathered everything up. "And I have to admit, your fishing skills are a bit of a turn on."

"Yeah?" Mia caught her bottom lip between her teeth and sent him a come-hither look so sultry, it was a miracle he didn't tear a hole through his jeans.

He set the bucket down and drew her into his arms. "Yeah," he whispered before leaning down to claim those lush lips. Damn, she had the sexiest full lips. He'd never grow tired of kissing her, not a chance in hell.

With a soft gasp, she slipped her arms around his neck and plastered herself against him. Jack ached with the need to make her his, to bury himself deep inside her, to love her until the rest of the world melted away and nothing and no one else mattered but the two of them.

The kiss intensified until Jack had to concentrate just to keep his balance. He plumbed the moist depth of her mouth, groaning as her tongue boldly met his with equal fervor. She nipped at his bottom lip and moved her hips against his straining erection.

He ended the kiss with a groan of frustration and

rested his forehead against hers while they both fought to catch their breath. "Mia—"

Someone cleared their throat, loudly, and Jack looked up to see a police officer heading their way, that Jared asshole right behind him.

"Jack Sutton?" the officer inquired once he'd reached them.

"That's me." He felt Mia tense in his arms as understanding dawned. "Something I can help you with?"

"Sir, I'm afraid I'll need you to come with me down to the station. I'm placing you under arrest for assault and battery."

Twelve

Mia shook her head in vehement denial as Jack muttered a curse and held out his wrists. She looked over at Jared and winced when her gaze landed on his black eye. "Please don't do this."

His bruised face pulled into a scowl. "Are you kidding me? This bastard attacked me, Mia. You think I should just let that slide?" Scorn laced his words as he eyed her with disgust. "I guess so considering you obviously have. Aren't you even the least bit afraid of what he might do to you?"

"I'd never hurt a woman—most especially this woman." Jack turned back to the cop. "Can I speak with my sister before we leave?"

"Sorry, you'll have to wait 'til we get to the station to call her." He slapped the cuffs on and led Jack away as he read him his rights.

No idea what to do or how to fix this, Mia turned to Jared. "Please, I'm begging you to drop the charges. It was my fault what happened. I should have told you I was seeing someone."

Jack stopped and turned back to face her, a slight frown marring his brow. "I'm to blame for this mess, not you. I lost my temper. Can you do me a favor and let

Sam know what's going on? And don't worry, I'll be home soon."

Mia swallowed hard and nodded. She bit her lip in an effort to hold back the tears as the officer gave Jack a tug to get him moving again. This was partly her fault and she knew it. If she'd just had a little faith in him instead of using Jared to soothe her battered pride, this whole mess could've been avoided.

Though, Jack's reaction *had* been way over the top. He'd hurt the guy pretty badly and should be held accountable for his actions. She could only hope he was able to swallow his pride and offer Jared the apology he deserved. Then maybe he'd drop the charges and they could all move on.

After explaining the situation to Kat, who agreed that they should post Jack's bond, Mia asked her to lock up the house and meet her by the car. She was halfway up the stairs that led to Jack's apartment when glass shattered with a deafening crunch and a huge male body flew backwards out Jack's living room window.

Holy shit! Mia raced up the stairs without thought. After the stabbing in the garage and the incident outside by the shed, there wasn't a doubt in her mind the incidents were connected. And Sam could very well be lying up there hurt or worse.

She nearly got knocked on her ass as the blonde fury burst through the door. She reached out a steadying hand, then cast a quick glance over the railing. A violent curse flew from her lips as the man flipped over onto his stomach and stumbled to his feet. He didn't even look back as he took off like a shot into the copse of trees and disappeared from sight.

Sam started after him, but stopped cold when Mia hurriedly announced, "Jack's been arrested."

"What? Why? What the hell happened?"

Loathe to admit she was the 'why,' Mia gave her the short version. "He got into a fight earlier today with Jared Winston, whose father owns the marina. Kat and I plan to bail him out if Jared doesn't drop the charges."

Frustration etched Sam's brow as she watched her attacker escape. That she wanted to give chase was evident. Fisting her hands, she smacked them against the rail, then muttered, "Fine. Let's go."

"What the hell are you doing here?" Jack rubbed his wrists as the cell door closed behind him. Bastard cop must be a friend of Winston; he'd clasped the cuffs a lot tighter than necessary.

"I've been arrested for Sherry's murder."

Stunned, he strode forward and plunked down on the cot beside Kent. "Shit, that's crazy. What the hell kind of reason could they have for—"

"Her brakes were cut. Someone wanted Sherry dead, and since the whole goddamn town knows my personal business, I'm their prime suspect."

Jack silently digested that shocking tidbit. "Any idea who'd want your wife dead?"

"Not specifically, no. Could be someone she was sleeping with. Could be the pissed off wife of someone she was sleeping with. Hell, could've been anyone for all I know. Sherry and I barely spoke to each other unless it was about Zoe. I can't even remember the last time we had a civil conversation. 'Bout the only thing we had in common was our love for our daughter."

Drawing his leg up, Jack rested his forearm on his knee. "Well, they can't charge you with murder just because you had an unhappy marriage. What evidence do they claim to have?"

"You mean besides the fact that my new cousin, who did time for murder, happens to run an auto garage?"

Fuck.

Jack leaned back against the concrete wall and closed his eyes. Thanks to his mere presence in town, the police had enough circumstantial evidence to arrest Kent for murder.

"Ah, hell, man, I'm sorry about the way that came out. None of this is your fault. I'm just…scared to death. I didn't kill my wife, but if the cops can't find another lead, I may end up spending the rest of my life in prison."

That sobering realization had Jack sitting back up with a start. "No way in hell that's going to happen. Not if I can help it." And if that meant going to Whitlow for help, so be it.

Kent gave his head a sad shake. "I've got a bad feeling about this, Jack. If someone *did* set me up, it's only a matter of time before the so-called evidence starts piling up." He leaned forward and cupped his head in his hands. "I want you to promise me something. If I do end up going to prison or…well, my mom's going to be a wreck. She'll need you. She—"

"Someone's trying to set you up for murder, and you're already resigned to your fate? No way, you hear me? You're going to fight this. You have a daughter who needs you. She's already lost one parent. You gonna let this bastard, whoever he is, make Zoe a complete orphan?"

Angrier than he'd been in a long time, Jack shot to his feet and started pacing. He'd done seven hard years in prison on a bogus murder charge and barely survived. His cousin might not be so lucky.

"Look, I realize this situation hits a little close to home for you, and I'm sorry about that. But I'm trying to be realistic here. Of course I plan to fight this. I just want to be prepared in case...well, in case the cocksucker who set me up did a damn good job of it." He combed his fingers through his hair and slumped back against the wall. "Now, tell me, what the hell are you doing here? Aren't you on probation or something?"

Shit. With everything else going on, Jack had managed to forget that fact. Hopefully, Garrett could help him out with this one. "I got in a bit of a fight earlier. Caught one of the guys from the marina about to kiss Mia. We've been sorta seeing each other. Bastard ran his mouth, I lost my temper and slugged him. He came back a few hours later with a cop.

"You must mean Jared." Kent chanced a small grin. "He's been trying to get a date with Mia since she and her sister moved here. The Winstons are a decent bunch. I doubt he knew she was seeing someone."

"Well, he knows now. And he'd better stay the fuck away."

Concern etched his cousin's brow. "You'd better learn to control that temper, or you're going to find yourself doing another seven years. This time by your own hands."

Kat copped an attitude as soon as she realized Sam

would be joining them. Mia was well used to Kitty Kat's instant dislike of people, but she genuinely puzzled over her aversion to Jack's sister. She practically worshipped the ground he walked on, so why risk his displeasure by treating his sister so poorly?

They rode in silence, neither she nor Samantha commenting on the window incident. Sam would obviously have to explain what happened since Jack would need to have his window replaced. Mia also wrestled with whether or not she should tell him about the night he got stabbed. She could probably do so without revealing her full part in it, but there'd be so many questions. Not to mention, he might end up hating her for lying to him all this time. The thought brought the sting of tears to her eyes.

She pulled into the parking lot of the Shelbyville PD, and they all hurried inside. The station room was surprisingly small, and as she quickly scanned every square inch, she realized Jack was nowhere in sight. The thought of him sitting in a jail cell broke her heart.

Samantha strode right up to the first officer in sight and demanded, "Where the hell is my brother?"

He quirked a brow and nodded for her to take a seat, his double chin quivering with the motion. Sam remained standing, hands on hips, glaring at him as if the whole situation was his fault.

Mia sighed, cast Kat a 'let it go' look, then strode forward and smiled at the officer. "I'm very sorry, but my friend is just a little upset. Her brother, Jack Sutton, was arrested a short time ago, and we're here to post his bail."

"Sutton's cooling his jets in a cell. You'll have to wait until he goes before the judge for bail to be set."

Sam slapped her hands on the officer's desk. "This is bullshit, I...mmmph!"

Her eyes widened with panic. It looked as if she were trying to speak, only her lips wouldn't open. Mia cast her sister a suspicious glance; the little shit smiled with smug satisfaction, but released the spell when Mia narrowed her eyes.

"What the hell...?" Samantha fingered her lips with comical dismay.

Hard-pressed not to laugh, Mia returned her attention to the officer and schooled her features into one of deference. "Do you happen to know when that might be? We could wait—"

"I wouldn't waste your time," he advised. "Judge Matthews is gol—gone for the day."

"Well, why didn't you just say that in the first place?" Sam demanded. "And you were about to say golfing, weren't you? Lazy ass judge in this little hick town."

The cop poked a stubby finger at her. "You watch your mouth, young lady, or I'll throw you in the cell right next to your brother."

Mia placed a restraining hand on Sam's arm and to the officer said, "Thank you for the help. I don't suppose there's any chance we could see Jack, let him know we'll be back tomorrow?"

"I'm afraid not, miss. But the judge will be here bright and early tomorrow morning. You can come back then."

"Thanks." She tried leading Samantha away, but the stubborn chick wouldn't budge.

"He at least got his one phone call, right? Everyone's supposed to get one phone call."

Exasperated, the officer wrestled his girth from the chair and rose to his feet. He waggled his chubby finger again. "Someone really needs to teach you some manners, missy. Of course he received his phone call. Which he made before he was led down to his cell. Happy?"

"Ecstatic." Samantha spun about and stalked from the police station.

Mia heaved a sigh of immense relief and followed her out.

Right on her heels, Kat muttered, "She's an idiot. I don't know why you brought her with us."

"Kitty Kat, I have enough on my mind right now. Please don't add to my stress."

"Whatever. You're just being nice because she's Jack's sister."

Mia shot her a quick look. "Of course I'm being nice because she's Jack sister. It's called respect. Once we get to know her better, I'm sure we'll genuinely start to like her."

"Which means you don't like her any more than I do," Kat pointed out with a smirk.

"I barely know her, and neither do you. What have I told you about making snap judgments on people? Besides, you adore Jack. You can't honestly believe he's going to appreciate the way you've been treating his sister."

A slight pout tugged at the corners of the young girl's mouth. "Hmph. I don't even believe she really is his sister. They don't look at all alike."

Mia chuckled. "As Jack pointed out to me when I made the same observation, neither do we."

"Well...I'd be a much better sister than that-that *sleazebag*."

Stunned, Mia stopped and grabbed Kat's wrist. Samantha had already reached the car, so hopefully she hadn't overheard any of their conversation. "All right, that's it. One more word and…" The truth suddenly dawned on her; the reason for Kat's dislike of Samantha made perfect sense. She was jealous. Jack had become like a big brother to her, and now she had to share him with his real sister. Understanding washed over Mia in a great wave of compassion. She let go of her wrist and wrapped an arm around the bristling teenager.

"Don't worry, honey, we'll get Jack out of that jail cell tomorrow. And we'll make him a celebration supper, how does that sound? We'll fry him up the crappie we caught today, and you can make him your awesome potato pancakes to go with them."

Seemingly mollified, Kat nodded and leaned into Mia as if for support, her tough girl façade dissipating if only for a short time.

"Come on. We'd better get home and clean those crappies before Mudcat finds them."

"Dammit, Whitlow, I told you to go take care of Sam." Jack shot to his feet and crossed the cell. "What the hell are you doing here?"

Kent had been released an hour earlier. Luckily, Uncle Jerry had been able to locate the judge, who happened to be a fishing buddy. Bail had been set, and Kent was back at home where he should be, comforting his daughter. Zoe would need her father by her side tomorrow when her mother was laid to rest. The last tenuous thread of Jack's faith in the justice system would have snapped had Kent not been able to attend his wife's funeral with their daughter.

"Hey, pup, show a little gratitude. Mr. J. here sprung your sorry ass. Got that punk to drop the charges and everything. Though *I* think he shoulda let them call your parole officer."

"Dudley, that's enough. I appreciate your loyalty, but I'll thank you to show respect when speaking to my son."

The chauffeur bobbed his head and clasped his hands in front of him in a seemingly respectful manner. "Of course, sir. My apologies."

Jack met his father's gaze, and though it nearly killed him to do so, he swallowed his pride—along with a few choice words for Dudley—and thanked the older man for taking care of him. Truth was, it felt damn good to have someone out there who actually gave a shit about him. "Look, I really do appreciate what you did for me, but I'm worried about Sam. She's been alone at my place for hours."

"Don't worry, Jack, she's fine. Dudley and I stopped there on our way here. I even found someone willing to replace your window first thing in the morning, though the SOB charged me an arm and a leg—"

"Broken window? What the hell are you talking about?"

John's brow knit in puzzlement. "The window off your kitchen, right next to the back entryway."

The clip of footsteps on the concrete floor preceded one of Shelbyville's finest as he came around the corner and marched their way. He cast all three of them a dubious glance before unlocking the cell door. Jack silently swore he'd never do anything to land himself in jail again. Even if that meant taking anger management classes. The thought of losing Mia, not to mention his newly found freedom, was sobering. He stepped out of the cell with a silent sigh of relief.

"What happened to my window?"

"No idea. Sam said she'd explain later, that you needed me more than she did. And she was right. If your parole officer had been called before I'd had a chance to get that young man to drop the charges, you'd already be on your way back to Green Bay Correctional."

"Like I said, I'm grateful. I truly am. Now, would you mind giving me a lift home so I can find out what the hell happened to my window?" Although he was afraid he already knew, and if he was right, Sam was going to require a lot more protection than he could provide.

The sun had already set by the time they arrived, but the skies were clear, so there was plenty of moonlight to be able to recognize Sam sitting on the hood of Jack's car, watching as the limo pulled into the driveway. He couldn't make out her expression, but her body language hinted at defensiveness. He wondered if she'd been sitting there since the broken window incident, like maybe she was afraid of his reaction.

Or afraid to go back inside.

"You don't look any worse for wear," she called out as soon as he stepped from the limo.

"Thanks," he said as he strode her way. "Your concern warms my heart."

She slid off the hood without further comment, hands on hips, her gaze glued to something behind him. Jack wasn't sure if Whitlow was the recipient of her narrow-eyed stare, or Dudley, and at the moment, he didn't care.

"What happened to my window, Sam?"

She transferred her scowl to Jack. "Relax, bro. Daddy dearest is taking care of it."

"I don't give a damn about the window, Slick, I care about you. And much as I hate to admit it, looks like you're no more safe here than you were in Green Bay."

She crossed her arms over her chest. "No shit, Sherlock, didn't I try telling you that? Still, you dragged me here, so here I stay until we figure out what the hell's going on."

Whitlow smiled his relief. "I agree."

One perfectly arched brow shot upward. "And who asked you?"

He chuckled. "Such a firecracker. I'm only trying to help you, Samantha."

"Yeah, well...I don't need your help."

"Okay," Jack announced, "this is getting us nowhere. Sam, I think Whitlow's right. He has Dudley here to help keep you safe. I have to work, so I can't keep an eye on you twenty-four seven."

"You talk about me like I'm some lollipop-licking little girl! I'll bet you each a hundred bucks I can kick your asses." She smiled in challenge. "One right after the other."

She relaxed her stance as if getting ready to back up her boast. Jack gave an exasperated shake of his head while Whitlow and Dudley exchanged grins, obviously enjoying her show of bravado.

"Put your hackles down," Jack told her. "No one is questioning your ability to take care of yourself. But until we figure out who's targeting us and why, we can't take any chances. Better safe than sorry."

She rolled her eyes before turning her gaze on

Whitlow. "So, what kind of a place did you buy?"

Jack almost laughed over her about face. His apartment was sparse at best, barely habitable for him let alone a young woman. She'd be much better off living with Whitlow, who could afford to provide her with, at the very least, a comfortable bed.

And Whitlow certainly looked happy to do so if his three mile wide smile was any indication.

"My assistant found a nice tri-level that's been sitting empty for a couple years. Needless to say, it needs some work. Mainly just a good airing out and a top to bottom cleaning. I have a crew coming in tomorrow, then it's just a matter of furnishing it."

"So we have to sleep on the floor?"

Whitlow's face screwed up in comical dismay. "Of course not. We're staying at the Kerrington until the house is habitable."

She shot a quick look at Dudley. "Well, I'm not sharing a room with either of you, that's for damn sure."

"I'll book you your own suite, of course," Whitlow assured her, beaming.

Jack barely resisted the urge to roll his eyes. Going from no family to more family than he knew what to do with in a matter of a week was going to take some getting used to. Not that he minded all that much. In a weird way, he was enjoying the kooky bunch.

Less the homicide and murder attempts.

"Good." Seemingly appeased, his sister shot him a conspiratorial wink before heading around back to the apartment.

"Hold up. I still haven't heard how my window got broken." Jack started after her, with Whitlow and Dudley bringing up the rear.

She sprinted up the darkened stairway, but stopped at the door to turn and face him. The ornery old sensor lamp decided to work, illuminating them with light.

"I was standing next to the counter eating a cupcake when someone attacked me from behind; wrapped an arm around my throat. I reacted, flipped him on his ass, we fought for a minute, then I gave him a kick that sent him through your window." Her gaze touched on each one of them before landing back on Jack. "Sorry."

"I don't give a damn about the window. I'm just glad you're all right." A shiver danced along his spine as another fleeting memory from the night he discovered that scar on his stomach flashed in his mind. *"...wrapped an arm around my throat."* He propped his hands on his hips and looked at Whitlow. "They must have attacked her within minutes of me getting hauled away." Which meant they'd been watching his place all along. Whoever the hell *they* were.

"As you can see, I'm fine." She held her arms out, as if for inspection. "But you might want to check on your girlfriend. She was kinda freaked over the whole thing."

"Mia saw what happened?" *Sonofabitch.*

"She must have been on her way up the stairs when I kicked the asshole through the window. I ran out to finish the job and nearly mowed her down on the stairs."

Jack scowled, his blood freezing at the thought of what could have happened had Mia arrived a minute earlier.

"Don't wet yourself. She was fine by the time we got to the station. She's tougher than she looks." Sam shrugged as if to say 'who'da thunk it?'

"Hurry up and grab your stuff," he said. "The sooner you're away from this place, the better."

"My thoughts exactly."

As soon as she dashed inside, Whitlow climbed the last few steps and placed a hand on Jack's shoulder. "Son, I don't want you staying here either. It's not safe. The window won't be replaced until tomorrow, and you can't stay up all night—"

"I'll be fine. I'm sure Mia won't mind if I crash on their couch."

The older man frowned, unconvinced. "Please, Jack. You'll be a whole lot safer at the Kerrington. I could book you a suite as well."

"I appreciate the offer, but I need to keep an eye on Mia and Kat. What if whoever's behind the attacks goes after them? I'd never forgive myself if something happened while I was twenty miles away at some fancy hotel."

"I can book a room for the sisters as well."

"Again, I appreciate the offer, but the sisters and I will be fine. Just take good care of Sam."

Whitlow swiped his fingers through his thinning, blond hair before giving a curt nod. "Of course I will. And please, call my cell if you need anything. Oh, and I know it's just a formality, but we'll need to set up that DNA test so I can get my legal ducks in a row. Particularly in light of everything that's happened."

"Mr. J," Dudley interrupted, "maybe you could hurry that girl of yours up? It's getting late, and I have a few phone calls to make when we get to the hotel."

"That *girl* is a woman, meathead," Sam corrected as she stepped outside, her suitcase in one hand and her duffle bag hooked over her shoulder.

"Females," Dudley pronounced, crossing his meaty arms over his chest.

"Dudley, please help Samantha with her bags."

Sam gawked at Whitlow, incredulous. "You're just gonna let that gorilla talk to me that way?"

Whitlow let out an audible sigh. Jack almost felt for the guy. Slick was a handful, no question, and Dudley didn't seem to be cowed by the fact she was the boss' daughter. He was quite happy to not have to listen to those two bicker half the night. He'd get more sleep on Mia's threadbare couch, no doubt about it.

Dudley reached past Whitlow to grab Sam's suitcase, but she yanked it out of his reach.

"I can carry my own bags. Just get out of my way."

She surprised Jack with a quick hug and a promise to call the following day, then shot Dudley one last, withering look before elbowing her way past him down the stairs. The chauffeur spit over the railing and muttered a curse before following after her.

Jack shook his head. He turned and met Whitlow's gaze, whose brow creased with worry.

"I'll be fine," he assured him. "If I were you I'd be more worried about Sam and your chauffeur. I think they may kill each other before the night is through."

A reluctant twitch of the old man's lips proved the humor wasn't lost on him. "It isn't Samantha I'm worried about. Dudley's knees have been giving him trouble lately. The old boy isn't as spry as he thinks he is."

"Just keep 'em separated and Sam won't have any reason to kick his ass."

Whitlow nodded, but his expression grew serious again. "Please don't forget about the DNA test, Jack. It's very important—to me and to the future of Whitlow Industries."

He reached up to massage the back of his neck. "I have a couple of jobs in the morning, and somewhere I have to be around ten, then I'm free. Where do I need to go for the test?"

"A couple of jobs? It's a miracle you can pay your bills. Why don't you let me set up an account for you so—"

"Forget it, Pops. Just tell me where to go to take the test before I change my mind."

"As stubborn and proud as the day is long." Whitlow gave his head a rueful shake. "The tests can be taken right at the hospital here in Shelbyville."

"I'll meet you there around noon."

Whitlow nodded and left without another word.

After the day he'd had, Jack needed a hot shower in the worst way. He made it a quick one, brushed his teeth, and threw on a clean pair of jeans and a black T-shirt before heading next door.

Mia flung the door open just as he lifted his fist to knock, her face lit up with relief at the sight of him. At least he hoped he was the reason for her pleasure. She threw her arms around him and squeezed tight, chasing away any and all doubts.

"Thank God you didn't have to spend the night in a jail cell."

He closed his eyes and inhaled deeply. The fresh scent of her flowery shampoo filled his senses, as intoxicating as any drug. He pulled back just enough so he could gaze into those luminous dark eyes. *God, she's beautiful.* As if drawn down by force, Jack brushed his lips across hers, once, twice, in just the lightest of caresses. A tiny hum of pleasure assured him Mia wanted more.

"I'm sorry," he whispered, nearly shaking with the need to crush her in his arms, kiss those soft lips until both of them were mindless with desire. "I never meant to worry you."

"You have nothing to apologize for."

"Of course I do. I let my temper get the best of me, I scared you. And while I still think he's a schmuck, your friend didn't deserve what I did to him."

She gave a reluctant shake of her head. "No, he didn't. And I wasn't scared—not truly scared." She let out a soft sigh and stepped back. "Come in. I made a pot of coffee, would you like a cup? It's decaf."

"Thanks, I'd love one. Kat isn't already sleeping, is she? It's barely nine-thirty."

Mia pulled a mug from the cupboard and poured him some of the steaming brew. "She conked out about an hour ago. It was a long day for all of us."

Guilt ate at him as he accepted the mug. Thank God her sister hadn't walked in while he and Jared were going at it. It would have killed him to see stark fear replace the adoration that usually shone from the young girl's eyes whenever she gazed up at him. Jack had never had anyone look up to him before, and he just now realized how much her approval meant to him. He wanted to be someone Kat felt safe with, not someone she feared.

After stirring in a spoonful each of sugar and powdered cream, he finally met Mia's gaze. "Please tell me Kat didn't see me get arrested."

She carried her own coffee mug to the table and sat across from him. "Don't worry, she didn't see a thing. Though she did come with us down to the station. Kat's tough, trust me. And a lot more level-headed than...well, she's mature for her age."

He grinned. "You were going to say Sam, weren't you?"

She tried to hide a smile by taking a sip of her coffee, but Jack caught it. She set it down with a thunk and admitted, "Okay, yeah, I was. But she really does need to work on her—"

"Temper?"

"Exactly. She needs to learn to control her tongue. It's a miracle they set bail for you the way she was carrying on. Which is one of the reasons Kat got so upset. My sister adores you, you know."

Jack reached across the table and grasped her hand. "The feeling is mutual, I hope you know that."

Her beautiful face lit up again, warming him from the inside out. She gestured toward the plate of sugar cookies on the table. "Have one. Kat and I baked them earlier, after cleaning the fish. We didn't expect to see you tonight, so they're supposed to be tomorrow's dessert."

A comfortable silence fell as they sipped their coffee and ate cookies. Jack devoured nearly the entire plate, much to Mia's amusement.

He let out a low chuckle. "Sorry, guess I was hungrier than I thought."

"You want me to fix you something? A sandwich, a plate of leftovers maybe...?"

"The cookies were enough, thanks. But I do need a favor."

"Name it."

"Mind if I spend the night?"

Thirteen

Mia's heart thundered in her chest at his softly spoken request. And not just because of the erotic images her mind immediately conjured. Now that she knew Tim Mallick was holed up in town somewhere, just waiting for another opportunity to grab Kat, Mia had been worrying herself sick each night, waiting for him to make his next move. Having Jack under their roof, even if only for the night, meant she might actually get a few hours of sleep.

"Of course not. But what about Samantha? After what happened earlier, I can't imagine you'd want to leave her alone. Which, by the way, we need to talk about."

"Don't worry. She's safe and sound sleeping in a comfy, king-sized bed at the Kerrington. And she already filled me on what happened. I'm so glad neither of you were hurt."

Mia took a sip of her coffee. "It's pretty obvious Sam can handle herself. But why aren't you there with her?"

"Because I wanted to make sure you and Kat were safe. There's been a lot of crazy shit going on the last few days. I'd never be able to sleep knowing you two were here all alone."

"I have to admit, I'm glad to have you here. And Mudcat will go crazy if anyone tries to break in, give us a little advance warning."

"He wasn't much help the other morning when that freak walked right into your house and scared the hell out of Kat," Jack pointed out.

"Mastiffs aren't attack dogs, they're barkers. And to be fair, he was outside with me when...when that guy broke in." She wrapped her arms around herself and gazed up toward Kat's bedroom. Even now, Tim could be lurking outside, just waiting for a chance to steal her baby sister away. The only comfort she found was in knowing Mudcat slept at the foot of her bed and would bring down the roof barking if anyone tried to break in.

She heard the slide of Jack's chair a few moments before his hands gently cupped her shoulders. His crisp masculine scent washed over her, as soothing as a cool breeze on a hot, muggy day.

"I'm sorry," he murmured, his sexy voice rumbling up from deep in his chest. "I'm supposed to be comforting you, not worrying you."

She closed her eyes and leaned into him, wanting nothing more than for him to crush her in his strong arms and kiss her until the rest of the world melted away. "I'm okay, just a little...wound up."

He leaned in close, his warm breath tickling her ear as his fingers started a gentle massage of the tender flesh between her neck and shoulders. A soft gasp escaped her as his thumbs worked just the right spot.

"I'm no expert, but I think I might be able to work out some of those knots."

"You have no idea how good that feels," she whispered. In fact, she was about three strokes away from dissolving into a puddle right there on the floor.

Clearing her throat, desperate to get herself under control, Mia reached back and grasped his fingers, then turn around to face him. Those gorgeous hazel eyes crinkled at the corners, his gaze smoldering with promise. All she had to do was say the word and he'd make all of her fantasies become reality.

"The sofa in the living room is a surprisingly comfortable pull out bed. I should probably go set it up for you."

"Let me. Those things are pretty heavy."

Mia grabbed the old blue comforter and two pillows from the hall closet while Jack pulled out the sofa bed and stacked the cushions against the wall. She tossed him the fitted sheet and bit back a grin as he wrestled it onto the thin mattress. After, she helped him spread the comforter across the bed before tossing on the pillows. They had an awkward silence as they stood facing each other, Jack with his hands shoved into his pockets, Mia with her arms crossed.

Finally, she asked the question she'd meant to ask earlier, choosing her words carefully since, thanks to her, Jack had no memory of the stabbing incident, or the confrontation the other night when he took out the garbage.

"Jack, what happened earlier at your apartment? Do you have any idea who that guy was or why he was attacking your sister?"

He reached back to massage the back of his neck, a move she'd come to recognize as his sign of discomfort. Too bad. This was the third attack she knew about, and if there was even the slightest chance her and Kat could become targets, she needed to know. Between Tim and this unknown threat, Mia was already riding the edge of panic.

Jack sank down onto the sofa bed with a grunt of resignation and clutched the edge of the mattress with both hands. "A few days ago I found out my father had been a sperm donor. My mom…she was in love with a woman, they wanted a child, so…" He gestured with his hands, as if he didn't quite understand himself. "My mother never told me, and as you know, she died before she had a chance to."

Mia sat down beside him and laid her head on his shoulder, wanting him to feel her support, to know that she understood his pain. He wrapped an arm around her and continued.

"When I got home the other day, there was a limo parked in my lot. Some rich dude got out and said he needed to talk to me—told me he was my father. I thought he was nuts, since I'd been told my father was dead, but I couldn't discredit his story without looking into it."

"I remember him. And his creepy chauffeur. Guy's a perv, I swear."

Jack pulled back to eyeball her, a slight frown marring his forehead. "Did he say or do anything to you?"

"No, geez, relax." She smiled reassuringly. "I just caught him staring at my chest while I was handing him his change. Not like he was the first, and I'm sure he won't be the last."

"I really wish you hadn't tacked on that last part."

He looked so put out that a rueful smile pulled at her lips. "Sorry."

He gave her a quick squeeze. "I'll be taking a DNA

test tomorrow so dear ol' dad can legally claim me as his kid. I told him there's no need, not like we're gonna start going to ballgames or anything. But he has some legal reasons for wanting to do it. Anyway, there's something I haven't told you because, honestly, the details are pretty sketchy. Remember the morning I came in for aspirin? I'm pretty sure I was attacked the night before."

Oh, no... "My God, what happened?"

He breathed deep, then gave his head a disbelieving shake. "I have no clue. I know this is gonna sound crazy, but I woke up on the floor in the garage with no memory of how I got there. When I reached my apartment, I realized my shirt had a tear in it, and I had a long red scratch on my stomach, and when I went back down to investigate, I found a puddle of blood, which couldn't have been from the scratch. Then Whitlow—that's the man claiming to be my father, John Whitlow—told me I had a sister and three brothers. He traveled up to Green Bay to meet my sister, and it turns out her roommate was killed the night before. She'd been sleeping in Sam's bed."

"Are you saying the killer was actually after your sister?"

"Looks that way. So, I drove up and talked her into returning to Shelbyville with me, figuring at least I could look after her here."

A slight grin stretched the corners of her mouth. "If anyone can take care of herself, it's your sister."

"She's a capable woman, no doubt about it. But even Sam can't stop a bullet."

Mia blanched. "She's not alone at the Kerrington, is she?"

Jack pressed his lips to the top of her head. "No.

Whitlow and his chauffeur are there, too. Whitlow bought a house in town. He plans to stay until whoever is behind the attacks is caught. He can afford to hire a bodyguard for himself and Sam. Not to mention, it's a good excuse to get away from his soon-to-be ex-wife for a while."

Mia would never admit it since she'd feel like a bit of a hypocrite, but on some level, it hurt she was just finding out all of this now. "What about you? Who's protecting you?"

Jack tilted her chin up and brushed her lips with his. "I can take care of myself, don't worry. Little sister isn't the only one in the family with martial arts training."

Which didn't help you at all the night you were stabbed, she wanted to point out. Of course she had no choice but to keep that thought to herself since she was the reason for his loss of memory.

They cuddled for a while in silence before Mia reminded herself she had to get up to bed. Not that sleep would come easy for her, but she had to get up early to open the shop. She stood up reluctantly and met his questioning gaze. "Well, I'd better get up to bed. I'll see you in the morning. 'Night."

"Sweet dreams, Mia."

Oh, her dreams would be far from sweet tonight. They'd probably set her damn sheets on fire.

After washing up and slipping into her favorite, oversized Chicago Bears T-shirt, Mia settled into bed. Not that she was the least bit tired. Her mind and body were restless with erotic thoughts of Jack—sleeping right below her, shirtless, pantless, lying there in only his...would he wear boxers or boxer briefs? Did guys even wear briefs anymore?

Her skin grew hot and clammy just thinking about him down there all alone, and she flopped onto her stomach in frustration. He was easily the sexiest man she'd ever known; all hard, sinewy muscle with raw sex appeal oozing from his pores. Not to mention those gorgeous bedroom eyes that seemed to bore straight down into her soul. Even his big feet were sexy. How unfair was that? She smiled. Thank God the man couldn't read her thoughts.

It struck her just how little she still knew about him. He was a complete mystery to her, yet sometimes she felt as if she'd known him forever.

And oh, how she wanted him. With an intensity that both thrilled her and scared the hell out of her.

A soft sigh escaped her as she watched the minutes tick by, her frustration mounting as sleep evaded her. She decided to head downstairs for a soothing, fragrant cup of herbal tea.

The silence was deafening as she crept down the stairs, careful to step around the creaky spots. Jack was probably already sound asleep after the day he'd had, but she decided to take a quick peek into the living room, just to make sure he was comfortable.

Yeah, right. She wanted to get another look at him, and that was the plain and simple truth. Maybe catch a glimpse of that incredible body, the cause of her restless—

"Can't sleep?"

Mia spun around with a yelp. Her heart lodged in her throat and she slapped a hand over her mouth, thankful she'd managed to keep from screaming bloody murder. Jack stood directly in front of her, barefoot, bare-chested, and more handsome than any man had a right to be. His hair was slightly mussed, as if he'd done a bit of tossing and turning himself, and her fingers itched to smooth those wavy locks back into place.

"I'm sorry. I didn't mean to scare you."

She heaved a sigh of relief while waving off his concern. "I'll live. I just figured you'd be sleeping by now."

A slow, sexy grin curved his lips. "I could say the same about you."

Praying her cheeks weren't nearly as flushed as they felt, Mia shrugged, running her fingers through her hair. "I guess I'm more worried than I thought."

With a softly muttered curse, he strode forward and took her into his arms. "I'm so damn sorry. I never meant to drag you into this." He pressed his lips to her temple. "I swear I'll keep you and Kat safe. You can count on it."

"I feel safe right now." She snuggled into his warmth with a lusty sigh of contentment. This was exactly what she wanted, and exactly where she wanted to be. Rational thought went right out the window as she plastered herself against his broad chest, twined her arms around his neck, and gazed up at him.

Jack didn't hesitate—he took her lips with such fervor Mia gasped her surprise. He kissed her, passionately, thoroughly, pulling her into the cradle of his hips, letting her feel his hardened length.

Tongues tasting, teasing, lips moving together in perfect harmony. Never had a man kissed her with such devotion, such adoration. Mia couldn't get enough of him. Her skin blazed everywhere they touched, her pulse thundered in her veins. By the time he scooped her off the floor and carried her into the darkened living room, she nearly cried out her relief.

"God, how I want you," he whispered as he laid her gently on the sleeper bed. "It scares the hell out of me how much." He lied down beside her and gathered her in his arms.

Her throat too thick to speak, Mia smoothed her hands over the hard planes of his back, reveling in the way his muscles quivered beneath her touch, in the low, sexy growl that escaped him. Her oversized T-shirt bunched around her waist, and though she knew he couldn't see them, Mia was unexpectedly self-conscious of the plain, white cotton panties she'd chosen to wear. Darn it, why couldn't she have thrown on the tiny black lace thong she'd dared to purchase online a few months back?

"I need you, Mia."

His work-roughened hands worshipped her body, slowly caressing her from shoulder to knee, making her tremble with anticipation.

She'd never imagined she could become so lost in a man's touch. No one had ever made her feel as desirable as Jack did. A flood of heat pooled at her core, and it was all she could do not to grind herself against his rigid length.

"Jack…" She pulled him down for another kiss, meeting the soft rasp of his tongue, tentatively at first, becoming more aggressive as her need for him grew. She hungered for the taste of him, ached to feel him deep inside her. The knowledge that he wanted her just as much was as heady a feeling as she'd ever known.

Jack drew her nightshirt up, breaking the kiss only long enough to whisk it over her head and toss it aside. Naked except for her panties, a wave of vulnerability washed over her as he gazed down at her moonlit curves.

But the reverence in his expression chased away any and all doubts. He reclaimed her lips, rolling so that he was more atop than beside her.

Mia looped her leg over his, desperate to get as close to him as she possibly could.

He trailed his free hand up from the tender spot behind her knee to one aching breast. Cupping it, he lifted its weight before circling the pebbled peak with his thumb.

He broke the kiss again to whisper, "I've been imagining this moment since the day we met."

"So have I," she admitted, grateful for the darkness that hid her burning cheeks.

Jack released her breast to gently palm her face. She could barely make out his handsome features, but his eyes glittered down at her. "I don't share, Mia. If we make love, you're mine. Understand?"

"I only want you, Jack. Only you."

He gave her a slow, toe-curling kiss, one she suspected was meant to stake his claim and seal their fate. The thought pleased her. She'd never desired another man the way she did Jack, never felt this all-consuming need to give herself so completely to another living soul. And she knew instinctively she never would again.

She stroked his back as he trailed a moist path across her cheek to nip at her earlobe, down the gentle curve of her throat, to her waiting breasts. He lifted one heavy globe and traced her aching nipple with his hot tongue before closing his mouth over the pebbled tip. Still mindful enough to suppress a groan, since the last thing she wanted to do was wake up her sister, she clamped her bottom lip between her teeth and ran restless hands through Jack's stunningly soft hair. She closed her eyes, reveling in his touch, his spicy masculine scent, desperate for him to treat her other breast to the same exquisite torture.

As if reading her mind—or maybe they really were that in tune with each other—he switched his attention to her other breast, caressing, licking, suckling. Every inch of her burned for his touch, every nerve sizzled to life as he worshipped her body, her breath growing more and more labored as her need for this sexy man soared to a fevered pitch.

He gave her tender nipple one last lick before tracing a molten path of fire from between her breasts, across her trembling stomach, to the thatch of black curls at the apex of her thighs. "I could come just *thinking* about tasting you," he murmured in a low rumble.

Mia couldn't have spoken to save her life. His raw admission nearly sent her over the edge. She wanted him to…oh how she wanted him to. But no man had ever… She swallowed, hard. "Jack—"

"Shhh." His warm breath feathered over her heated flesh like a silken caress. "Let me. I want to make you go up in flames."

Flames? Hell, she was on the verge of internal combustion. Mia swallowed her inhibitions and met his twinkling gaze with as much confidence as she could muster. "I mean…if you insist."

His low chuckle flowed over her nipples like a deliciously cool breeze, tightening her aching buds into painful peaks.

"I insist."

He slipped his fingers beneath the waistband of her panties and stripped them off, leaving her completely naked...and oddly vulnerable. She watched him through heavy-lidded eyes, a flood of desire pooling between her thighs at just the thought of what he planned to do...Oh, *God*.

She held her breath in anticipation as he pressed his mouth to the spot just above her bellybutton and his fingers found their way through her course curls. He slowly circled one finger over her swollen nubbin—once, twice—then pressed through her slick folds, and slid into her hot passage. Mia arched her back with a loud gasp. She drew her knees up and squeezed her eyes shut as Jack slowly stroked her molten core.

"You okay?" he whispered.

Clutching the blanket in a death grip, Mia forced herself to relax and opened her legs a bit more, giving him better access. "I think I'll die if you don't...get on with it."

He chuckled. "Such a romantic you are."

"It's your fault, you're driving me crazy," she informed him, her embarrassment dissipating in the face of her urgent, base needs.

Jack knelt on the floor and positioned himself between her thighs. His breath feathered across her belly as he slid his hands beneath her butt and literally lifted her off the mattress. The first touch of his tongue on her sensitive flesh drew another gasp from her. Never could she have imagined how good this would feel. And the sexy sounds he made—as if she were a succulent feast—only intensified her pleasure. Mia tried to hold herself still, but instinct took over, and she moved her hips in urgent rhythm as he loved her with his mouth.

She was on the brink of explosion when he stopped

suddenly and stood. She barely held back a sob of frustration. "Jack...?"

His handsome face, bathed in moonlight, was taut with need. Naked, wet, and throbbing, Mia watched in fascination as he reached for the button of his jeans. Her heart pounded as Jack slipped out of his jeans and boxer briefs. His erection was every bit as impressive as the rest of him, just as she knew it would be. She wanted to touch him, stroke him, bring him to the brink of ecstasy just as he had her.

"I have protection," he told her, his tone adorably sheepish as he grabbed his wallet off the end table and pulled out a small square package.

She sat up and knelt in the middle of the bed, her blood pumping through her veins in eager anticipation.

Jack joined her on the bed and took her in his arms with a deeply murmured, "Come here."

Cupping the back of her head, he captured her mouth again, his tongue demanding entrance, his need for her evident in every touch, every caress. His hardness pressed into her belly, and she reached between them to grasp it. He groaned, deepening the kiss as she eagerly explored his thick length.

Mia experienced a brief moment of panic when his declaration of earlier replayed in her mind—reminding her of Jack's brutal attack on Jared—but she quickly pushed it aside. She ached for this man, craved him in a way she didn't fully understand. *He's your soulmate,* that little voice reminded her. *And he would never hurt you.*

Jack grasped her ass with both hands and broke the kiss with a softly muttered curse. "God, yes. Touch me, sweetheart. Feel what you do to me."

His sex was silky smooth, yet hard as granite—satin over steel. She stroked his thick length gently at first, moving faster with each groan she wrung from him.

Mindless with need, Mia gazed up at him, so turned on she could barely think straight. "I need you...inside me. *Please.*"

With a softly muttered "Yes, ma'am," he tore open the condom packet and quickly sheathed himself. Mia slid her arms around his neck as he lowered her to the bed. Holding his gaze, she grasped his stiff erection with one hand and guided him to her slick passage.

"You're so beautiful," he whispered, his voice achingly tender.

Her throat too thick with emotion to speak, Mia wrapped her legs over the backs of his thighs and braced herself as Jack sank into her with a hoarse groan. Their lips melded, their hips moving together in perfect rhythm, straining, aching for release. The man was magnificent in every way, and Mia met each thrust with a hunger she never knew she possessed, writhing beneath him in mindless need.

She clutched his back as passion consumed her, each slow stroke drawing a gasping cry from her as their hips surged together. Oh, God, she was so damn close—

Jack rolled them swiftly to the side, gripped the underside of her knee and held her leg aloft while thrusting into her. Her nipples tingled and her clitoris throbbed as their new position heightened her pleasure, hurtling her right over the precipice. With a soft cry, she exploded. His guttural moan mingled with hers and they rode out the wave of sweet release, undulating together until the last shuddering spasm rocked through her.

Once their heartbeats slowed back to normal and they

caught their breath, Jack gathered her in his arms and pressed his lips to her temple. "You have no idea how good you feel in my arms."

God help her, she wanted to stay in his arms forever. Or, at least for the rest of the night. But she couldn't risk Kat coming downstairs and finding them like this.

"I have to get back upstairs. If Kat were to come down and find us sleeping together, the questions would never end."

Jack chuckled, a deep, masculine rumbling, and released her. "I was hoping you'd stay down here with me, but I get it. One of these nights, I want to sleep with you in my arms."

Mia collected her nightshirt and panties off the floor and pulled them on before casting him a cheeky grin. "Such a romantic you are."

"Is that a problem?" He gave her backside a playful slap.

"No, it's a date."

Alexandra Whitlow pitched her cell phone across the room and threw herself onto the four-poster bed with a furious curse.

That idiot! First he went off chasing after those sperm donor brats of his, and now he was moving to that hick town indefinitely?

Considering John's money and influence, she wouldn't be able to fight the divorce forever. Her lawyer had already suggested she take John's "generous" settlement offer and consider herself lucky. But she didn't want that pittance amount, dammit, she wanted it all. If only he'd been able to get her pregnant, like a real man.

Her alternative plan had been working like a charm, until John decided to find out if he'd had any bastard kids. The drops she'd been sprinkling in his coffee every morning for the past three months had made him so sick he literally puked the moment he rolled out of bed in the morning. And just as she'd been promised, his doctor hadn't been able to find anything wrong with him.

Her cell phone rang and, with another curse, she shot off the bed to retrieve it. She glanced at the display before answering. "What the hell are we supposed to do now?" she demanded. "It's bad enough I won't be able to dose him for a while. But if we don't get rid of those brats, it won't goddamn matter anyway!"

"Calm down," her brother instructed. "I'm going to take care of it, I told you that."

"You haven't done a very good job so far," she snapped, checking her reflection in the mirror. For thirty-eight, she looked fabulous and she knew it. Long, auburn curls, big brown eyes, and her mother's amazing genes were just a few of the reasons she's been able to hang onto John as long as she had. She'd been leading him around by the dick since day one. Until his cow of a sister stuck her uppity nose where it didn't belong.

"Hey, shit happens, all right? I swear these people have nine fucking lives. But don't worry, no one's that damn lucky. I'll get rid of the bastards one way or another, then we'll take care of your husband. Permanently."

The thought brought a smile to her face. Once John and his newly found brood were eliminated, she'd inherit his fortune and kick the rest of his useless kin out on their asses.

Fourteen

Jack watched from the back of the funeral parlor as one person after another paid their condolences to Kent, Aunt Pat, and Uncle Jerry. Although Sherry Kingston wasn't exactly well liked by the townsfolk, according to the buzz he'd been hearing since her death, the Kingstons were highly respected in the community. The room was packed with everyone from the little old lady who ran the coffee shop in town, to the post office workers, to Mayor Johnson.

Glancing around, Jack finally spotted Zoe, sitting quietly on the beige loveseat in the far corner of the room, her shiny black shoes barely hanging off the cushion, her eyes huge in her pale little face. Jack gave Mia's hand a quick squeeze. "I'll be back in a few minutes."

Zoe watched him approach, her expression guarded. When he got close enough, he realized two silent tears were sliding down her cheeks. Damn. He'd give anything to be able to take away her pain, to carry it inside himself instead. He sat down next to her and propped his hands on his knees, not quite sure if he should try to speak to her, or wait and see if she wanted to talk.

"My mommy's in that big box," she murmured almost immediately. "Daddy said she's taking a nap before her trip to heaven."

"Your daddy's right. It's a long journey."

She gazed up at him, and Jack could've sworn a spark of anger flashed in her eyes. "Then how come she didn't say goodbye? Mommy always gives me a kiss goodbye when she goes somewhere."

Ah, hell. His heart shattered into a million jagged pieces, paralyzing him with grief for this precious little girl. He swallowed, searching for just the right words, fearful of saying the wrong thing and adding to her anguish. "She couldn't, peanut. Please don't be mad at her. Your mom would've said goodbye if she could have. That I promise you."

Her bottom lip quivered, but she bravely held his gaze. Jack wrapped a gentle arm around her shoulders, and she surprised him by leaning into his side. They sat in silence for a few minutes until she let out a sigh so quiet he almost didn't hear it. When she looked up again, the tiniest frown marred her forehead. "Is my mom gonna be an angel like Aunt Karen?"

Jack hated the doubt that crept into his mind. But then, who was he to judge? "I'm sure she will. In fact, I bet our moms become best of friends. Just like you and me. I mean, if you want me to be your friend."

A smile tugged at his lips as he watched her think about it for a moment.

"Can cousins be friends?"

"Well, sure, why not? Your daddy is my cousin, and he's also my friend."

"Okay, we can be friends, too."

This time his smile won out. It quickly faltered,

however, when a familiar figure caught his gaze, heading in Mia and Kat's direction. His jaw clenched. *Jared Winston. Great, just frickin' dandy.* Jack's first instinct was to rush across the room and wrap a possessive arm around Mia's waist. Instead, he remained seated next to Zoe, silently offering his support while her father and grandparents spoke with those who had come to pay their last respects. Kent caught Jack's eye and nodded his appreciation.

He tensed when Jared, instead of moving on to speak with the Kingstons, grasped Mia's hand and spoke in an almost urgent manner. What the hell did that asshole think he was doing? Her gaze darted around the room before landing on Jack in silent concern. For herself, he wondered, or because she feared his reaction? He plastered a smile on his face to let her know all was well. He'd never cause a scene here, especially not in front of Zoe. The little peanut sitting beside him was the most important person in the room right now, and Jack intended to help make sure her mother's funeral wasn't sullied by any ugliness.

His will was sorely tested when Jared cupped Mia's elbow and appeared to be trying to coax her outside. She attempted to yank her arm free, but the asshole held tight.

Reaching the end of his patience, Jack caught his aunt's attention and gestured her over. "I have to go talk to Mia," he explained to Zoe. "Your grandma's on her way over, but I'll come back when I'm done, if you'd like me to."

"Okay."

He gave her shoulder a gentle squeeze, then stood and spoke with his aunt. "I just need to go check on Mia.

Looks like she might have some unwanted attention."

Aunt Pat shot a quick glance over her shoulder, frowning when her gaze landed on Jared. "Please, Jackson, no scenes. Not here."

He gave her a wry smile. "News certainly travels fast."

"It's a small town," she reminded him. She squeezed his hand and added with a reassuring smile, "You'll get used to it."

By the time he reached Mia's side, Jared's voice had started to rise. Jack wrapped an arm around Mia's shoulder. Taken by surprise, Winston dropped her hands and stepped back. Frustration twisted his features as he processed Jack's possessive actions.

"I think it'd be best if you leave."

"I don't give a damn what you think," Jared pronounced, his superior tone daring Jack to cause a scene.

With as cordial a smile as he could muster, Jack nodded and started to lead Mia and Kat away.

"Mia, this guy's making a fool of you, and you're letting him," Winston insisted in a furious undertone. "Your skin should be crawling just from letting him touch you."

She stopped and spun around, her mouth tight with anger. Thank God she had the presence of mind to keep her voice down. "Look, Jared, I'm sorry about what happened the other day, and so is Jack. I should have told you I was seeing someone."

"You're not just seeing *someone*, Mia. This guy's a killer. Jesus, I'm afraid for you."

Fuck. Jack glanced back at Uncle Jerry, who kept his expression carefully bland. He'd hoped the older man would keep quiet about Jack's time in prison. It's not like he had anything to gain by spreading such news about his own wife's nephew. Unless he was hoping Jack would race back to Wisconsin with his tail between his legs.

"Okay, now you're completely out of line and I want you to leave. *Please*. This is Jack's family. You have no right—"

"Dammit, Mia, he's a murderer. He just got out of prison like two months ago. Go ahead, ask him if you don't believe me. It's easy enough to verify." Jared cast a meaningful look in Uncle Jerry's direction.

Kent strode forward and joined them. "Winston, I'm not sure why you chose my wife's funeral to cause a scene, but I don't appreciate it. My daughter just lost her mother. Show a little respect and get the hell out of here."

Seemingly remorseful, Jared propped his hands on his hips and blew out a hard breath. He cast one last glance in Uncle Jerry's direction before murmuring an apology and heading for the exit.

"You all right?" Kent asked, giving Jack a light thump on the back.

He gave a curt nod, embarrassed, angry, frustrated. Mia gazed up at him, those big brown eyes bursting with anxious curiosity. Kat frowned her annoyance, though he didn't think it was directed at him. At least he hoped not. He'd planned to tell them both about his time behind bars once they figured out who was behind the attacks on his family. But thanks to Uncle Jerry, Jack had some explaining to do right now.

"Look, I appreciate you coming," Kent told him. "And it meant a lot to my mom and Zoe, too. But maybe you ought to just take Mia and Kat home. I'll give you a call tomorrow."

"You sure? I hate to leave like this."

"You should stay," Mia told Jack, her tone cool. "Don't worry about us; we can catch a ride with someone."

"No way am I letting you two leave alone. Besides, we need to talk."

"You think?" She grabbed her sister by the forearm and led her out of the funeral home.

Jack muttered a curse. He'd never intended for Mia to find out about his past this way. He should have been the one to tell her, dammit.

Kent gave him another thump on the shoulder as Jack followed the Grey sisters outside. They stood beside his car, Mia staring off into the distance. Lord only knew the kind of thoughts running through that gorgeous head of hers. Was she mentally chastising herself for falling into bed with an ex-con? He swallowed the familiar bitterness as he dug his keys from his pocket.

She looked up, and he was taken aback by the hurt and uncertainty swimming in those mesmerizing brown eyes. He'd expected fear, disgust, maybe even contempt the way she'd marched out of the funeral home. A glimmer of hope tightened his chest.

She cast her sister a quick glance before spinning around to climb into the car. Kat gave her head an exasperated shake. She smiled as he approached, and if Jack didn't know any better, he'd swear the younger girl was offering him silent support.

They drove home in silence. Kat sat in the back with her legs and arms crossed, staring gloomily out the window, while Mia did the same in the front. Jack pulled into their driveway and shifted the car into park, letting it idle.

"Look, I have to meet Whitlow at the hospital for that DNA test, but I was hoping we could talk when I get back…?"

Mia barely spared him a glance. "Sure. You know where I'll be." She jumped from the car and stormed off, turning once to throw her sister a 'let's go' look.

Kat opened the door, but hesitated a second. "She's just surprised," the younger girl assured him. "I'm sure once you explain…"

Her words trailed off, and Jack met her gaze in the rearview mirror. "I hate that you guys found out this way. I promise, I'll explain everything once I get home."

With another reassuring smile, she swung the door shut and took off after her sister.

Jack decided to run up to his apartment and change out of the only decent pair of slacks he owned and into his work clothes. He backed out of Mia's driveway and pulled into his own, surprised to spot a van parked just off to the side of the garage, enough so that he hadn't seen it from the road. McCutcheon Windows & Siding.

He headed around back just in time to see two men heading up the stairs with what he assumed to be the replacement window. Well, one thing he could say about his old man—he sure knew how to get things done.

After exchanging a few brief words with the men, he changed clothes and headed to Shelby Memorial Hospital. Forty-five minutes early, he grabbed a bottle of water, unsure if he could eat or drink before the test, and grabbed a seat in the lobby. His newfound family arrived exactly at noon, with Dudley bringing up the rear, keeping a short distance between himself and Sam, who looked as if she were in desperate need of coffee. Jack met them at the nurse's station.

"Well," he said eyeballing Dudley, "I don't see any bruises or broken bones. Guess you were smart enough to keep your mouth shut last night."

The chauffeur's eyes narrowed, but he crossed his arms over his chest and remained silent.

Sam stalked past him to lean against the wall. She glanced around with barely concealed uneasiness. "So? Can we get this over with? I'd like to head into town, see what kind of fun awaits me here in hickville."

Whitlow walked up and awkwardly placed his hand on her shoulder. "Samantha, we can do anything you'd like to do today, go anywhere you'd like to go. I'd love to explore Shelbyville with you. Which, by the way, has quite a bit of historic significance, including one of the few last remaining wooden bridges in America. And did you know the dishwasher was invented here back in 1886 by a lady named Josephine Cochran?"

Sam's face screwed up with disbelief. "Are you serious right now? Who knows that kind of shit?"

"I read a few pamphlets in the hotel last night," he informed her, looking somewhat affronted.

She turned back to face Jack. "Why are we even in this tiny ghost town anyway?"

"I came here looking for my aunt. She's the only family I have…well, had. Until a few days ago."

"Yeah, love you, too, bro."

Jack grinned. "You know what I meant. Geez, someone's a real crabass today."

"Try every day," the chauffeur muttered.

Sam flipped the old guy the bird.

A nurse walked up before Dudley could respond in kind. "If you'll all follow me, please?"

The actual mouth swabbing took all of ten minutes. The nurse told them the results would be ready in five to ten days.

"That'll be fine," Whitlow said, surprising Jack. He'd half-expected the old man to slip the nurse a hundred dollar bill to hurry the tests along.

"So, what do you say I buy us lunch?" The old man clapped his hands together, smiling as if he'd just offered to take them all on some great adventure.

"Sorry, I have to get back to work." Jack realized if he didn't need to get home to Mia, he wouldn't mind sharing a meal with them. "But have fun."

Sam cast him a 'get real' sidelong glance before turning and heading for the exit.

Dudley reluctantly followed after her.

"I'll let you know when I get the results back," Whitlow told him. "Give me call if you need anything."

Jack gave a curt nod, still a little uncomfortable with the whole father-son thing.

The old man thumped him on the back, then followed the others from the hospital.

Figuring it must be around twelve-thirty, Jack headed back to his place eager to find Mia so he could explain…well, everything. After the incredible night they'd shared, it killed him to think she might not want anything to do with him now that she knew about his prison stint.

His car stalled at the corner of Vine and Abel, and Jack smacked the steering wheel as he cursed his crappy luck. A quick look under the hood revealed no answers, though he was fairly certain the alternator needed to be replaced. Since there was nothing he could do at the moment, and not a chance in hell he could push the fucker up the hill, he pulled it off to the side of the road and started walking back to the garage. Thankfully, he had less than a mile to go.

As soon as he strode around the bend in the road, he stopped short. Unless his eyes were playing tricks on him, Mia and Kat were dragging someone onto their front porch by their arms. *Well, shit.* He gave his eyes a quick rub, but nope, the image was still there.

He crept around the side of the auto garage and came up on the other side of their shop. Once he had a clear visual of their front porch, he watched in stunned amazement as Mia started the same odd ritual she'd performed on that bird the other day. Kat knelt on the other side, her gaze sweeping the area every few seconds as she kept watch.

Suddenly, the guy heaved a hard breath and sat up, clutching his head. Eyes wide with horror, he looked from one sister to the other before attempting to scramble to climb to his feet.

Mia wiped her forearm across her sweaty brow, then propped her shoulder under his arm to help him up. "My God, Mr. Bilsky, are you all right?"

"I-I think so. What happened?"

The sisters exchanged a quick glance before Mia explained, "You slipped on a rotten apple as you were climbing the steps, and hit your head on the railing."

"Huh. It's the strangest thing, I can't remember it." He reached out and steadied himself for a moment, shook his head, then turned and wobbled down the stairs without another word.

Jack fingered the scar on his stomach, and a flash of

memory returned with stunning clarity. *I* was *stabbed!* That night he'd been about to close shop; someone had come up behind him and plunged a knife in his gut. He'd fallen to the ground, they'd robbed the place...or made it look like a robbery. Once they left, he'd managed to crawl to the phone, but had no memory of dialing 9-1-1. He must have passed out at that point. Then...an angel's voice—

"Dammit, Kitty Kat, I warned you!" he heard Mia reprimand in a furious whisper. "You could have seriously hurt him. Or worse."

"I didn't mean to! He just makes me so mad, always blaming my dog for pooping on his lawn. And now chewing up his rose bushes? Mudcat was in the house when we left for the funeral, and he hasn't been out of my sight since we got back."

"I know it's frustrating, but you can't keep losing your temper over every little thing. You should've let me handle it. I would've explained to Mr. Bilsky that Mudcat hadn't left our property all day, and short of videoed proof—which he would have shown us if he'd had it—he would've left in a huff, and that would have been the end of it. But you made apples rain down on his head. My God, do you have any idea how badly he could have been hurt? What if I hadn't been here?"

The younger Grey sister's face screwed up, and she started crying softly. Mia rubbed her own eyes before exhaling a sigh and enfolding her little sister in her arms.

Torn between wanting to throttle them, and wrap his arms around them, Jack decided to compromise and simply demand some answers. They both had a lot of explaining to do, and if Mia tried to work some mystical mind tricks on him again, he'd be ready for her.

He waited until they disappeared into the store before following them inside. The bell jingled, announcing his arrival, and Mia spun around as if startled. She quickly whispered something to Kat, who scurried off toward the bathroom, Mudcat, as usual, right on her heels.

"We need to talk."

She schooled her facial expression into a mask of nonchalance, but Jack knew better after what he'd just witnessed.

"We certainly do. But this isn't a good tim—"

"This is a perfect time, lady. You have some serious explaining to do. You and your sister both."

"*We* have explaining to do?" she shot back, hands on hips. "You failed to mention you spent seven years in prison for murder. You don't think that's something I should have been told before I...*slept with you?*" The last words were spoken in a harsh whisper, no doubt so her sister didn't hear.

"I was set up—I didn't kill anyone. Even the cop who testified against me thinks I was framed."

Her knit brow conveyed her skepticism. "Then why did he testify against you in the first place?"

"Because he had no choice. His partner—the prick who set me up—sent Jamison to check out the warehouse where he found me and my supposed victim. Said a call had come in claiming they'd heard a shot. He found me lying unconscious next to the guy I supposedly killed, gun in hand."

She ingested that bit of information before asking, "Why were you unconscious? I mean...that doesn't make any sense."

"Seems you and I are the only two who find that odd. And they couldn't do residue testing because it's inadmissible in court. Add a lousy public defender who was no doubt on the payroll, and I didn't stand a chance."

Her features softened, her eyes glowing with sudden compassion. "I'm so sorry you had to go through that."

He shrugged, feeling somewhat uncomfortable with her concern. Was she trying to scramble his memories again?

"Mia, I need a straight answer. Who the hell are you? *What* the hell are you?"

She visibly swallowed, stiffening as the bathroom door opened and her sister appeared. Kat headed their way, but slowly, as if on her way to face a firing squad.

Mia wrapped an arm around the younger girl and pulled her to her side. Protective, as always. One of the very reasons he'd been so drawn to the two of them. Mudcat plunked down beside them and let out one, very loud bark. If Jack weren't mistaken, the dog was letting him know where his loyalty lied.

"That's a long story. One best explained in privacy, not out in public."

He cocked a brow and ran his gaze around the empty store. "Pretty sure you have nothing to worry about on that score."

Kat raised her chin and smiled cockily. "We're witches."

He stared at her for a moment, then looked to Mia. "Excuse me?"

She raised her chin a notch as well. A note of pride etched her voice. "It's true. My sister and I are what most people would call witches. We have...certain abilities."

"Like mind control and making shit move?"

"Among other things."

It took him a moment, but the truth dawned on Jack with the force of a gale wind. "Holy fu...You *were* there. The night I was stabbed. I heard a voice call out to me, but I was so weak, I...I passed out, didn't I?"

They shared a look, then Mia admitted, "Yes."

"And you...?" He fluttered his hands the way he'd seen her do when she'd healed that bird. And Mr. Bilsky.

A grin broke free, but she suppressed it before repeating, "Yes."

"You saved my life."

A nod this time.

"Thank you."

"I'm just glad I ran over when I did."

He bounced a glance between the two of them, unsure of what the hell to think. To say that all of this was bat shit crazy would be the understatement of the century. Yet, he had no doubt every bit of it was true. Hell, he'd seen it all with his own eyes. But he needed more answers, especially what went down the night he got shot.

"Tell me everything that happened that night, Mia. And no mind games."

When she hesitated, Kat turned to face her. "We can trust him, Mia, I know we can. You know it, too." The younger Grey sister turned big blue eyes on him. "We'd be trusting you with our lives."

Mia gave her sister a pat on the shoulder. "As dramatic as that sounds, it's true. If people were to ever find out about us, it could be catastrophic."

"As annoyed as I am with the two of you, I would never put your lives at risk. I care about you. Both of you. But I need some answers. And…" He hardened his expression. "I need you to both promise me you'll never use your 'abilities' on me again. You had no right messing with my head like that."

Kat nodded, her eyes growing suspiciously bright.

"I'm truly sorry, Jack," Mia said. "I hated doing it. But I couldn't let you discover our secret. I've been protecting Kat and myself for so long, it's become second nature. I can never let my guard down or…" She shrugged, but then he didn't need for her to finish the sentence to grasp her meaning.

And just like that, his heart swelled with love for both these amazing young women. They'd obviously been on their own for a while, taking care of each other while trusting no one. The thought of how lonely they must have been before he came along caused a lump to form in his throat. He swallowed past it and reached out to grasp both of their hands.

Kat's face screwed up as if she were on the verge of tears. She swayed his way, and Jack wrapped his arms around the young girl, his protective instincts like a rush of adrenaline. She cried softly, as if some enormous weight had been lifted from her shoulders.

Mia brushed at her eyes before mouthing the words, '*Thank You*.'

He nodded, and she leaned in to give Kat a kiss on the top of her head.

"Honey, why don't you go into the house and get supper started. The chicken needs to be washed, the mushrooms sliced, and the pint of strawberries washed and quartered for dessert."

When she pulled back and looked up at him, the most beautiful smile stretched across the young face. She nodded at her sister and flounced off, Mudcat on her heels.

Once the back door shut behind her, Mia wrapped her arms around his neck, plastered herself flush against him, and murmured, "You, Jack Sutton, are the most amazing man on the planet."

Unable to resist, he leaned down and kissed her. A slow, deep kiss that had his pulse pounding and his heart racing with anticipation. She moaned, a breathy, sexy little gasp of air, and Jack grew instantly hard. He couldn't imagine ever wanting a woman as much as he wanted the one in his arms.

He frowned suddenly and pulled back, eyeing her with suspicion. But his memories were intact, he quickly realized, and he breathed a sigh of relief.

"I promised I wouldn't scrub your mind anymore, and I meant it. Doesn't seem to work on you anyway," she admitted with a slight frown of her own.

"What do you mean?"

She dropped her arms and stepped back, then made her way behind the counter. After filling two small paper cups with the coffee she always had sitting on the warming plate, she pushed one toward him, then proceeded to add lots of cream and sugar to her own. "When I scrub someone's mind, it's permanent. Always. Well...until you. For some reason, it seems to wear off on you."

Jack thought about that for a minute. He walked up and leaned a hip against the counter. After a couple of cautious sips of the hot brew, he said, "The first time you...*scrubbed* my memory was the night someone stabbed me, right?"

"I had to," she said simply.

Though he didn't agree, Jack admired her courage and conviction. "I guess I can understand, since you didn't really know me at the time," he conceded. "Now, please, tell me already."

As Mia explained everything that had happened, starting from the time she saw the two men enter his garage through the back door, Jack's own memories of that night returned in full force. His blood ran cold as he realized the danger Mia had put herself in when she decided to come investigate. Though he thanked God she had, or he'd be in the city morgue right now, with his newfound family never the wiser. To think how close he'd come to death...

A chill raced up his spine and he took another gulp of his coffee.

"I hated leaving you there, lying alone on the cold concrete like that. But I didn't know what else to do. If I'd have called 9-1-1, they would've had tons of questions for me. Questions I wouldn't have had answers for. I knew you'd have a killer headache the following day, but I also knew you'd live."

"And the night those two men showed up with guns?" Jack watched as her cheeks grew flushed. "Yep, I remember, though I didn't at first. Did you make those oars...?"

She shook her head. "Kat. Her telekinetic abilities are ten times stronger than they should be at her age."

"How do you know? I mean...are there more like you? Were both your parents...?" Good God, was he really having this bizarre conversation?

"My mom. She had healing abilities like me, though not as strong. Her strength was as a seer. After my father died, she needed to make a living, so she started telling fortunes. A couple of Hollywood A-listers came to see her, and the next thing she knew, she was 'Madame Lena, Psychic To The Stars.' She became so famous, European royalty started to seek her out."

Psychic To The Stars? The notion seemed crazy. Though his definition of the word was definitely changing. "I'm sorry about your father. So he wasn't a...?"

She smiled sadly. "No. He worked for the railroad. Died of cancer when I was five. I don't have any memories of him, but my mom loved taking pictures, and filled six photo albums by the time he passed."

"So you and Kat are half-sisters. I kind of figured, but you have the same last name, so I wasn't sure."

"After my mom passed, we needed to basically disappear, so we started using her maiden name." She polished off her coffee and tossed the cup in the trash. "A few years after my dad died, my mom met Tim Mallick—Kat's dad—while doing a reading for a client in their room at the Hilton. He worked room service. She really fell hard for him. Though I was still pretty young, I remember how excited she was the night she introduced us, the joy that lit up her face."

Mia's eyes misted over with the memory of her mother, and Jack wanted nothing more than to gather her in his arms and squeeze tight.

"Tim was tall, handsome, charming," she continued. "But once he discovered her secret and realized my mother possessed true psychic abilities, he changed. Greed took over, and suddenly the only thing he cared about was getting filthy rich. My mom was already making lots of money as a psychic, but Tim wanted more—a huge mansion in Beverly Hills, to rub elbows with all those stars he'd once served while working at the hotel. I remember him vowing that all those 'pompous assholes' who wouldn't look him in the eye, would soon be begging him to make appearances at their parties. The man was delusional, he really was."

"Sounds like a real jerk to me."

"And then some," she agreed. "A couple years after Kat was born, my mom caught him having sex with our nanny. She kicked him out and filed for divorce, but he lawyered up and contested, so it dragged on for years. Until he realized Kat had started to develop strong telekinetic abilities and kidnapped her during one of his visitations."

Jack let her talk. Something told him she'd needed to unload for quite some time, but could never let her guard down with anyone for fear her and Kat's secret would come out. "His own kid? What a piece of shit."

She nodded, her loathing of her stepdad evident in the scowl twisting her beautiful face. "He figured if he couldn't use my mom to get rich, his daughter would have to do. But he hadn't counted on just how strong Kat's abilities were, and one night while he was sleeping, she used her gift to unlock the door of the hotel bedroom he'd locked her in, then ran down to the lobby and demanded someone call the police. By the time they arrived, Tim was gone. He popped up a time or two after that, but never approached us, just watched from a distance, as if biding his time."

"You and your sister have been through so much." He shook his head, wanting to take her in his arms and let his support seep into her bones. He held back, however, knowing she needed to get it all out. Never again would they have to worry about someone discovering their secret. Even if it meant moving from one town to another for the rest of their lives, Jack would keep them safe.

"My sister's a trooper, trust me on that. But she's also young and vulnerable. We've been in hiding from her father since my mother died, which is when we started using Grey. I...I'm pretty sure he poisoned her, but I don't have any proof. Neither did the cops, so after a brief interrogation, he was released, and my mother's death was ruled a suicide. That was three years ago. Kat and I spent a few weeks here and there as we made our way across the country. We both felt a connection to Shelbyville, so here's where we decided to stay."

"Good thing for me." He smiled and leaned in, propping his forearms on the counter.

She grabbed a pack of gum from the display, unwrapped a piece, and stuck it in her mouth. She met his gaze after some power chewing and said, "Jack, I need to tell you something. It's about that guy who ran out of here with his hair on fire."

The truth dawned on him almost immediately. "Tim?"

"Yep. He tried to catch Kat unaware, but thankfully, she heard a squeak on the stairs as he crept up to her room. Kat's abilities are useless if she'd blindfolded and her hands are tied, and Tim knows it."

Great. So, not only did he have his own crazy family to worry about, but Mia's, too. Thankfully, his old man could help out in the security department. Jack would keep the Grey sisters safe no matter what the cost. Even if it meant forging a relationship with dear old Daddy Warbucks.

"Look, I don't want you to worry. I'm going to take

care of everything. I just need you and Kat to be extra careful until this Tim asshole is out of the picture."

Her beautiful face screwed up with fresh concern. "Jack, I appreciate your help more than you'll ever know. But Tim isn't going to just leave. If he can't snatch Kat, he'll alert the media about us. But he certainly won't just walk away now that he's found us."

Fifteen

"I hate that I have to tell you this, Mr. John, but...your son was shot. He's at the hospital, and it doesn't look good."

Whitlow gripped the phone so hard it's a miracle it didn't crack in two. *Dear God...Jack?* "Dudley, are you sure? What the hell happened?"

"I don't know. By the time my guy showed up, the house was surrounded by yellow tape and swarming with cops. He said he overheard Scott's sister talking to a neighbor. She heard several gunshots."

Scott, not Jack. John felt an overwhelming sense of relief, followed by immense guilt. He knew they hadn't known each other very long, and how Jack felt about him was still up in the air. That his own flesh and blood had been so viciously attacked, and quite possibly because of his connection to the Whitlows, was something he'd have to live with for the rest of his life.

Though, Lord only knew how long that would be.

"I'm devastated. I simply cannot believe this is happening. Who would want to see my offspring..."

His words trailed off as one particular person came to mind. He hated himself for even thinking it, dismissed it almost immediately as absurd. But it would have to be looked into. Only he wouldn't bother Dudley with this one. John would investigate his beloved sister personally.

"What is it, Mr. John. Whatcha thinking?"

"Nothing. Just trying to wrap my head around…everything. Listen, *please* make sure you have security in place for the rest of my children. It kills me that I can't do something for Scott's family." Except pray.

"You got it, sir."

John tossed his cell phone aside and stalked over to the window, his mind a jumble of unwanted thoughts. *Carol.* He loved his sister dearly, had always been close with her; his only sibling. No one had ever been as supportive and loving as his big sister.

But things had started to change in the last few years. She'd grown more and more frustrated with Whitlow Industries' very specific by-laws concerning who can be CEO, and had voiced her displeasure when he'd proclaimed his intentions to find out if his donations had produced any offspring.

He'd had major doubts concerning Carol's oldest son, Phillip, since the first time he'd caught the boy banging his secretary, pants around his ankles, the young woman bent over his desk.

John had lost his temper, something he rarely did, and Carol had been just as horrified at first. But after firing the young woman and giving her randy son a good tongue-lashing, Carol had proceeded to place the blame all at John's feet, claiming he made his nephew feel like an outsider instead of a respected member of the family.

Respected members of the family didn't bend their

secretaries over their desk in the middle of a work day, but he'd kept that observation to himself.

The light clip of his sister's designer pumps brought him out of his reverie. He turned, slowly, hating the inkling of suspicion that she may have had something to do with the attempts on three of his offspring's lives. He simply couldn't imagine her ever being capable of such violence. But he knew how desperately she wanted Phillip to helm the family business. And if the boy could keep his mind on business instead of his penis, John might have eventually supported him as his successor. Unfortunately, he'd lost faith in his nephew after the *third* time he'd caught him screwing the office help.

Though, he couldn't envision Jack in a three-piece suit, let alone as CEO of a company the size of Whitlow Industries, so he had no idea what the future would hold for the family business.

Carol stepped inside and smiled with what seemed like true pleasure at the sight of him. "I was hoping to find you in here. I take it your meeting went well?"

John had flown home to meet with the owner of an up-and-coming new company he wished to acquire. "It did." He didn't elaborate, and knew she didn't expect him to.

"Wonderful. How would you like to join me for a movie?"

"Empty house tonight?"

She shrugged on slim shoulder. "Phillip flew to New York with a client for a ball game, and Michael is in Cabo until Sunday."

"Ah, Cabo, I'd forgotten. One last hurrah before college, hey?"

"A family tradition he had no intention of skipping,"

she said, laughter in her tone. "And Gregory took Elizabeth and the kids up to his parents place in Houghton so they could meet their new granddaughter."

"Well, I'm sorry you're on your own tonight, and any other night I would love to join you. But I have to fly back to Shelbyville. I left Samantha and Dudley alone together, and I'm quite worried about the old boy."

He watched her face closely, but not so much as a twitch betrayed anything other than mild concern. In fact, a reluctant grin curved her mouth.

"After meeting the young lady myself, I understand your concern."

"Raincheck?"

"Always." A note of sadness tinged her reply.

John stepped forward and enfolded his sister in his arms. He silently berated himself for suspecting her capable of hurting anyone, let alone his children. She was a kind and gentle soul, and nobody knew that better than him. "You're welcome to come with me, you know."

She gave him a pat on the shoulder, then pulled back and teased, "If I were to join you, who would be here to keep an eye on that...*woman* holed up in the guest house?"

A groan escaped him. He'd almost forgotten about the soon-to-be ex-Little Missus. "She hasn't been giving you any trouble, has she?"

Carol waved a delicate hand. "I haven't even seen her in almost a week. But I hope you plan to evict her soon. I can't stand the thought of that terrible woman taking advantage of our generosity any longer than necessary."

John let out a silent sigh. "I promise, just as soon as

my business in Shelbyville is complete, I'll march back to that guest house and take out the *trash* myself."

Tim Mallick set his drink down on the bar with a thunk of disgust as his gaze traveled around the dimly lit hole-in-the-wall tavern. God, how tired he was of this place. His mind drifted back a few months, to the first night he'd walked in. He'd seen a pretty blonde sitting in a corner booth all alone, so he'd taken a drink over to her and flirted her up. Forty minutes later, she'd let him take her back to his motel room, where she'd fucked and sucked him to within an inch of his life. Hell, she'd been so good he'd had a hard time believing she wasn't a prostitute.

It wasn't until the third time they'd slept together that she admitted she was married with a kid. Frankly, to his way of thinking, that had made the situation even better. He could screw her, then send her home to her clueless schmuck of a husband. Last thing he wanted or needed was some clingy woman pushing him for a commitment. He'd just wanted some…companionship while he searched for his darling daughter and her bitch of a half-sister.

Though he'd started to wonder if he'd ever find them. Tim had been searching for them since the day after Lena's funeral. He'd planned to sue for custody of Katarina now that—good riddance—his ex was gone. But his step-daughter was far savvier than he'd given her credit for, and they'd disappeared before their mother was even cold in the ground. He often wondered if Mia had the same abilities as Lena and had 'seen' what he'd done to their mother.

And what he planned to do to her once he had his daughter under his control.

But his search had proven futile those first six months, until he remembered something Lena had told the girls when Mia asked where her father was buried. He'd had family in Tempe, Arizona, and they'd insisted he should be buried in the family plot, which Lena agreed to. Though she'd later told Tim in confidence that her ex-husband's family had shown little interest in either her or Mia, and she hadn't seen them since his funeral. Maybe, he reasoned, Mia had gone in search of what family she might have left.

So he'd headed to Tempe and shown the girls' pictures to everyone and anyone willing to speak to him until someone finally recognized them. A waitress at a Denny's. She remembered them specifically because they came in for lunch several days in a row, whispered a lot, and the younger girl always seemed angry. She claimed she heard them talking about Illinois, so he assumed Lena must have been telling the truth about her ex's family wanting nothing to do with his kid.

Tim had drained what little bit of money he had in his checking account, and headed for the Land of Lincoln. Illinois was a big state, but at least he had a lead. He ran out of cash several months later while working his way through the south suburbs of Chicago. He followed route 45 down to Kankakee and farther, working odd jobs until he finally landed in a little town by the name of Mattoon. Another waitress in the small town's diner gave him fresh hope when he showed her the pictures. Said her boyfriend had taken her boating on Lake Shelbyville, and she remembered both girls from a little bait shop they'd stopped at, though she couldn't remember their names. He'd headed to the town of Shelbyville, and met Sherry that first night.

The first time she complained about 'those evil Grey sisters' who ran the bait shop down by the marina, Tim had nearly pissed himself with excitement. He'd tried not to get his hopes up, but the description he'd gotten out of her was nearly spot-on. So he'd driven past the place, and couldn't believe his eyes when he recognized his daughter playing catch out front with some beast of a dog. After two years, he'd finally found her!

Though, oddly enough, he hadn't been in as big a hurry to snatch her away as he'd once been. Truthfully, he'd yet to tire of Sherry Kingston's considerable charms, so he'd bided his time, enjoying the best sex of his life while waiting for just the right moment to put his plan into motion. Unfortunately, he got drunk one night and blabbed, and the next morning she attempted to blackmail him into killing her husband so they could be together. They'd get married, he'd be a wonderful step-father to Zoe, and they'd also have a few kids of their own. Uh, no fucking thanks. Been there, done that, got royally screwed out of millions. So he'd done what he had to do—eliminated the bitch.

Again.

The very next day, he made his first attempt at grabbing Katarina, waiting for her sister and that beast of a dog to head outside before slipping in the front door. Which turned out to be a major bust when the little witch nearly incinerated his ass. And that new neighbor had been hanging around every damn night since, making it almost impossible for another opening. If he wasn't there, a cop seemed to be driving by every fucking ten minutes.

All he could do at this point was be smart, stay out of sight, and wait for an opportunity.

Jack finished his last job and closed up shop, opting to clean up in the morning so that he could join the sisters for supper. He hated leaving them alone even for a minute now that he knew about Kat's crazy father and the danger the guy presented. But they had a business to run, and he knew how stubborn Mia could be. She'd never agree to stay in the house all day with the doors locked.

After a quick shower, he dressed in a pair of faded jeans and a black T-shirt, then grabbed his keys and locked the place up. He hoped Mia would invite him to spend the night—not for sex, but for protection. Though he *was* hoping for some alone time with her. The woman was incredible, and he wanted her with every fiber of his being.

He had just lifted his fist to knock when the door suddenly flew open. Kat stood several feet back from the entryway, grinning. Obviously, now that he knew their secret, the little minx felt like showing off a bit. He stepped inside and purposely shut the door before she had a chance to pull another Sabrina.

"Hi," Mia said as she finished rinsing a cup. She turned off the faucet and dried her hands on a dish towel before rushing over and twining her arms around his neck. Her shy smile enchanted him, but she cast an uncertain glance at her sister.

Kat rolled her eyes as she pulled plates from the cabinet. "Good God, kiss him already."

Mia shook her head, but surprised him by pulling his head down for a quick peck. She cleared her throat, then went back to the sink to finish washing dishes. "I hope you like pepper steak."

"*I* don't," Kat chimed in as she set the table.

"So just pick the peppers out and quit complaining," Mia shot back. "I don't like corn dogs, but I make them for you at least twice a month."

"Yeah, yeah, you're a goddess."

Jack smiled, loving the banter between them. It amazed him to think about how much they'd come to mean to him in such a short time. "I've never had pepper steak," he admitted. "Is it hot?"

"No, it's made with bell peppers and stewed tomatoes. I serve it over rice with biscuits on the side."

"Sounds awesome." He'd have to make sure to start doing sit-ups or he'd look like Santa Claus by the time the first snow fell.

Jack discovered with the first bite that pepper steak was just as delicious as everything else Mia had made for him. He ate with relish, wolfing down the huge serving she'd piled on his plate, plus several buttered biscuits, and two glasses of milk. Mia grinned at him in that knowing way he'd come to love. He ached to pull her into his arms and become lost in her warmth.

"Why don't you two go sit down by the lake, watch the sunset. I don't mind doing the dishes."

"Um, Kitty Kat, are you feeling okay?" Mia teased with a lift of her brow.

With a scowl, little Grey shot up and started gathering the dirty plates. "God, I was just trying to give you two some privacy. Forget it."

"And I appreciate it, honey," Mia quickly assured her. "You just took me by surprise."

"It was a thoughtful offer. But I have no intention of leaving you alone in the house until your...until Tim is in police custody."

The young girl's face screwed up with a combination of panic and fear, but she quickly masked it.

Jack knew she wasn't nearly as indifferent as she put on.

"I have a better idea, why don't all three of us go down by the lake and watch the sunset? If I remember correctly, you still have some popsicles in the freezer."

"I call the last blue one!" Kat exclaimed as she shot up and threw the freezer door open.

Mia rolled her eyes. She took the box from her sister and pulled out two more. "Green or red?" she asked him.

"Either one. I don't have a preference."

"Yeah, right. Everybody likes blue best," Kat crowed as she waved her prize under his nose.

Jack chuckled. God, how he adored the little shit.

The three of them took their treats outside into the fading sunlight and headed down to the docks. They sat there watching until the sun disappeared into the western horizon, talking about anything and everything: school clothes for Kat, fishing, swimming, flowers, family.

Everything but the subject on all three of their minds—Tim Mallick.

Kat lied back in the grass, and within minutes, soft snores poured from her mouth.

"Guess someone was pretty tired," he said in a soft tone.

Mia smiled down at her sleeping sister. "It's been a long day." She gave her a slight shake. "C'mon, sleepyhead. You're too big for me to carry into the house."

Kat roused and ground her fist into her eye. "I can't believe I fell asleep."

"I can. You've been up since five."

The little stinker shot her a look of feigned disgruntlement. "Well, whose fault is that?"

Mia winked at him over her head as she hustled her back toward the house. "I know, I know. I'm a slave driver. But it'll be worth it when it's time to shop for school clothes."

"I want a new pair of combat boots. Black. And a fatigue jacket."

"Not exactly the look I was picturing, but...maybe with a cute skirt."

"Ugh."

As Mia followed Kat up the back porch, Jack thought he heard the crunch of gravel. Who would be visiting either of them at this time of the evening? He wondered. "Hey, I'm going to go check and make sure I locked the front garage door. Lock the door behind you, just to be safe."

Mia's eyes narrowed the slightest bit, as if she didn't quite believe him.

"I'll just be a second, promise. Can't be too careful, right?"

With a reluctant nod, she followed Kat into the house and shut the door. Once he heard the lock click, he slipped around the side of the house and made his way up front, being careful to stay close to the building. No headlights shone against the grass...maybe he was simply hearing things. After all that had happened, a little paranoia wasn't exactly surprising.

He was about to head back when a thump, quickly followed by a softly uttered curse, reached him. Moving in closer to investigate, Jack realized a car had pulled into his driveway, one he didn't recognize. Careful to stay in the shadows, he inched closer, his Spidey senses tingling. When he saw a hulking, dark figure trying to peer into his garage windows, Jack's pulse kicked into overdrive. What he wouldn't give to have a weapon, any damn thing.

Picking up the largest rock he could find, he crept closer until he was less than ten feet away from his would-be...hell, was he there to rob him, or attack him?

The guy stepped back and turned around, and Jack frowned as recognition dawned.

"Dudley? That you?"

His father's chauffeur spun around and clapped a hand to his chest. "Jesus, pup, you scared the shit out of me."

"Mind telling me why you're looking in my windows?" Jack demanded without preamble.

"Your old man sent me. Wanted me to check on you and the sisters, make sure everything is copacetic. He's worried. Got news today that one of his other kids was shot."

Shock gripped him. "Not Sam?"

"Nah. One of the boys. The one living in Minnesota."

Not Sam, thank God. "Is he all right?"

"Sounds like he's gonna make it. But Mr. John thought I should come check on you since the cops don't know who shot him or why."

His suspicions abated, though for some reason, Jack still didn't trust the guy. "Tell Whitlow I appreciate his concern, but I'm good."

"You gonna stay next door with that hot, little—"

"Dudley, if you want to leave here with your teeth intact, you won't finish that sentence."

The old guy crossed his arms over his chest and cocked his head, but then a grin broke free. "Didn't mean no disrespect. Just wanted to know so I could ease Mr. John's mind."

"Tell Whitlow he can rest easy. I plan to sleep next door. On the *couch*," he added, wanting to knock that knowing look off the old bugger's face.

"Whatever you say, pup." Dudley chuckled as he strode past. Over his shoulder he added, "Make sure you lock the doors. Never know what kinda riff-raff's roaming around at night."

Sixteen

"Don't forget to grab a box of frosted flakes. We're almost out. And ice cream…mint chocolate chip."

Mia glanced up from her grocery list and frowned. "How can we be out of ice cream? I just bought two half-gallons last week."

Kat cast her a cheeky, over the shoulder glance. "Mudcat and I snuck downstairs for sundaes last night. I can't believe you didn't hear us."

Mia managed not to show a reaction. She hadn't heard because she'd been in the middle of yet another erotic dream starring their sexy next door neighbor. "I was tired. And you know you shouldn't be giving that dog ice cream. It's a miracle he didn't…have an accident all over the house."

Her sister blanched, as if she hadn't thought of that possibility. "Well, he didn't. And don't worry, I won't give him anymore."

They strolled down the aisle, grabbing the cereal and a box of chewy granola bars. As soon as Kat reached the end, she stopped dead in her tracks, her face growing white as a sheet.

"What is it, Kitty Kat? You look—"

Her sister gave the cart a quick shove, then rushed

around to Mia's side. "It's Tim!" she announced in a furious whisper. "He's standing over by the frozen aisles. Think he saw us?" The younger girl's eyes grew wide. "Think he's watching for us?"

Heart hammering in her chest, Mia grasped Kat's elbow and firmly escorted her to the opposite end of the aisle. A quick left and then a quick right brought them to the entrance to the restrooms. She pushed opened the door and pulled Kat in after her.

"Geez, panic much?" Miss Smartmouth snapped as she rubbed her arm.

"Don't make light of this. You were as scared as I am."

Kat's expression sobered, but her show of bravado was far from over. "I ain't afraid of him."

Mia pressed her ear to the door. "Well, I am. So we're going to hole up in here until he leaves."

"I don't want to hang out here all night," her sister complained, pulling a complete one-eighty. "Who cares if he sees us? It's not like he doesn't already know where we live."

Mia heaved a sigh as she walked over to the sink. After washing her hands and splashing a little cool water on her face, she dried both with paper towels while trying to decide how best to handle this. Of course, Tim already knew where they lived. Didn't mean she wanted to have a confrontation with him in the middle of the grocery store.

She opened her purse and rummaged inside, cursing when she came up empty.

"What is it?"

"I must have left my cell phone in the car."

Before she could react, Kat inched the door open and

peered outside. "Crap...he's still there. Why the hell won't he leave?" She glanced over her shoulder and an almost evil grin pursed her lips. "Want me to make those soup cans fall on his head? That would distract him for a while."

"It would probably do more than that, Kitty Kat."

"So?" She propped her hands on her hips in defiance. "I don't care. I hope he dies."

"Kat—"

"I hate him, Mia. He killed mom. You know it, and so do I."

"We don't know anything for sure, honey. I have my suspicions, but I could be wrong. He's your father. Not that I'm trying to defend—"

"Don't call him that! He's nothing to me, hear? I don't care what you say—he's responsible for mom's death. And one of these days, I'm going to make him pay."

Jack glanced at the clock, surprised to discover it was already almost four o'clock. The afternoon had flown by thanks to a string of oil changes. He needed to check in with Sam and Whitlow, make sure everything was all right. After Dudley's odd behavior last night, he wasn't so sure the guy was working with a full deck.

He took a quick shower, and had just pulled on a pair of jeans when the phone rang. He grabbed the old receiver off the wall. "Hello?"

"Hey, Jack, it's Kent. I...You got a minute?"

Sounded ominous. "Sure. What's up?"

"Well, your neighbors came in shopping about an

hour ago. I happened to be watching when they started acting…hell, I don't know…strange."

Jack almost laughed. Had that little shit decided to show off her magic again? Maybe float a head of lettuce across the store? "Describe strange."

"They kind of ducked out of the way like they didn't want to be seen. Mia grabbed Kat's arm, and the two of them rushed into the restroom. That was thirty minutes ago, and they're still in there."

"You must have just missed 'em."

"I don't think so. Their half-filled cart is still sitting in aisle nine where they left it. If they suddenly had to leave, I can't imagine they wouldn't have at least put the cold items back. Or asked someone to do it for them."

Jack's pulse sped up as worry for those two settled into his chest. "Did you have someone go in and check on them?"

"I sent my sister in right before I called. Figured if they needed a ride home or something…"

"I appreciate it. And thanks for keeping an eye on 'em. I'll be there in ten minutes."

He actually made it in seven, rushing inside as several scenarios played in his head—none of them good.

His cousin met him by the front doors, as if he'd been watching for him.

"They haven't come out yet, and I'm sure Chelsea would have told me if it were something serious."

Jack nodded and followed along as Kent led him to the back of the store in the far right corner. He hadn't met any of his other cousins yet, and if memory served, Chelsea was the one who looked like his mother. An anxiousness that had nothing to do with the sisters nearly overwhelmed him. He cleared his throat and waited while Kent inched the Ladies Room door open and spoke to his sister.

"Hey, Chels, just wanted to make sure everything is okay in there…?"

A young woman stepped out, the same familiar face that had stared back at him from the photo his aunt showed him. Only she wore her makeup a little heavier than what Jack perceived to be normal. And she had a nose piercing, which he'd bet hadn't gone over well with her parents, regardless of her age.

Somehow, Jack thought it suited her.

"Yep, no worries. Kat just got her period."

Relief deflated Jack's chest like a popped balloon.

Chelsea grinned, as she knew her announcement had made both of them uncomfortable. "Her first. Trust me, *not* a fun time for a girl."

Kent cleared his throat and cast Jack a sidelong glance. "Chelsea, I'd like you to meet our cousin, Jack. Jack, this wiseass is Chelsea, my youngest sister. She does most of the ordering in the dairy and freezer aisles."

Her eyes lit up with genuine excitement. At least, he assumed it was genuine. She cocked her head to the side and studied him for a moment, as if sizing him up. He couldn't help but think that she and Samantha would get along famously.

"Hey, cousin, it's about time. Thought I was going to have to come looking for you. Growing up, you were like this phantom family member I never actually thought I'd get to meet."

She didn't put out her hand, or lean in for a hug, but

her smile—that oh-so familiar smile—was enough to put him at ease.

"The stuff of legends, hey?"

"*Hey?*" She mimicked with a laugh. "Yep, you're a cheesehead all right."

He grinned. "Nice to meet you, too, FIB."

"Oh, I can't believe you went there." She glanced at her brother with what had to be feigned outrage. "I can't believe he went there."

The bathroom door slowly opened, and Jack's gaze was drawn to Mia. Beautiful as ever, except for the creased forehead—which made him anxious to get her alone and make sure there wasn't something else going on.

He stepped forward just as Kat followed her out of the restroom.

The younger girl met his gaze for a brief moment before pretending interest in her nails.

Jack grasped Mia's hand and gently tugged her forward. "You guys all right? Need a ride home?"

"Kat… Well, you heard. And I have my car, thanks."

He cast a quick glance at her little sister, who continued to evade his gaze, then turned to Kent. "Thanks for giving me a call. I appreciate it." Then to Chelsea, he said, "Glad I got to meet you. Hope we can get to know each other better soon."

"No worries on that score. I'm sure mom will be inviting you over at least once a week for supper."

Somehow, he doubted that would go over well with Uncle Jerry. "I look forward to it."

"Crap, I forgot about the groceries." Mia looked to Kent. "We have milk and pork chops in the cart. I'm sorry. I'll go pay for them so—"

"No worries. After I called Jack, I put the milk and the chops in the back cooler. They're fine. You just take care of your sister."

Mia smiled. "Thanks, Kent. If you want to push my cart into the stock room, I'll come back for everything in the morning."

"Will do. Take care."

Jack escorted the sisters from the store and followed them to their car. He met both of their gazes before announcing, "I'd appreciate the truth as soon as we get home."

They pulled into her driveway ten minutes later. Once he had them safely inside, he said, "All right, let's have it. What happened?"

"Tim was in the store," Mia replied without preamble.

He cursed under his breath. "Did he see you?"

"No. Kat noticed him first, thankfully. But it was weird. He just stood there, arms crossed, as if he didn't have a care in the world. I don't know if he knew we were there or not. It seems odd that he would wait for us out in the open if he did. Yet…why else would he be there? He wasn't shopping."

"Okay, until this nutjob is gone or behind bars, I don't think you two should go out alone anymore."

Mia strode forward and wrapped her arms around his waist. She gazed up at him, attempting but failing to mask her fear. "As much as I wish we could just hide from the world, it's not possible. Life goes on. School will be starting soon. We have to shop for supplies and clothes, and Kat has a physical and eye appointment next week."

Frustration gripped him. He wrapped his arms around

her and clasped her tight, the beat of her heart a small comfort. "I'll take you wherever you need to go. I'm not taking any—"

"Jack, I appreciate you wanting to take care of us. It means…a lot. But sooner or later we're simply going to have to deal with him." She disentangled herself from his embrace and stepped back. "I'll have the restraining order renewed, which'll help."

He swiped his fingers through his hair and cursed again.

She frowned, but didn't scold him for his language.

"There's no guarantee you'll get one," he pointed out, growing more frustrated by the minute. Stubborn woman.

"I can't see why we wouldn't. But if not, we'll…well, we'll have to think about relocating."

"No fucking way."

"Jack, I know you're upset, but please don't use that kind of lang—"

"There's no way in hell I'm letting you go. I'll take care of Tim—one way or another."

Kat gasped. "Do you mean you'll…?"

Mia's eyes grew wide. "Of course he doesn't! Please tell her you didn't mean…*you know*!"

"I'll do whatever it takes to keep you two safe. And here, in Shelbyville." He pulled her back into his arms, ignoring her weak protest. "I just found you, sweetheart," he whispered against her cheek. "It would kill me to lose you."

He glanced over her head at Kat. Tears swam in the young girl's eyes.

"You both love this town. You belong here. We all belong here. I'm not letting that SOB chase us away."

Kat rushed forward with a soft cry and wrapped her arms around them both. Jack reached over and gently patted her back.

"Mia, I don't want to leave," she insisted, a tremor in her voice. "You know I don't. And I hate Tim. I don't care if Jack... Tim killed mom, I know he did! And so do you. He doesn't deserve to live. I should have taken care of him myself before we moved here."

The vehemence in the young girl's voice was a tad startling. Not that he didn't understand, knowing what he did. But it broke his heart to hear how jaded life had already made her.

"Oh, Kitty Kat, please don't say things like that. You aren't a killer. You can't even let a sick bird die, let alone hurt your own father."

"He isn't my father!" the younger sister insisted. "Fathers are supposed to love you, protect you. Not kidnap you and slap you and—"

"Calm down, honey," Jack said in a soothing tone. "He won't ever get the chance to hurt you again. I swear it."

He held them both tight, his protective nature coming out in a rush of fury. The thought of anyone trying to hurt either one of them made him postal.

After a minute, Kat pulled back and let out a half-uncomfortable laugh, half-throat-clearing. "I'm hungry."

He and Mia chuckled. She stepped forward and opened the fridge. "Hmm. Well, I froze all of the crappie. How about grilled cheese sandwiches and canned soup?"

The sisters looked at each other and both burst out laughing.

"Am I missing something?"

Mia winked at him. "Inside joke."

After three grilled cheese sandwiches and a bowl of tomato soup, Jack stood and stretched, damn near ready for a nap. "I don't know how you do it," he told Mia, "but you can even make a grilled cheese and tomato soup taste like the best meal ever."

She set the washed and rinsed pot in the strainer, then swung her head around and gave it a 'yeah, sure' tilt. "If you're trying to butter me up, taking the garbage out would work a whole lot better than flattery."

He chuckled as he carried his plate to the sink and handed it to her. "No problem. It's the least I can do after you fed me again." He pulled the bag out of the can and opened the back door.

Mudcat scrambled to his feet and followed Jack outside. The monster dog let out a *'hello world'* "Woof," then took off to do his business.

Jack decided he'd never tire of the view across the lake at sunset. He tossed the bag in the big garbage bin, then stood for a moment, enjoying the slight breeze blowing in off the lake. Yep, he'd made the right choice when he decided to head down to Shelbyville and look up his family. Though, he still had plenty of kinks to work out—namely Uncle Jerry. Patience was key...not that he'd had much experience on that forefront. But he'd come to care about his mother's family in the short time he'd know them. And he still had plenty of family yet to meet.

With a shake of his head over his wayward thoughts, Jack turned back toward the house. A loud thud had him swinging his head back around. The sound had come from down by the lake...one of the boats hitting the dock? After a quick glance toward the house, he decided he'd better go investigate.

He'd just stepped onto the dock when a dark figure rose up from behind the boat bobbing in the first slip. Jack recognized his father's chauffeur even in the last few rays of fading sunlight. Dudley pulled a gun from his waistband and pointed it at Jack's head.

Obviously, the old boy wasn't there to check up on him this time.

"Now, why am I not surprised?" Jack muttered, keeping his tone as even as possible. Inside, he was seething. He'd always had niggling doubts about the guy, though Whitlow seemed to trust him implicitly.

"Hey, it's nothin' personal, kid. My sister and I've worked too hard and long to let some sperm donor reject waltz in and steal Whitlow's money out from under us."

"You and your sister? Who...? Ah. The almost ex-wife." Amazing they'd managed to keep their connection a secret from the old man all these years. "Whitlow isn't exactly elderly. Are you and your bimbo sister *that* patient?"

"Hell, didn't he tell ya? He's sickly. Been going downhill fast for about a year now." Dudley let loose a soft chuckle. "My *bimbo sister* is a lot smarter than anyone's given her credit for. She's been slowly poisoning him with eye drops, if you can believe it." Another chuckle. "And not a single one of those stupid doctors ever caught on. They run test after test, but everything comes back negative.

"Meanwhile, he's puking, shitting his brains out, dizzy, can't breathe. Won't kill him, but he's become so weak, one good push down the grand staircase should break his neck. Fuckin' genius if you ask me. It had to be slow so as not to look suspicious to anyone. 'Specially that nosy bitch of a sister of his. I tell ya, I'd like to put a bullet between *her* eyes. Guess it'll be sweet enough when Alex kicks her snooty ass out of the mansion."

Jack's pulse shot into overdrive. This crazy idiot was going to kill him…and then Sam. "Where's my sister? I swear, if you hurt her, I'll—"

"You'll what? You're gonna be dead in about five seconds, so don't waste your breath on empty threats." Dudley gave a quick nod toward the house. "Or I'll kill your girlfriend and her mouthy little sister right after I waste you."

Thinking fast, desperate to catch him off guard, Jack looked out across the lake, widened his eyes and yelled, "Holy shit!"

When Dudley swung his head around, Jack dropped to the ground and rolled forward, taking the guy's legs out with a maneuver he'd learned in prison. The chauffeur went down with a curse, his back hitting the wooden dock with a loud thud. Jack delivered a quick blow to his gut before attempting to wrestle the gun from him.

"You little bastard!" Dudley bellowed as he fought desperately to hang on to the gun. But Jack had learned plenty during his seven years behind bars. He'd never lost a fight, and this was the most important battle of his life.

He landed another blow, this time to the guy's meaty face. He bucked up with a roar, tossing Jack completely off him. Stunned, he dove right back and grasped Dudley's wrist. They grappled for control of the gun, rolling back and forth across the wooden planks, grunting and cursing. Until a shot rang out.

Seventeen

"Mia, Jack should be back by now…don'tcha think?"

After a quick glance at the clock, Mia craned her neck toward the back door. She'd been trying not to worry, but her sister was right. He'd been gone almost fifteen minutes. "I'm sure he just got sidetracked, made a phone call or something. I'll go check and make sure—"

A muffled blast made them both spin toward the door. A gunshot? And it sounded as if it came from down by the lake. Her heart leapt to her throat as she cast a quick look at Kat—the young girl's eyes grew huge with fear. She rushed to the door and pulled the curtain aside.

"I'm coming with you," her sister insisted, slipping into her flip flops.

"No, you're not. And don't even waste your breath," she added when Kat's mouth shot open. "We have no idea what—or who—could be out there."

Before the stubborn girl could launch an argument, Mia stepped outside and quietly shut the door behind her. She hurried down the steps and ran over to Jack's place. Both the garage and apartment above were dark. She sprinted up the stairs and knocked on his back door.

After testing to see if the door was locked, she spun around and rushed back down the steps. She was heading for the docks when a scream split the air, freezing the blood in her veins. *Kat!*

Mia jerked around and raced back to the house. When she threw the back door open, her gut twisted with fear. Tim held a struggling Kat in front of him, her arms pinned behind her back. Tears slid down the young girl's cheeks, but her mouth tightened with contempt for the man who had never been anything more than a monster in her nightmares.

"Let her go," Mia insisted, trying desperately to keep her voice from quavering. She took a step forward. She could see Tim had Kat's hands bound with some sort of zip tie.

Tim pulled a gun on her, and she froze. Had he shot Jack, leaving her in the position of having to save either the sister she adored, or the man she loved? She could only pray Jack wasn't lying in a pool of blood somewhere as the life drained out of him.

Just as it almost had the night she'd healed him.

Would she get the chance to save him a second time?

As much as it killed her, she had no choice. Kat had to come first. She'd never be able to live with herself if anything happened to her little sister.

She tried to convey to Kat with her eyes that everything would be okay before slicing her gaze back up to Tim.

"Let her go," she repeated with feigned bravado. "Take me instead. My powers are twice as strong—and I'd be a hell of a lot more useful to have around than a little girl."

His eyes narrowed, and he seemed to waver, no doubt

considering every angle of her statement, the pig. Mia would die before letting this murdering scumbag lay a hand on her, but she steadily held his gaze, hoping her boastful claims and subtle innuendo were enough to tempt him.

"Mia, no. Please," Kat cried.

She caught her lips between her teeth, desperate to comfort her. She'd never wanted to hurt anyone before, but she'd gladly kill this man if that's what it took to keep her sister safe, to keep them both safe.

Finally, he shook his head and smirked. "Nice try, but you know what they say? Fool me once…"

Before she could think of a reply, Tim raised the gun and cracked Kat on the back of the head. As she crumpled in his arms, Mia let out a roar and lunged for him. But he fired, hitting her in the shoulder. She flew back, hitting the wall with a thud before dropping to the floor. Tears burned her eyes. The pain was nearly unbearable, like someone had set fire to her.

And the bastard knew she couldn't heal herself.

"Please, no!" she screamed as he dragged her unconscious sister from the kitchen into the living room. Tears of frustration pooled in her eyes, blurring her vision. When she heard the front door open, Mia summoned all her strength and pushed herself to her feet, using the wall for leverage.

Once she had her footing, she swiped at her eyes and staggered after them, fueled by a rage she'd never known before. When the screen door flew off its hinges and sailed into the yard, she reeled back in shock. Since Kat was incapacitated, she had to have done it herself. Had fear for her sister unleashed powers she hadn't known she possessed?

She staggered out the door and faced a stunned Tim. He turned and struggled to get the silver sedan's driver's side door open where it was parked at the end of the gravel driveway.

Mia managed to make it down the steps without falling over.

"Let her go," she demanded for a third time, with as much confidence as she could muster. Her shoulder throbbed and her vision blurred, but she fought with everything she had to stay focused and alert. She took a couple steps toward them. "I'll kill you if I have to, you piece of garbage."

Tim dropped Kat on the ground like a sack of potatoes and spun around to face her. "Bitch. Think you're better than me, don't you? Just like your mother. Think you can keep my own kid from me. Well, I shut her whining ass up for good, and I have no problem shutting you up as well."

Was that a confession? Did he just admit to killing their mother?

He raised his gun and took aim. Fueled by anger and the cruel satisfaction of his admission, Mia lifted her hand and mentally summoned the weapon. It tore free of Tim's grip and flew across the yard, landing in the grass beside her. She sliced her arm through the air, sending Tim airborne. He crashed into the tree and fell to the ground with a sickening thud.

Tears spilled from her eyes as she rushed forward and dropped to her knees beside her sister. Her pulse tripped when she spotted the puddle of blood beneath the young girl's head.

"Kat? Sweetie, please wake up." Afraid to move her to search for the wound, she cupped her palms together, and then held them over her sister's head to heal the unseen gash.

"Mia…?" Kat moaned and tried to sit up just as Mia's strength started to diminish.

"Shhh. It's okay. Tim can't hurt—"

A savage growl made her spin around, and a scream froze in her throat when she saw Mudcat slowly approaching Tim, fangs bared, as if stalking his prey. Mastiffs were docile by nature, but fiercely protective when it came to those they loved.

Tim scrambled for the gun, and Mia tried to will it away again, but she couldn't budge the damn thing. Healing her sister must have sapped her powers.

He rolled and snatched it up before pointing it at their protector. Mudcat leaped, and Tim fired. The massive dog dropped to the ground with a sharp yelp.

Kat cried out and, hands still bound behind her, half-crawled, half-ran toward her best friend. She glared at her father, who groaned and clutched his shoulder. "You're a monster! I hate you, I wish you would die!" She tumbled down next to Mudcat and laid her head against his, cooing softly to him as tears streamed down her cheeks. "You have to save him, Mia. *Please.*"

She took one last, ragged breath before hurrying to her sister's side. "Honey, I'll try. But I'm pretty tapped after—"

"I know, I know. Just…try. You can do it. I know you can."

Sweat dripped off her forehead as she held her cupped palms over their beloved pet's chest. Kat wept softly as Mia concentrated with all her might—meager as that was. The massive dog let out a weak grunt as the small metal bullet was pulled from his body. It rose up through the hole in which it entered and fell onto the grass. Kat continued to stroke his head as Mia used every ounce of her strength to heal the wound. Mudcat's breathing was shallow at best.

So focused on saving the dog's life, Mia didn't realize Tim had crept up on them until it was too late. He stuck the gun in her face, then grabbed Kat by the hair with his free hand and yanked her back. Her sister cried out, helpless with her hands still bound, and Mia mentally kicked herself for not cutting the tie from Kat's hands when she'd had the chance. And dammit, she had no strength left to will the gun away from him again.

"All right, brat, let's go. I'm done screwing around. I've had enough of this backward ass town to last me a lifetime."

"I hate you, I hate you, I. Hate. You! I'll kill you the first chance I get, you hear me? Mia, *please*!"

Mia watched in horror as Tim dragged Kat back to the car. She let out a roar as she struggled to her knees, desperate to save her sister from the despicable man and whatever evil plans he had in store for his own daughter.

"Mallick!"

Jack!

Mia's heart swelled with hope as his voice rang out, clear and strong. She swung her head around and saw him rush forward, gun in hand and aimed at Tim. He didn't appear to be hurt, and her shoulders sagged with relief.

Never taking his gaze off Tim and Kat, Jack rushed to her side. "You okay? I heard a gunshot and nearly lost my damn mind."

"He got me in the shoulder. It hurts like hell, but I'll live. What about you? I was so scared." A sob escaped her as she gripped his arm. "I-I thought you were dead."

He cast her a quick, assessing glance; his eyes hardening when they landed on her injury. "I'll fill you in later," he promised, stepping in front of her, as if to shield her from another bullet. To Tim he said, "Give me one good reason why I shouldn't kill you right now, you sonofabitch."

Tim tightened his grip on Kat's throat. "I'd say the answer is obvious, convict. I'll kill the little witch."

"I hate you!" Kat cried again, struggling against her restraints and the man, whose only positive contribution in life was helping to create her. She arched away from him, almost as if giving Jack a bigger target and permission to shoot.

"Put the gun down and let her go," Jack quietly demanded. "If you leave now, you might make it out of here before the cops arrive."

As if to corroborate his statement, the faint wail of police sirens could suddenly be heard in the distance. They grew louder with each second as Tim and Jack continued their silent standoff.

"Jack, no! We can't—"

Tim fired, cutting off Mia's surprised pronouncement, but Jack had fired almost simultaneously, hitting Tim in the thigh. With a howling curse, he threw Kat to the ground and attempted to climb into his car. Jack rushed forward and grabbed him, spinning the guy around and landing two quick blows to the face.

Mia, having regained some of her strength, pushed to her feet and raced to her sister's side. "Are you all right?" she asked, looking her over, wishing she had something she could use to cut the zip tie off her wrists.

She cast a quick glance at Jack and saw that he had Tim pinned to the ground.

"I hate him, Mia. He sh-shot you. I can't believe…I mean, I always knew he was scum. But I never really believed he would hurt anyone. And he…he's my *father*."

Her heart breaking, Mia helped her sister to sit up, leaning her against the side of the car. "Shhh. Yes, you share DNA with him. But Tim is nobody's father."

Kat's eye suddenly grew round and filled with fresh tears. "Mudcat! Oh, my God, Mia, did you save him? Please tell me you were able to—"

"Relax. He'll be fine, I promise. He's probably going to sleep for a few hours, though."

The wail of sirens grew to a deafening level. Fear mingled with relief as two squad cars pulled into her driveway, kicking up gravel as they skidded to a stop right behind Tim's sedan. Would the police discover their secret? The thought made Mia want to pull Kat into a protective embrace.

As soon as they turned off their sirens, Jack said, "You two all right?"

"We're fine," she assured him, her heart swelling with love as she gazed at the most amazing man on the planet. "Thanks to you."

Car doors opened and slammed shut before three police officers rushed over and cuffed a belligerent Tim on the ground. Jack rushed to their side and called one of the officers over, who used a pocket knife to free Kat's bound hands. The angry red rings around her wrists renewed Mia's anger. But she simply wrapped gentle hands around them and let her healing powers do what they could.

Jack kissed her on the head and gave Kat a pat on the shoulder before walking off to speak with the officers. They'd all be questioned before the night was through, but Mia didn't mind. They were all safe, and nothing else mattered.

She helped Kat up so they could check on Mudcat. The big moose snored away, and would hopefully have no memory of being shot when he woke up. Kat stroked the big guy's head while Mia watched as Jack led one of the officers around back.

When they returned, he headed straight back to her side and wrapped a gentle arm around her waist, offering her his strength. The officer, she was shocked to see, escorted Jack's father's chauffeur. Blood covered half his shirt—and his hands were cuffed behind him. What the hell?

The officer shoved him into one of the squad cars while the other two hauled Tim to his feet. He whined like the pathetic whiner he'd always been. Mia's stomach knotted just thinking about how close he'd come to getting away with kidnapping her sister—for a second time.

Two ambulances pulled into the driveway, and suddenly four EMTs were on the scene. They spoke with the police, then dispersed. One headed her way, one knelt beside Kat, and the other two got to work on Tim and the chauffeur.

Mia argued when the young woman explained she would have to go to the hospital and have the bullet removed. She insisted they take it out right there, that she was a fast healer. No such luck.

Jack held her hand while they loaded her into the ambulance, along with Kat.

"I'll get Mudcat comfortable in the house, then follow behind." He kissed her on the lips, and suddenly the throbbing in her shoulder ceased to exist.

Tim grew belligerent as the EMTs were getting ready to transport him. He lifted his head and looked around, his gaze finally settling on Mia. "Are you idiots really that blind? Can't you see what she is...what they both are? Witches! Just like their mother."

She held her breath, her heart pounding in her chest.

The officer who'd cut the tie off Kat's wrist replied, "Yeah? Well, I'm the tin man, George there is the scarecrow, and Carl here is the cowardly lion."

Officer George chuckled, while Officer Carl's brow creased with feigned indignation.

The first cop shook his head as if to say 'nutjob,' then waved to the EMTs. "Take him to Oz, boys. We'll meet you there as soon as we finish up here."

Eighteen

As soon as Jack got Mudcat into the house, he pulled out his cell and gave Whitlow a call. He couldn't even imagine how hard this would be on him. The guy truly trusted and respected Dudley, had literally put his family's safety in his hands.

After filling his father in on everything that had gone down earlier, he kept his anger in check while explaining about Dudley and Alexandra's surprising connection…and how they had been poisoning him for months.

Whitlow was quiet for a few moments, no doubt having a hard time digesting it all. Not that anyone could blame him. What a kick in the teeth.

"Son," he finally said. "I don't know what to say. I'm just…I'm so sorry. Dudley and Alexandra, brother and sister? It seems so preposterous, yet…when I think about it, there were signs. He always sympathized with her whenever she and Carol had words. I just thought he felt sorry for her." A hard breath blew through the phone.

"They fooled everyone," Jack offered. "Hell, you probably weren't even their first con. Let's just be grateful we found out now, before they had a chance to follow through with their plan to…"

"Kill me?"

He gripped his phone tighter. "Yeah.

"Listen, you just take care of your young lady and her sister. I'm going to make sure Dudley and my lovely wife both spend a very long time behind bars."

Of that, he had no doubt. "And I want you to promise me you'll see a doctor. Make sure those eye drops didn't cause any serious damage."

Whitlow cleared his throat. "Jack, if I didn't know any better, I'd think you might care about your old man after all."

"Yeah, well, don't let it go to your head." Jack chuckled, though Whitlow was right. Somehow, he'd come to care about the guy. And, oddly enough, the thought didn't scare the hell out of him anymore.

Mia and Kat were released from the hospital just after one a.m. Jack's heart finally slowed to a normal pace once he had the sisters' home, safe and sound. He carried a sleeping Kat inside and up to her room, while Mia headed into the kitchen to check on Mudcat. She grasped his hand as soon as he returned, and silently led him into the living room. She didn't turn on the light or the TV, just sat on the couch and pulled him down beside her.

"You okay?" he asked, tracing the line of her jaw with his finger. She hadn't said a word since they left the hospital, and he wondered if she was experiencing some residual effects of shock. After everything she'd been through, he wouldn't be surprised. She'd held it together for her sister's sake, but maybe the magnitude of what happened, of being shot, was finally hitting her. "Are you in pain? Maybe you should head up to bed as well. I can carry—"

"I'm fine," she assured him, giving his hand a squeeze. "The bullet missed the bone, and the meds they gave me must be pretty potent, 'cause I can't feel a thing." She turned to face him, her eyes gleaming in the moonlight pouring in through the picture window. "It just hit me while we were driving home. I could have died without ever telling you."

"Without telling me what?"

A tear slipped from the corner of her eye, and Jack's pulse kicked back into overdrive. "Sweetheart, what is it? Tell me. Please."

"I love you, Jack. So much."

Stunned beyond words, he could only stare. This beautiful, incredible woman was in love with him? His heart swelled so big he feared it might burst from his chest. He'd dreamt of hearing her say the words; he'd hoped that someday she might come to care about him as much as he cared for her. But in the back of his mind, he'd had those niggling doubts that he wasn't good enough for the likes of her, and he knew it.

"I guess your lack of response says it all."

He cupped the side of her face and kissed her. A soft, reverent kiss meant to convey just how deeply his feelings for her went. "Are you kidding me? I'm so in love with you I can't think straight."

"Then why did you...hesitate?"

Surprised by the quaver of uncertainty in her voice, Jack kissed her again. "Because I was stunned. You're so far out of my league. I never really thought...I couldn't believe... Hell, I don't know."

Her beautiful face crinkled. "What a ridiculous thing to say. What's so special about me?"

"Do you really want to know?"

"No. What I want—" She leaned in and rested her hand on his thigh, just inches from his crotch. "—is you. Here…right now."

"You're killing me, honey." He grasped her hand and gave it a squeeze. His cock stiffened painfully, but he knew she wasn't in any condition for what she was asking. "I don't want to hurt you."

"You don't want to hurt me…or you don't want me?"

That damn vulnerable quaver again. He moved her hand so that she could feel the proof of his desire. "Does this answer your question? I want you more than you can possibly imagine. But I'm trying to be respectful of your injury. And you're not making it very easy."

A playful, sexy smile curved those luscious lips of hers. "I don't want to make it easy. I want it hard." She punctuated her words with a squeeze of her own.

Ah, hell. Good intentions be damned. He cupped her face and kissed her, needing her more than he'd ever thought possible. With a soft moan, she melded into him, her tongue slipping between his lips as her hand worked at the button of his pants. She unzipped his fly and freed his erection. He nearly came when she gripped him tight.

"Easy, baby. Or I'll never make it inside you."

She laughed softly and released him. "I can't help it. I've been thinking about getting you naked again since the other night. I want you so much," she added in a purr as she leaned in and started kissing and nipping playfully at his neck, driving him wild.

"I just—" He swallowed as she tugged on his earlobe with her teeth. "We need to be careful of your shoulder. I know you're feeling good right now thanks to the pain meds, but I'll feel awful if it starts bleeding again."

"I'll be fine," she promised in a silky whisper. "Now, are you going to strip, or am I going to have to beg some more?"

She hiked her leg over his lap so that she was astride him, then lowered herself and ground lightly against the rocket in his pants. Holy hell, had he ever been this stiff before? Felt like the damn thing was on the verge of explosion.

"Lift up," he directed, giving her hips a squeeze. Mia propped her hands on the sofa behind his and held herself aloft while he lifted his hips and quickly slipped out of his pants and boxer briefs. He kicked them aside before yanking off his T-shirt, and then his socks.

She lowered her still fully clothed self back onto his lap and continued her sexy little lap dance.

"No fair," he whispered, feeling oddly vulnerable sitting there completely naked while Mia hadn't so much as removed a shoe.

She kissed him, her soft mouth gently coaxing as she continued her seductive games, her moist, hot tongue sweeping back and forth across his lips, seeking entrance. Jack felt her love and desire for him in every soft gasp and whispered encouragement as she stroked him from his shoulders to his waist, and back up again, teasing his nipples, gripping his biceps, running her fingers through his hair. Working him into a melted puddle of sexual need.

And just when he thought he'd go up in flames, she whispered, "I'm going to need you to undress me."

"About damn time," he growled, desperate to bury himself deep inside her.

Mindful of her injury, he unbuttoned her shirt and gently slid it down her arms, then unclasped her bra and carefully removed it. Her lush breasts were more temptation than he could handle, and he eagerly cupped them both, teasing the nipples with his thumbs, as she had his.

Her head fell back, her back arching slightly in silent encouragement. He teased both pink tips into tight buds before taking one into his mouth. A soft moan was all the incentive he needed. Jack suckled first one swollen nipple, then the other.

Mia ran her fingers through his hair, tugging lightly, then slid off his lap with a muttered curse. Jack chuckled softly as he watched her shimmy out of her shorts and panties.

Fully naked, she murmured, "Hang on."

Hard and throbbing, Jack took deep breaths as he waited for what seemed like forever. She finally returned and tossed a couple of condoms at him, before resuming her place on the couch.

"I want to…do it like this. With me on top," she informed him in a breathy whisper before capturing his lips again in a searing kiss, leaving him no time to voice a complaint. As if he would. Her take charge attitude was an incredible turn-on. He'd never known a sexier, more desirable woman—not that he'd "known" all that many. But watching her shed her inhibitions was about the hottest thing he'd ever imagined. The fact that she already felt that level of comfort with him brought an ache to his chest.

Jack somehow managed to tear open a package and roll on the condom while she devoured his mouth, her hot little tongue mating with his own as her hands forged a hot new path across his shoulders, back, chest.

She grasped his shaft and lowered herself, taking him in slowly, inch by torturous inch, until his entire length was engulfed inside her slick, tight channel. Throbbing with anticipation, Jack couldn't take his gaze off her as the moon shone across her expressive face. She had her bottom lip caught between her teeth and her eyes half-mast, glowing with sexual energy. His breath caught. Never had he seen a more beautiful sight.

He settled his hands on her hips and gave a gentle squeeze. "I love you." His words came out much gruffer than he'd intended.

Wrapping her arms around him, she kissed him before whispering, "And I love you."

She rode him with slow, even strokes, her head lolling back on her shoulders as she moved up and down, that sweet tongue darting out to moisten her lips. Jack didn't think he'd last thirty seconds, but he forced himself to focus on her pleasure and found an inner stamina. He cupped her breasts, caressing and molding the soft globes, thumbing her nipples with light strokes. He closed his legs a bit when she increased her speed, her hips rolling in a steady rhythm as soft moans escaped those luscious lips.

His balls tightened, and he knew he couldn't hold back much longer. He released one breast and found the swollen little nubbin between her thighs, stroking circles over her slick flesh.

She cried out, and he nearly wept with relief as her inner walls clenched around his throbbing shaft, milking him as she climaxed. He grasped her ass with both hands and drove into her, his bare heels digging into the carpet as he followed her off the cliff. Her hips rolled as they rode out the wave together, until she let out a lusty sigh and collapsed on top of him.

Jack kissed her temple, enjoying being able to simply hold her in his arms. After a moment, she slid off his lap and leaned toward the kitchen as if straining to listen.

"What is it?" he whispered, stroking the curve of her back. She had such soft, silky skin. Like nothing he'd ever felt before.

She sat back down and cuddled against his side. "Nothing. I just wanted to make sure we didn't...you know, wake up Kat."

Though he could barely make out her features, Jack had no doubt a pretty blush stained her cheeks. "You *were* pretty damn loud, sweetheart. But she was exhausted, both mentally and physically. I can't see her waking up before late morning."

He got up and headed into the kitchen to dispose of the condom, then wet a paper towel and wiped himself off. As soon as he returned, Mia stood and pressed her soft curves against him, twining her arms around his neck. Gazing up at him, she purred, "In that case, are you ready for round two? You can be on top this time. Or we can be a little more creative." She turned in his arms and ground her sweet little backside against his already straining erection.

She truly would be the death of him. "Honey, as tempting as that is, I think I'd better let you get to sleep. I'm afraid once those pain meds wear off, you're going to be in quite a bit of pain. And I'll feel guilty as hell."

"Are you thinking about heading home?" Disappointment laced her words.

Jack pulled her across his lap and cupped her cheek. Gazing down at the most amazing thing that had ever happened to him, he said, "Actually, I was thinking I *am* home."

Epilogue

"Happy birthday, Samantha!"

His arm around Mia's waist, Jack watched as Whitlow handed his daughter a small gift box topped with a pink bow. The enthusiasm in the old man's tone had him curious. Probably bought her some ridiculously expensive diamond earrings that will make Jack's own present of a charm bracelet seem lame by comparison. Not that he minded. Little sister knew he couldn't compete with their father in the gift-giving department.

When Sam opened the box, her eyes widened and her mouth dropped open. "Seriously?" she exclaimed, doing a little shimmy Jack had come to recognize as her 'happy dance.' "You bought me a freakin' car?" She gazed up at dear old dad with something akin to hero worship.

"Holy shit," Mia whispered. "Talk about making up for lost time."

Jack chuckled and gave her a quick squeeze. Sam had decided to give small town living a try, and moved in with Whitlow, who spent more time here in Shelbyville than he did back in Madison.

The weather was surprisingly warm for late October, nearly seventy degrees, so the old man had decided to have one last cookout since Sam's favorite meal was anything grilled and slathered with barbecue sauce.

Mia and Kat had brought several homemade salads, a crockpot full of baked beans, and a couple of ice cream pails full of a drink Mia called brandy slush. The Kingstons had insisted on supplying dozens of fresh-baked buns, plus a beautiful, multi-tier birthday cake that looked as if it belonged at a wedding reception, also made from scratch in their store's bakery. Jack sprung for the soda and a full keg of beer, while his father provided enough meat to feed an army: brats, hotdogs, hamburgers, chicken, steak, ribs, and pork chops. Plus everything else needed for a proper cookout, such as condiments, paper plates, plastic cups and silverware.

At first, Whitlow had insisted on reimbursing everyone as he'd spent his entire life footing the bill for everything. But he'd finally conceded once he realized things were done very differently in a small town. Everyone contributed, everyone helped out, *everyone* showed up.

For the most part anyway. Jared Winston and his mother were still holding a grudge, though his father and three brothers had all come down for the party. Jack suspected one or more of them had hopes of snagging Samantha, though ironically, she seemed to have eyes for Jared. Jack wasn't sure how he felt about a possible romance between his sister and the guy who'd had him thrown in jail not that long ago that. But since the jerkoff wasn't there, it wasn't something he needed to worry about at the moment.

Uncle Jerry had his yearly fishing trip with his brothers down in Tennessee. That bit of news had actually been a relief if he were being honest. Though the older man tolerated him, Jack knew he still had his doubts, though Aunt Pat assured him it was just her husband's way. The man was a "stubborn mule" by nature, but she was convinced he'd come around.

Everyone followed Whitlow as he led Sam to the pole building out back. He slid the door open with a flourish, and revealed a cherry red Jaguar convertible. Little sister let out a squeal that had everyone laughing. She ran inside and slid into the beautiful sports car. Tears filled her eyes, which Jack knew had to frustrate his tough as nails little sister, but she merely swiped them away and bestowed their father with the most dazzling smile he'd ever seen. Hell, he had no idea she was even capable of smiling so wide.

"She'd radiant," Mia said as she snuggled into his shoulder. "It's a good look for her."

Jack kissed the top of her head. "Agreed. The old man seems to have chosen just the right gift."

"Well, to be fair, a red sports car is 'the right gift' for pretty much anyone." She laughed softly. "I could use another drink, you?"

"Sounds good. Though since one of us has to drive home, we'd better grab some food as well." He polished off his beer and led her back to the house.

The last of the sun's rays were just disappearing into the eastern horizon when they said goodbye to the last of the guests, which left only Jack, the sisters, Kent, Chelsea, and Dillon, who Jack suspected had a crush on Kat; his young cousin hadn't left her side since they'd arrived. Zoe conked out after hours of running around outside, but when Kent mentioned it was time to get her home, Aunt Pat insisted he and Dillon stay and visit since she was ready to head home anyway.

Whitlow saw the ladies out to the car, and when he returned, he handed Jack a manila envelope. "Open it," he insisted when Jack merely stared at him.

He bent up the little metal prongs, lifted the flap, and pulled out the document, which appeared to be…his pulse sped up as he met his father's gaze. "I…don't know what to say. I-I can't accept this."

Whitlow's smile disappeared. "Of course you can. You're my son, and I want to do this for you."

Jack stared down at the deed in his hand, more torn than he'd ever been. To own the garage outright was his dream. But he wanted to buy it himself, to earn it. Not have his rich new father hand it to him on a silver platter. "I appreciate the thought, I really do. This is…more than generous. But you don't owe me any—"

"This isn't about me owing you anything, Jack. You are my son, regardless of how that came to be. You've had a hard life, first losing your mom, then spending all those years behind bars for a crime you didn't commit. Despite everything you've been through, you managed to grow into the kind of man anyone would be proud to call son. I happen to have more money than I could spend in ten lifetimes, so please, let me do this one, small thing for you."

Jack had to clear his throat before he could speak. He glanced at Mia, whose eyes glistened with unshed tears. She nodded her support. He slid the deed back into the envelope and held out his hand. "I…thank you. I accept your generous gift."

Whitlow clapped his palm against his and shook his hand, then thumped him on the shoulder, his smile so wide Jack felt as if he'd just handed the old man a moonbeam. His chest grew tight as he realized he'd truly come to love the guy. Hell, maybe a ballgame was in their future after all.

A tipsy Samantha stood and hooked an arm around both their necks. "Group family hug!" she announced giving them both a squeeze and air kisses. Jack grinned at the smile of adoration on the old man's face as he beamed at his mirror image of a daughter.

"Hey, wanna go for a ride in my new car?" Sam asked as she pulled back and dug the keys from the front pocket of her jeans.

Jack plucked them from her hand and held them up out of her reach. "Yeah, I don't think so, Slick."

She scowled and made one jumping attempt to reach them, then froze as something behind him caught her attention.

Jack turned and recognized the officer from Sherry's crash site the night she died. He strode up and offered nods all around, then made eye contact with Kent.

"Hey, Hal. You out on patrol, or are you here to join us?"

"I have some news."

"Good news?" Kent asked with a lift of his brows.

"Great news," the officer confirmed, smiling. He glanced around, as if unsure whether he should speak to Kent there or in private.

"You're welcome to speak freely, Hal. This is all family…or soon to be family." He winked at Mia, who cast Jack a suddenly shy smile.

The officer nodded again, though he did seem a tad uncomfortable. "This actually concerns the Grey sisters as well."

Kat and Mia exchanged looks. "Does it have to do with Tim?" Mia asked.

"It does." He walked around and sat down next to Kent. "Turns out some pretty compelling evidence has surfaced regarding your wife's accident."

"That right?"

"You know that motel out on route 9, about a mile down from O'Shay's Pub?"

"The Shamrock Inn." Kent closed his eyes for moment as if he knew what was coming next. "She was meeting someone there, wasn't she?"

"'Fraid so. The Shamrock has video surveillance of the outside of the hotel. Turns out Mallick had been renting a room there for months. He met Sherry at O'Shay's, and they started…seeing each other."

He glanced at Kat, who archly informed him, "I'm not a baby. I know why people meet up at motels."

He cleared his throat, returned his attention to Kent, and continued. "She'd been going there twice a week for at least a couple of months. Every Tuesday and Thursday."

"Tuesday was movie and dinner night with her mom, and Thursdays she took a writing class." Kent stared off into the distance and scrubbed a hand across his face, as if trying to get his emotions under control.

Mia gave Jack's hand a quick squeeze, as if sensing his concern for his cousin. He lifted her hand and pressed a kiss to her palm.

"The night Sherry died, they have footage of Mallick carrying her out of his room and putting her into the car. She appears to be unconscious or…"

"Dead?" Kent finished for him.

"Sorry, man. But yeah. According to the coroner's report, her official cause of death is asphyxiation by manual strangulation."

"Well, why did it take them so long to figure this all out?"

"It usually takes a good month, month and a half to get the final report back from the coroner. And we had no reason to connect Mallick to Sherry, but we got lucky while investigating him. After examining the video footage, the DA believes they have an airtight case against Mallick in her murder." He gave Kent a quick thump on the back. "That's all the info I have for right now. Just wanted to let you know. I know how hard this has been on you and your family."

"I appreciate it, Hal. Tell Lydia and the girls I said hello."

"Will do."

Once Kent's friend left, his shoulders slumped with relief. "This is unbelievable."

"It's great news, though. All around. Once he's behind bars for good, Mia and Kat'll never have to worry about him again."

Kent nodded and cast Mia a reassuring smile.

"I'm so sorry," Mia said to him. "I feel responsible for…everything. It's bad enough we've had to deal with that man all these years. But knowing that monster killed your little girl's mother because we brought him here? I'm just…so sorry."

Kent frowned. "Hey, now. None of this is your fault. Mallick is responsible for all his own actions, as is…was my wife. She put herself in that situation willingly. Her choice, her consequence. I'm sorry for my daughter, but nothing that man did is in any way your fault. You understand?"

Mia's eye grew bright as she nodded, her smile of gratitude heartwarming. Jack hugged her to him.

Damn, his cousin was pretty frickin' amazing.

As he escorted his two favorite ladies home later that night, a shooting star soared across the skyline, making them both squeal with excitement.

Jack had a feeling it was a sign…a sign there'd never be a dull moment in Shelbyville.

Author's Note

I hope you enjoyed the first book in my new series, which takes place in the beautiful, small town of Shelbyville, Illinois. Jack Sutton was first introduced in MEANT TO BE, Book 2 of my Jamison Family Series. I knew right away Jack would have to have a story of his own—and my readers agreed.

Thanks for reading!

Turn the page for a couple of fun excerpts from my Jamison Family Series, set in my hometown of Green Bay, Wisconsin!

There's Only Been You

Jamison Family Series, Book 1

Lies destroyed their past—will the truth end their chance at a future?

Sara Jamison has no clue where Mike Andrews' been all these years, but she knows where she's been—busy raising their son. Two weeks after he accused her of cheating and disappeared from her life, Sara discovered she was something she never expected to be—an unwed pregnant teenager. But with the love and support of her annoyingly alpha-male family, she's managed to make a good life for herself and her young son. She even owns her own business, Sara's Bakery, which she's built into a thriving success. Sure, she works too hard and her social life is nonexistent, but for the most part, she's content.

Until the day Detective Mike Andrews walks into her bakery and back into her life…

"THERE'S ONLY BEEN YOU *is a heartwarming story of family and a second chance at love. This is the first of what we hope is many novels from this talented new author. Reading Donna Marie Rogers is like coming home."*

~ Tori Carrington, Bestselling, award-winning
author of *SOFIE METROPOLIS*

"Love lost and found is the basis of this wonderfully heartwarming read. Throw in a years-old lie and a strong sense of family and it only gets better and better. A subplot concerning a dirty cop adds a nice mystery to spice up the story."

~ 4 Stars, RT BOOK Reviews

Excerpt

Of all the bakeries in town...

Sara blew out a frustrated breath as she faced the troublesome machine. "Couldn't have waited 'til Monday, could you? Rotten appliance."

Ten minutes later, she smiled with triumphant satisfaction as the sweet aroma of vanilla coffee filled the bakery. First thing Monday morning, she'd call the dealer and ask when they could deliver a new machine.

The bell above the door chimed. "See, Amanda. You just have to show this devil who's bos..." The words died on her lips.

Legs braced apart, a disdainful scowl curling his lip, Mike stood just inside the door. Her heart lurched and her breath caught.

This isn't happening, this isn't happening, this isn't happening—

"You sound just like that arrogant brother of yours."

Deep breath, compose yourself. "I'll take that as a compliment." She narrowed her eyes. "Now get the hell out."

"You need to work on your people skills, lady." He strode forward and stopped in front of the display case, looking around in obvious astonishment. "Well, I'll be dipped. When I saw the Sara's Bakery sign, I said to myself, no friggin' way. But morbid curiosity got the better of me. So a bakery, huh? Not much of a surprise, really—"

"What do you want, Mike?"

He turned toward her and she finally got a good look at the side of his face. My God, had Garrett done that? She couldn't help feeling a measure of satisfaction. Oh, who was she kidding? She hoped it hurt like hell.

He must have realized where her gaze rested because he reached up and fingered his jaw. "Don't get too excited, he sucker-punched me." He leaned over and tapped the glass above her jumbo chocolate muffins. "I'll take one of those and a large coffee. Regular, not that flavored crap."

With an angry huff, she stalked over to pour him a cup. Why did he have to look so damn good? Was it too much to ask for a receding hairline and a donut around the middle?

He wore his thick, blue-black hair shorter than he used to, which only made the resemblance between him and Ethan more pronounced. He'd put on a good twenty-five to thirty pounds of solid muscle as the black T-shirt stretched tautly over his chest could attest to. And those eyes—cobalt and incredible—had continued to haunt her over the years.

Ethan's were the exact same color.

Closing her own eyes for a brief moment, she prayed for strength. She turned around and set his coffee on the counter. She felt like she should say something about his father. "Sorry to hear about your dad."

"Don't be, I'm not. I hope the bastard suffered."

Her gaze flew to his. "My God, you're cold." She shook her head, surprised by his callous words despite…everything.

"My old man deserved a lot worse than what he got, and you know it. Or maybe you think I deserved what I got…?"

She gasped. "I can't believe you'd even say that to me." No child should have to go through what Mike had. Parents are supposed to love and protect their children, not abuse them. Unfortunately, it seemed Mike had inherited his father's cruel streak. A chill ran up her spine at the thought of him putting his hands on Ethan in such a way. She'd die before allowing that to happen.

Using a sheet of waxed paper, she snatched a muffin off the tray and stuffed it into a bag. "It's on the house." She dropped the bag next to his coffee. "Now, get the hell out."

Mike flipped a folded five-dollar-bill on the counter. "Something tells me you can't afford to give out freebies. Not with the way you treat your customers."

That got her hackles up. Jackass. She flicked the bill off the counter using her thumb and middle finger.

His jaw worked back and forth. He didn't bother to pick up the money.

"Look, I'm on my way out," she finally said. "So if there's a reason for this visit other than to ruin my weekend, get the hell to it."

He glared at her for what seemed like forever. "You sure fed your brothers a line of bullshit, didn't you?"

"What in the world are you talking—" Before she could finish, the bell above the door chimed and Amanda walked in, humming softly.

Mike shot an impatient glance over his shoulder.

"You did a beautiful job, Amanda. Thank you."

The young woman walked behind the counter and stuck the bottle of cleaner and paper towels back under the register. When she straightened, she gestured toward the coffee machine. "Fixed it?"

Sara nodded. "If it gives you any trouble, though, just turn it off and clean it up."

"I will. So how come Ethan didn't come with you?"

Sara's breath caught. The inquisitive teenager couldn't have known the inner turmoil she'd just caused. She flicked her gaze Mike's way before replying, "He was still in bed when I left."

"Ah. Well, I still need to package those pies. Thanks again, Sara." Amanda gave Mike a curious once-over before disappearing through the swinging door.

"Who's Ethan?" he asked as soon as the door swung shut.

Sara met his gaze dead on. "He's the love of my life."

Mike's eyes hardened. "Hope you and this idiot are happy together." He snatched up his bag and cup and strode out the door.

~*~

Available at your favorite bookstore or online retailer.

Meant To Be

Jamison Family Series, Book 2

She's running from her past, he's unsure about his future. Maybe together they can figure out what was MEANT TO BE...

Officer Garrett Jamison is at the lowest point in his life. He's lost faith in his ability as a police officer after unwittingly setting his sister up with a dirty cop. Garrett ended up getting shot, and his sister's son kidnapped right out of his own bed. He takes a leave from the force, in need of some time to make a decision about his future. Too bad he can't get a decent night's sleep thanks to his sexy new neighbor and her howling cat.

Jessica McGovern moves halfway across the country to start a new life in Green Bay, Wisconsin after her ex-husband is convicted of involuntary manslaughter in the death of their young son. Her new neighbor is as infuriating as he is handsome, but when her ex is released from prison early and shows up in town, Jessica discovers she's never needed anyone more.

"Witty and heartfelt, with an unforgettable cast of secondary characters, MEANT TO BE is a definite page-turner!"

~ Lori Foster, *NY Times* bestselling author

Excerpt

"Remember, you promised to be good," Garrett reminded his nephew as he pulled open the door to the restaurant. "Any sass-mouth and I'll take you right home. I mean it."

Ethan frowned, but wisely nodded his head. He stomped through the door and stood next to the PLEASE WAIT TO BE SEATED sign. Garrett couldn't help but grin. Even annoyed, Ethan had better self-control than his uncle.

The hostess, a busty, middle aged woman with a humongous salt-and-pepper beehive hairdo, walked up and winked at Ethan. "Hey, good-lookin', would you like a table or a booth?" She grabbed a menu, placemats, and a few crayons off the hostess stand.

"We'll take a booth," Garrett said. "In Jessica's section, if that's all right."

She cast him an appreciative once over and smiled. "She has a booth open in the corner. Follow me."

Ethan dragged his feet the entire way, then climbed in and crossed his arms, his little face screwed up in a mutinous scowl. Garrett let out a resigned sigh.

The hostess handed him the menu, set down the paper placemats, and dropped the crayons in front of Ethan. "Jessica will be with you in just a minute."

"I ain't no baby," Ethan muttered as soon as she walked away.

"You're seven, sport. There's nothing babyish about coloring when you're seven." Garrett flipped open his menu, hoping a decent meal might sweeten Ethan's disposition. Hell, who was he kidding? The only cure for his nephew's foul mood would be if Jessica disappeared from the planet. And *that* would surely put *him* in a foul mood. The thought of never seeing her again was enough to make his blood run cold. Damn, when did he become so attached?

He blew out a frustrated breath and glanced over the menu. "Hey, they have chicken quesadilla appetizers. Want to split an order?"

Ethan shrugged. "I s'pose." He picked up one of the crayons and started doodling.

Garrett felt a glimmer of hope. He certainly didn't need the little squirt's permission to date Jessica, but it would be nice if he could at least be civil to her.

"Well, I didn't expect to see you two here."

Jessica approached the table, and Garrett had to clear his suddenly dry throat. Jesus, what in the world was wrong with him? It hadn't been *that* long since he'd gotten laid.

He shrugged. "We have to eat lunch, and this is as good a place as any." *Did that sound nonchalant enough?*

"So, what can I get you?" She pulled the pad and pen from her pocket before craning her neck to see what Ethan was drawing. "Wow, that's amazing. A dog?"

His nephew looked up with utter disdain. "It's a horse. Don't you know anything?"

Garrett's face grew hot with embarrassment. He slapped his menu shut and yanked the crayon from Ethan's grasp. "That's it, sport, I warned you. No lunch and no movies tonight. You can sit in your room and pout until you learn how to treat people with respect." His gaze moved to Jessica. Jesus, what she must think. "I'm sorry. I honestly thought his manners would've improved by now."

Ethan's eyes grew red and his chin quivered. "But it's a horse! Anyone can see that!"

Garrett had had enough. He started to push himself to his feet when Jessica laid a placating hand on his forearm.

"Please, he's right. Anyone can see it's a horse. I don't know what I was thinking." She then turned to Ethan. "You know, we make one of the best cheeseburgers in the city, and it comes with a big plateful of curly fries. *And* if you finish your food, you get a free sundae. What do you think? Are you up for it?"

Ethan shrugged a shoulder, but remained silent.

"If you don't think you can do it..." Jessica added, letting her words trail off as if in silent dare.

Garrett watched in wonder as most of the hostility faded from his nephew's eyes. The thrill of possible victory even brought a smug grin to the little shit's face. A free sundae? There wasn't much Ethan wouldn't do for that.

"Well, sport, it's up to you. Do we stay, practice our manners, and have one of the best cheeseburgers in the city, or go home for some of Uncle Luke's Spam casserole?"

Ethan shivered in revulsion. Garrett and Jessica both laughed.

"I guess that settles it. And I think I'd like to try that challenge as well." He handed Jessica both menus as he mouthed the word "thanks".

She winked. "Okay, so that's two cheeseburger challenges. What can I get you to drink?"

Ethan glanced at Garrett who nodded. Those bright blue eyes lit up. "A large orange soda. And no onions on my cheeseburger."

"Make it two sodas." Garrett leaned back and laid his arm along the back of the booth. "And no onions on mine either." He returned her wink.

She rolled her eyes, but he caught a hint of a smile as she turned away.

Thirty minutes later, Jessica set two huge, cherry-topped hot fudge sundaes on the table with a flourish. "I have to say, I'm impressed. You boys sure can eat." Of course, she'd never admit she'd seen Garrett filching curly fries off his nephew's plate. The kid was, after all, only seven.

And while Ethan wasn't exactly smiling and friendly, he *had* managed to refrain from hurling insults at her. For that, she was grateful.

"Yeah, but nobody can eat as much as Uncle Danny," Ethan informed her. "I saw him eat a whole cake before."

Jessica widened her eyes dramatically. "No way! A *whole* cake? He must've had a bellyache for a week."

He nodded, warming to his subject. "Yep, and he puked his guts up, too."

"Ethan, we're in a restaurant," Garrett warned in a low tone. He met her gaze and shook his head. "Sorry."

Jessica waved his worry away. Although a typically

indulgent and caring uncle, Garrett didn't let the little stinker get away with bad behavior, which, she had to admit, was another check in the man's 'pro' column.

She slid the check face down onto the table and said, "Well, I'm glad you guys stopped in for lunch. Have a great time at the movies tonight. Eat some popcorn for me."

Garrett cocked a brow at his nephew whose little face screwed up in resignation. "If you wanna come, you can come," Ethan grudgingly invited. "But you have to eat your own popcorn."

He earned a wink and smile from his uncle, which seemed to please him.

Jessica knew the last thing Ethan wanted was for her to tag along, though, and decided there was no point in pressing her luck. They'd be neighbors for at least five more months, and it would certainly be easier for everyone if Ethan didn't think of her as the Wicked Witch of the West.

"Thanks. I appreciate the offer, I really do. But the last thing I want to do is intrude on a guys' night out."

Garrett raised both brows at his nephew this time, and Ethan set his spoon down with a resigned sigh. But when he glanced back up at her, his smile seemed almost genuine. "It's okay. My mom even comes with us on guys' night out sometimes. And she's a girl, too."

Jessica could barely hold back a giggle. She looked over and met Garrett's gaze with a you-don't-have-to-do-this look. But the truth was, she hadn't been to a movie theater since she was a kid, and, darn it, she wanted to go.

"Come on, it'll be fun," Garrett said. "We're going to

see that new superhero movie. And it'll be my treat, popcorn and all."

She glanced back and forth between them. "If you're sure I'm not intruding, I'd love to come. I haven't seen the inside of a theater in years."

Ethan shoved a heaping spoonful of ice cream into his mouth and shook his head. "We're not going to the theater," he said after gulping it down. "We're going to the drive-in!"

~*~

Available at your favorite bookstore or online retailer.

About The Author

USA Today Bestselling author Donna Marie Rogers inherited her love of romance from her mother. Romance novels, soap operas, *Little House on the Prairie*—her mother loved them all. And though it wasn't until years later Donna would come to understand her mother's fascination with Charles Ingalls, Donna's love of the romance genre is every bit as all-consuming.

A Chicago native, Donna now lives in beautiful Northeast Wisconsin with her husband and children. She's an avid gardener and home-canner, as well as an admitted reality TV junkie. Her passion to read is only exceeded by her passion to write, so when she's not doing the wife and mother thing, you can usually find her sitting at the computer, creating exciting, memorable characters, fresh new worlds, and always happily-ever-afters.

Visit Donna at:
www.DonnaMarieRogers.com